MOVING WITH THE SUN

Book Three in the Troop of Shadows Chronicles

By Nicki Huntsman Smith

Copyright © 2018 by Nicki Smith

http://www.MovingWithTheSun.com

ISBN-13:
978-1987652901

ISBN-10:
1987652908

Acknowledgements

I would like to thank the following:

Lori, my editor, proofreader, and grammar consultant extraordinaire. Thankfully, comma placement doesn't vex her as profoundly as it does me.

My beta readers, who provided advice, suggestions, and top-notch cheerleading. Al, your suggestions were especially helpful.

My friends and family, who have always accepted my eccentric interests and overt nerdiness with indulgent affection. If any of my children ever read my books, they will get mentioned by name. That's the deal.

Lastly and most importantly, my husband Ray, without whose constant encouragement, gentle nudging, infinite patience, and support on a million different levels, this book would never have been written. I owe him everything.

A Shadow

I said unto myself, if I were dead,

What would befall these children? What would be

Their fate, who now are looking up to me

For help and furtherance? Their lives, I said,

Would be a volume wherein I have read

But the first chapters, and no longer see

To read the rest of their dear history,

So full of beauty and so full of dread.

Be comforted; the world is very old,

And generations pass, as they have passed,

A troop of shadows moving with the sun;

Thousands of times has the old tale been told;

The world belongs to those who come the last,

They will find hope and strength as we have done.

--Henry Wadsworth Longfellow

Prologue — Anonymous

Dear Diary,

We destroyed the bridges today in an effort to make us 'safer.' Acquiring the explosives was no small task, but the placement and detonation was child's play. Bridges are easily demolished, unlike larger structures, such as skyscrapers and athletic stadiums. When it came time to topple them, it was over in less than five seconds. Rather anti-climactic, but still more interesting than anything else that happened today.

I admit, I have mixed feelings about being cut off from the continent. Of course, there will still be access via boat, or for those so inclined, an invigorating swim, but removing the bridge roads felt a bit like severing an umbilical cord. It's an appropriate metaphor; all the necessities of life for this baby island formerly came from the mother mainland.

Now we're truly on our own.

You have to see the irony, Diary. You do, don't you? They went to such extreme measures to secure their safety and well-being, blissfully unaware that already in their straw-hut midst is one who intends them more harm than any huffing-puffing wolf.

Chapter 1 — Tyler

"Little dude, that is not the way to do it. You can't rush these things. Pretend there's a school of mermaids swimming around out there. You don't want to fling that hook into a mermaid face or a mermaid breast. You want to lob it gently into the water so she'll notice it. She'll see the bait and swim up to it, all sexy and gorgeous with her long red hair streaming around her, then her luscious lips will latch on to it. When you feel that tug, that's when you go Rambo on her. Jerk the rod to set the hook. Got it?"

Tyler spoke to the fourteen-year-old standing next to him on the beach. The water looked like celadon silk, the late morning sky was an azure canvass painted with wispy horse-tail clouds, and the temperature was already a balmy ninety degrees.

"You just described The Little Mermaid. You want me to set a hook in the mouth of Disney's most beloved princess? What kind of monster are you? And a *Rambo* reference? Are you eighty?"

Tyler laughed. During college at the University of Florida, the movie star smile in the handsome face had compelled most members of the Zeta Tau Alpha sorority to drop their lacy panties. He doubted that many of those nubile young ladies were alive now. The Zetas were known for their blond hair and long legs, not their brains, and the scattering of survivors seemed to register very high on the intelligence scale.

"Never mind about Rambo," he said to the boy. "Just remember what I told you. You're smart. You can do this."

"For sure. But I'm a lover, not a fisherman," Kenny said, slipping into Tyler's surfer-dude accent. Tyler wasn't sure if the kid did that without thinking or if he were being made fun of. Kenny was one intelligent kid. And it was hilarious to hear a short, nerdy black teen emulating his speech pattern.

"Lover? Really? Have you even kissed a girl yet?"

Kenny smirked and waggled his eyebrows. "I'm not the kiss-and-tell type, pervert. Go bag your own woman."

"For sure, man. Just know that if you have any questions about...that kind of stuff...I'm here for you."

He had become attached to the orphaned teenager these past few months. There were a lot of brainy people in the Colony — himself included — but Tyler often wondered if Kenny weren't the smartest of all. When the boy had wandered onto the island while the bridges were still intact, he had been near-starving and suffering from PTSD. God knew what he must have witnessed out there in Mad Max Land. Tyler had offered up one of his bedrooms with the understanding that his fostering was temporary; at twenty-six, he wasn't ready to be a parent. But in the process of getting some meat on the kid's bones, the two had bonded. There would be no need to pass him onto any of the other Colonists at this stage.

"Dude, I know about sex. I'm fourteen, not four."

"Right. Sorry. But I'm just saying, I'm here for you if you have any questions. There's a lot more to relationships and romance than just the sexual act."

Kenny rolled his eyes. "Seriously. Stop talking."

"Okay, okay." Tyler smiled. "I think you have an interested mermaid. Do you feel it? Look at your line skittering as you reel in. See how it's darting a little to the left and right? That's what you're looking for."

"I think I do feel something," Kenny said, too excited to resume surfer-dude speak. His normal voice often carried a post-puberty break — much to his dismay — and the accent was pure Brooklyn. "Fuckbucket! I think I caught one!"

"Hey, that kind of language will not cut it. You know Rosemary's etiquette law. Nothing worse than 'shit' or 'damn.'"

"I can't help it. I have Tourette's."

"Horseshit. That Tourette's business might work on the others, but not on me. You're such a weirdo for doing that."

"Not a weirdo. Fake Tourette's allows me to say shit I wouldn't otherwise get away with."

"Yeah, there's nothing weird about that at all."

"It's brilliant, actually," Kenny replied, reeling in what might be a decent-sized fish, judging by the sweat glistening on the kid's face as he struggled with the rod. "The benefits are twofold: I get to make snarky comments with impunity, and I also get sympathy because I have a 'condition.' With sympathy comes cookies. It's simple causation theory. Oh wait...let me dumb that down for you, blondie. That means cause and effect. Ladies feel sorry for me, I get cookies. Holy crap! I think I hooked Moby Dick!"

"Amberjack, subspecies crevalle, more likely. Let me dumb that down for you, Moriarty. You snagged a jack. That's what you usually get in the surf. They're decent eating when smoked or diced up in corn fritters."

"Why did you call me Moriarty? Isn't that the bad guy in *Sherlock Holmes*? I'm not a villain. I'm delightful."

"I called you that because you're an evil genius."

"Let's keep that between the two of us for now, shall we?" Kenny said with a grunt, pulling the fish out of the water and flinging it onto the sand.

"You got it, little dude. Yep, it's a jack, all right. Good job," Tyler said, removing the lure. "This is a small one. They'll get three times that size a half mile out. Let's take it up to the Love Shack and have them put it on ice. Maybe you can use your fake Tourette's to score some cookies for us both."

It was a five-minute walk from the shore to the Colony's common house, aka The Love Shack. In its former life, the building had hosted parties and social functions for those locals willing to pay the hefty annual membership fee; it was a beach version of a country club, but without the golf or tennis courts. And it didn't need them. The 180-degree views of the ocean to the east and the inlet channel to the south were magnificent. The second story wrap-around balcony was one of the best places on the island to catch a cool breeze. Inside the first-floor great room lay the nucleus of the Colony. Two commercial freezers, three refrigerators, a six-burner stove, several microwave ovens, and anything else that required electricity and was necessary for comfort and survival, including a serviceable collection of books. Nobody had power at their houses, not after the Solar Harvest when every panel in the area had been collected and installed here. Outside, a herd of 12-volt deep-cycle marine batteries stored the sun's energy captured by the panels; a dozen nearby inverters transformed it from DC to AC. Everything was connected — panels to batteries, batteries to inverters, inverters to the Love Shack. The result was a miniature power plant, and it was vastly more efficient than the meager electricity formerly produced at individual homes.

The decision to create the Love Shack had been a pivotal moment in the evolution of their cooperative community. They would all fare better if they worked together, just like those hundreds of solar panels that lined the roof and grounds of the communal building.

There was strength in numbers.

"Hello, gorgeous," Tyler said to one of the people standing at the stove. The kitchen folks usually did the cooking in the early morning or at night, when it was cooler. All the windows were open and the temperature wasn't unpleasant at the moment. By late afternoon it would be sweltering, just like everywhere else on the island.

"Howdy, handsome. Hello, little boy," the woman replied without turning. Charlotte hadn't seen the kid, but she knew he was there. The woman was a hillbilly ninja, with her partially toothless grin and her innate ability to know everything that was going on around her. It was a bonus that she was the best cook this side of Appalachia.

"How do you do that?" Kenny said to the woman's skinny backside. "And why do you call me a little boy? I ain't little where it counts. *Huge cock!*"

The combination of the fake Tourette's done in Charlotte's Kentucky accent was almost too much. He bit his lip and punched Kenny in the arm.

"Sorry about that, Charlotte. You know how it is with him."

The woman turned around while stirring the large stock pot. Thin lips twitched at the corners. Tyler could picture a corn cob pipe poking out of that mouth and a ramshackle cabin in the background. She might look like a country bumpkin, but that wasn't a euphemism for stupid. And while he suspected Charlotte might have been a deep-south racist in her former life, she had grown as attached to the nerdy black teenager as had Tyler himself.

"You brung me a fish, I see. Not a big 'un, but it'll do. Gut it, scale it, put it in a baggie with some water, then stick it in the freezer on the right. Not the other one...that's for everything that didn't come from the ocean. When you done that, come back and I'll give you boys some cookies. I baked a fresh batch this morning."

"Whoop!" Kenny said, darting a pointed glance at Tyler. He was out the door the next moment.

"He know how to gut and scale?"

"Yep. I let him do that string of pompano I caught two days ago. He did a good job."

Charlotte nodded. Whatever bubbled on the stove smelled delicious. Tyler thought again how fortunate their community was to have her. She could make seagull edible.

"He doing okay? I fret 'bout that boy. Ain't right for a child to go through all that by hisself." She waved the soup ladle in the direction of the mainland and the aftermath of the plague. "He ever talk about it?"

"Nah. I've tried to get him to, but he clams right up. Maybe sometimes it's best to leave sleeping dogs lie. Know what I mean?" he said, maneuvering to get a spoon into the pot.

"You're lucky I like you. Otherwise, you'd be missing some fingers right about now. Go ahead. Tell me what you think."

He could see okra and bell pepper floating in the rich broth, and something else that might have been looking right back at him. The spoon paused on its trajectory.

"Don't worry. Thems frozen oysters from the spring. I know better than to serve summer oysters, even though I never seen seafood until I come here. If you'd hurry up and get that oyster farm going, we'd have a lot more. You marine biologists sure do move slow."

Tyler smiled, then sipped the liquid heaven. "Oh my god. You're a culinary sorceress. As for the oyster farm, these things can take a couple of years. It took weeks just to get the cages repaired and in place, then seeded with the...let's call them 'baby oysters'...from the aquaponics tank. They'll still take another year or two to reach maturity. In the meantime, we'll still have wild oysters during the winter months. Patience, my dear." He kissed the bony cheek before heading out to check on Kenny.

As he stepped back through the main door of the Love Shack, he heard a popping sound, then shouts coming from the side of the island that faced the Intracoastal Waterway and the continental land mass beyond. The western side of their diminutive paradise had been secured in several ways. The first line of defense was staying out of sight. Colonists were discouraged from going to the west side where they might be seen from the mainland — if there were no visible inhabitants, there was no one from whom to steal food. Second, a discreet watchtower had been constructed in a copse of royal palm trees in which a sentry stood guard twenty-four hours a day. Third, a series of cadavers, long dead and past the smelly stage, dangled from wooden crosses near the shoreline, signaling a clear warning: stay away or this will happen to you. Their fourth line of defense for the persistent would-be intruder: a percussion tripwire installed near the water's edge. Anyone who swam or boated across the waterway and trudged upon the sandy beach of Jupiter Inlet Colony would encounter it. The tripwire wouldn't kill; its purpose was to announce a breach of their perimeter. The ball bearings from the shotgun shells had been removed, leaving the harmless caps that would explode with a loud pop when triggered.

"Come on, but stay behind me!" Tyler said, sprinting past the boy, who had already dropped the half-gutted fish.

"Should I arm my dart gun?" Kenny reached into the back pocket of his baggy cut-off shorts as he ran.

"No! I told you to leave that stuff at home. You could accidently hurt yourself or someone else with those things." The two sprinted down residential streets on their way from the Atlantic side of the tiny island to the Intracoastal side.

"You never know when there might be a pirate invasion. My wolfsbane darts are ready for those eye-patched, parrot-shouldered bastards."

"Put them away. Now."

"Damn it, you're pissing in my Wheaties again." He slid the gun back into its pocket.

"Where are the darts?"

"They're in a Tupperware container. Don't trouble your pretty head about them."

"You're a scary little bastard," Tyler said, as they jogged around a corner.

"You don't know the half of it. Hey, you're not supposed to say that word!"

They reached the western shore moments later.

"That's no pirate," Kenny said, as they approached two Colonists huddled next to a young woman. "She might be the Little Mermaid all grown up."

Chapter 2 — Rosemary

Rosemary was at her wit's end. If she didn't get the well treatment process off the ground soon, they would run out of potable water. July had been exceptionally dry and hot. They couldn't blame that on man-made climate change now that mankind had almost perished from the planet. Who knew if the damage had already been done prior to Chicxulub, though? What she did know was that the rain shortage wasn't normal for summer on the Florida coast, and it had thrown a potentially deadly wrench into the gears of their fledgling island community.

Before, you could set your watch by the brief afternoon thunderstorms which would blow up and disappear within a fifteen-minute period, dumping an inch of rain before they moved out. But that wasn't the case this year. As a result, their rainwater reservoir systems were empty, and residents were relying solely on Ingrid's well for their drinking water. Wells on the island were unheard of, but Ingrid was a far-thinking, suspicious, gloom-and-doom curmudgeon who had installed a 150-foot well on a section of her pricey real estate two years before the end had come.

And thank god she had.

The well water was pumped by wind power and then manually filtered and treated by hand in small batches using time-consuming, inefficient processes. At the current pace, people were already going thirsty. In her former life, Ingrid had used the water for irrigating her opulent tropical landscape. Its source was a surficial aquifer filled with undrinkable, salt-tinged brackish runoff, which is why she had also purchased a commercial-grade reverse osmosis system at the time the well was built...just in case. She had never even opened the boxes stacked in her cavernous garage. Now the well and its briny water were the only game in town.

And the old woman knew it.

"I realize the filter and carbon block must be changed out every twelve months," Rosemary said, keeping her tone reasonable.

"And the membranes every twenty-four months." Ingrid's silver cotton-candy hair was pinned to the top of her head, and the hazel eyes burned with intelligence above the perfect cheekbones. She had been no sun worshiper; her flawless, alabaster skin was an anomaly in an ocean of leathery brown Floridian retirees. The German immigrant must have been a knockout when she was young, Rosemary thought, and the woman's intellect rivaled her own.

"And when the time comes that they need to be replaced, how will that be done, hmmm? Since you people destroyed the bridges, we can no longer easily get to the mainland, where we might have been able to procure replacements." The German accent was faint. Most people might not notice it, but Rosemary did.

Rosemary noticed everything.

"We've been over this. We'll send a team by boat, just like we do when we need other things that we don't have here. As we've discussed before, the decision to destroy the bridges was not taken lightly, and it was voted upon. The majority of our citizens chose increased safety over easy access to the mainland."

"Hmmph," Ingrid replied.

"So what do you say?" The survival of their community depended on this cantankerous old broad. If she didn't acquiesce on her own, they would be forced to take extreme measures. She hoped it wouldn't come to that.

"What about the rain harvesting? My tank is still half full."

Rosemary sighed. "I told you. The communal reservoir is almost empty, and everyone's individual systems are the same. Your cistern is larger and there's only you to provide for. This must be the driest July on record."

The older woman made a clucking sound with her tongue. "Bunch of short-sighted idiots. They didn't build their collection tanks large enough."

Rosemary had realized more than a year ago that 'idiot' was one of Ingrid's favorite words, along with 'twit,' 'cretin,' and 'dummkopf.'

"Please, Ingrid. If we don't install the RO system on your well, people are going to become dehydrated. Sick people can't work. If we don't have workers, we can't grow all those fresh vegetables you love. Besides, we're providing you with a new battery-charging wind turbine in the bargain. That well will operate on solar-powered electricity instead of this dinosaur." She indicated the archaic windmill. "You'll be getting a free upgrade, compliments of Jupiter Inlet Colony. What do you say?"

"What I'm hearing is, 'Ingrid, we're going to start pumping out a lot more of your water, and oh-by-the-way, we need your RO system too. You weren't using it, after all.'"

Rosemary kept her expression neutral. She watched the still-lovely face as it struggled with the concept of sacrificing a significant piece of her own far-sighted preparedness to help others.

"Don't forget that in return, the community offers you security, companionship, and a much better variety of produce than you're growing in your little victory garden. Can you imagine going out to sea on a fishing boat? Or scaling a coconut palm for that milk you so love? You're no fisherman, and you're no tree climber." A sarcastic tone had crept in which did not go unnoticed. Ingrid was no fool. She had read the subtext of the speech: fish and veggies in exchange for more well water.

The old woman nodded. "Fine. I want Hector to oversee the work. Once it is in place, I want time limits on when people can traipse around my property. I don't want anyone here before eight in the morning, nor after eight at night. Agreed?"

Rosemary flashed her a smile. "Agreed. Thank you, Ingrid. We'll make this as painless as possible."

The old woman turned and marched back into her home, a house valued at ten million before the end of the world. Now it was a forlorn-looking, two-story dwelling on which salt erosion had begun its relentless assault.

There was a time when Rosemary fantasized about owning such an opulent house. It had been her goal before Chicxulub to breech the stodgy, old-money society of Palm Beach and make her fortune on its back. She had been running a long con when the end of the world ruined her plans. The bad news: she would never achieve that dream. The good news: she could now have her choice of any unoccupied multi-million dollar home in in the Colony.

The best news of all was that no one alive knew about her past.

Instead of the opulence she had previously desired, she had chosen for her new life a modest bungalow two blocks from the beach. She wasn't sure what that said about her, and she didn't care. She no longer struggled with the juxtaposition of her former life as a grifter and her current life as the leader of a small, post-apocalyptic community. Nobody's 'former' mattered now. All that mattered were the skills, expertise, and experience they brought with them. Rosemary possessed many useful talents, but foremost were her matchless intellect and her ability to get people to do what she wanted. Both served her quite well in this new leadership role.

A popping noise emanating from the west shattered her introspection. Her feet were already moving, sprinting toward the Intracoastal, before her brain had given them the order to do so.

An invader had attempted to enter their paradise.

Chapter 3 — Amelia

"You might be the most vexatious creature on the planet." The man who spoke was short in stature but leviathan in all non-physical ways. Blue eyes, bright now with anger, blazed from within the bearded face. The facial hair was a rusty Brillo-pad version of that which sprouted above. The follicular flames springing from the head seemed to defy gravity in their upward reach; it would forever remain a mystery to all who knew the man how such lofty heights were achieved in a world without hair-styling products.

"Perfect," the equally small woman replied. "If I can't be helpful, vexatious is the next best thing. And besides, extolling that I'm the most of anything on this culled planet isn't saying much. There are only a few million people scattered about the globe these days."

Amelia loved when Fergus smiled at her like he did now. The smile said: *I love all women, but I love you best.* And since he was the love of her life (but not her only lover), the smile made her feel special. Which of course she was, as were all those who had survived Chicxulub, the pandemic that had annihilated most of humankind. She and Fergus were especially so, however, as members of an ancient race that lived in what amounted to a cavernous hyperbaric chamber hundreds of feet below the nondescript plains of Kansas. The name of their home, *Cthor-Vangt,* translated in modern English to "Home of the Ancients." In the past, Fergus and Amelia (and others much older) had experienced historic events in person when they traveled up to observe humanity's progress. They had witnessed other momentous occasions from home, below ground, utilizing their *scythen,* an inherent talent similar to telepathy. All the ancients possessed the ability to *scythen,* but in various degrees, and a few of the people above ground could tap into it as well – they just didn't know it yet. The true nature of people like Amelia, Fergus, and their brethren who lived below the Great Plains, was unknown to the current race of humans. Perhaps the survivors wouldn't care if they knew, being preoccupied with the business of staying alive in their post-pandemic world.

"So we're at an impasse," he said.

"It would seem so."

She no longer braided her silver-shot dark hair into two side braids. Because of the balmy breezes and high humidity of Jupiter Island, she coiled one thick braid onto the top of her head and off her neck, where it had been making her sweat. She adored this gem positioned off the Atlantic side of the Florida coast, but it was damn hot and muggy in the summer. She could cut her hair short, but alas, she was a prisoner to some minor vanity...and also Fergus adored her long hair.

"You've been here six months now. I think it's time for you to go home. Every day that you linger is another day older. Don't you want to go home where your increasingly decrepit body will cease to age?" She gave him a sly smile.

"Decrepit, you say. That's not what you called me last night. I believe your words were, '*You magnificent stallion!*'"

"I said no such thing. But you're right. You outdid yourself last night. Now back to the matter of your leaving."

"I'm not leaving yet" Fergus said. "And you can't make me. I have been mentoring some exceptional people, and I'm not ready to abandon them. I intend to stay a few more months until I'm certain this group will survive on its own. I don't want to walk away at a critical moment and disappoint those who have come to depend upon me, and also those who have fallen in love with me and with whom I have fallen in love." The blue eyes became misty.

"Yes, I know how you felt about abandoning Dani and Sam, but it was for the best. Those two are quite capable. Perhaps better than most."

"Yes, yes. I just miss them."

"I know, darling. And I miss Maddie, and Pablo, and Jessie. Such is the nature of our existence: to mentor and teach, become attached to our students, then leave them with our hearts broken. It's not fair, but it is what we signed up for."

"True. So dearest, please allow me the pleasure of your company for a few more months. More significant than my selfish happiness, though, is the mentoring. Also, I'm working on a bitchin' tan. When I go home, I intend to look like a bronzed Greek god."

"More like a sunburned leprechaun."

Fergus pulled her into his arms. "So it's decided. No more nagging until at least October. Agreed?"

She sighed. "Very well. Come October though, the nagging shall commence in earnest. So let it be written...so let it be done."

"Aha! So you did watch some of those old movies. I thought you hated them. That Yul Brynner...now there was a manly man for you."

"He can't hold a candle to you, my love. What's on your agenda for today?" As she spoke, she shuffled around the ground-floor, ocean-front condominium which was Amelia's home now. She had made it cozy and inviting, despite no running water or electricity. Such was the reality of their new world. If Curly Sue the poodle had come with her, it would have been perfect, but the shameless hussy was in love with Bruno, a handsome German shepherd living with her dear friends Pablo and Maddie in Liberty, Kansas. Curly Sue had decided to remain with them; Amelia's *scythen* had told her as much. It was for the best. Amelia had barely managed to stay alive with only herself to take care of on the thirteen-hundred mile journey. Nothing would keep her from reuniting with Fergus — not miles, nor near-starvation, nor bad gasoline. She had made it to Florida and her beloved, and it had been worth the hardships.

Perhaps she would find another pet to take the poodle's place — a feral cat she could domesticate, or a homeless mutt nobody else wanted. Since she could never return to their below ground home with Fergus (having committed the unforgiveable violation of direct interference in a human conflict), she would make Jupiter Inlet Colony — a tiny section of land at the southern tip of the snakelike Jupiter Island — her home for the rest of her natural days. Why not make it as pleasant as possible?

Fergus stretched and yawned as he stood by the open window, allowing the balmy morning breeze to cool his sunburned face. The hot weather demanded he abandon his trademark army-green jacket, the one Dani called his 'magic coat' for all the useful items withdrawn from its mysterious interior. He now sported a sun-yellow Hawaiian shirt and some khaki cargo shorts; the type with a multitude of pockets.

The man loved his pockets.

"I think I shall see about the water treatment business. There's nothing more crucial to our little nuggets than having clean water."

"You just want to gawk at Rosemary's breasts. I don't blame you. They're magnificent."

"Yes. Yes, they are. But that's just a bonus. I want to talk to her about some other things too. The woman's mind is remarkable. She's an excellent leader for this colony. Next to you and Dani, I think she may be the most extraordinary female I've ever known."

"That's because you've never met Cleopatra, Sacagawea, or Katherine Johnson. I've conversed with all three, and Rosemary could hold her own with any of them. But back to her breasts..."

"Never mind her breasts," he said, irritated now.

Amelia smiled. She adored Fergus, even on the rare occasions when he became cross. She would never admit to him that she found his bushy red eyebrows especially adorable when they were furiously frowning – they looked like a pair of wooly bear caterpillars on a date.

"It's not me you have to worry about when ogling her bosom; it's her handsome partner who may not appreciate it. Just keep your eyes on her face and you'll be fine. Lucas is as muscular as he is good-looking. I'm fairly sure he could kick your ass, if he felt so compelled."

Fergus grunted, then nodded. "I believe you're right. Duly noted, my dear. I'll make sure my lust is well-cloaked. See you at dinner." He gave her a lingering kiss, then was gone.

Amelia felt a rush of happiness as she watched him through the window. He trudged down the sidewalk of their building, past the communal fire pit everyone in the complex used for cooking, then down a street running along a white sand beach. The ocean lay beyond, the water looking like turquoise glass this morning. When you could end your days here in paradise, who cared that you had given up eternal life? That lightness of being, knowing that she wouldn't live thousands of years, or perhaps tens of thousands, felt natural. Felt like a gift, even — the casting off of the burden of immortality.

"I think I will visit Hector this morning. I'm concerned about his arthritis," she said. She talked to herself often these days. It also felt natural and right.

She gathered her medical bag and a bottle of water. Here in her new home, she had continued her masquerade as a midwife. It was the role she had chosen for herself when she first met Pablo and Maddie in Arizona, and it suited her well. After all, she knew more about human anatomy and biology than most, having lived all those thousands of years. Still, it never hurt to expand one's education, so she had made several trips to the mainland's public library before they had destroyed the bridges. An impressive collection of medical journals populated the bookshelves in her living room. Since there was no doctor nor even veterinarian on the island, the task of keeping everyone healthy had fallen to her. She embraced it. With her considerable skills and knowledge, the talents of Fergus (for now), and a bit of luck, their tiny seaside community of fifty-two people would thrive.

She had committed to make it so.

Chapter 4 — Ingrid

Ingrid didn't consider herself a 'prepper.' She thought of herself as a pragmatic realist with a cynical view of government and humanity in general. Prior to the plague, she had known the country teetered on the brink of a horrific world-shifting event. Would it be societal collapse spurred by the crash of the financial markets? A terrorist attack on the nation's power grid? Natural disasters wrought by climate change? She had put all her eggs in the baskets of the former two, because her beloved island would not be the optimal place to live if the polar ice caps decided to melt completely. Since that wasn't likely to happen for several more decades, she dismissed elevated sea levels as a potential harbinger of the apocalypse; she expected it to arrive much sooner.

When the end did come, just as she had known it would, she wasn't surprised. She had been ready.

With any catastrophe, survival comes down to two things: water and food. Before Chicxulub, she had installed the well and an impressive rain collection system. She had also purchased commercial-grade reverse osmosis products and many years' worth of shelf-stable food, stored in a secret butler's pantry off the kitchen. The room had been modified for the purpose of hiding it; nobody but her, and now Hector, knew it existed. It hadn't taken long after the supply chains collapsed for her to develop an utter loathing for shelf-stable food. But it had kept her alive, barricaded in her mansion, until the world sorted things out. She was happy when the stench of rotting corpses diminished. The Colony's prior population had only been four hundred souls, many of whom were not full-time residents. When the end came, it took all of her neighbors. She had no idea why she had survived when almost everyone else perished; and because she could never know, she banished it from conscious thought. That is the nature of the pragmatist.

After some months, other survivors began migrating to her island home, recognizing the inherent security of living in a place that was only accessible by water and two bridges. Of course, it had been necessary to destroy the bridges to increase their safety, but it had broken her heart. How many times had she been stuck on the Beach Road drawbridge waiting for a tall-masted boat to sail down the Intracoastal Waterway below? She had such wonderful memories of this place...her island...her sanctuary before and after Chicxulub. She loved it like the child she never had. And while she had allowed Rosemary to take over leadership of her fiefdom – at seventy, she didn't have the energy for the job —

she intended to stay active in all aspects of their community. She felt it was her due as the oldest resident. And now, as a supplier of water to the colonists, her position as unofficial overlord to her vassals was strengthened. Water equated to life – not a small thing. And as long as she maintained the proper balance between 'imperious' and 'accommodating,' everything should be fine.

She was an old woman, but she was no fool. If they wanted her water, they would take it with or without her permission. But since Rosemary seemed determined to preserve the niceties of civilized society, they would continue to dance around each other in a subtle power struggle. In truth, it was more like a chess match, and she suspected Rosemary relished it as much as she did.

She heard a noise at her back door, snapping her out of her reverie.

"Hector, is that you?" Her raised voice echoed off the marble tile.

"Not Hector. It's your other Latino boyfriend, here to clean your pool and trim your shrubbery."

Ingrid laughed, waiting for the man to appear around the corner, her heart beating faster than normal. The thought made her feel both foolish and giddy. To have a wildly inappropriate affair with her gardener would have been scandalous twenty years ago. Now, it didn't matter who she slept with. And she very much enjoyed sleeping with Hector.

"Ahhh, you are a vision, my darling." The salt and pepper hair was still thick and lush. She admired it as he bowed over her hand, planting a kiss on her fingers. Most men Hector's age were either bald or well on their way to it. She considered it a symbol of his virility, since there was also nothing lacking in the nether regions.

"Why don't you move in with me?" she said, suddenly. The thought had just occurred to her. "It's absurd for us to keep up this pretense."

Hector's eyes opened wide in surprise. She adored the tiny flecks of gold in the chocolate brown irises. In her old life, she had never had a conversation with any of her landscape workers intimate enough to discern their eye color.

"I would not compromise your reputation," he replied in his accented voice. The sincerity was unmistakable.

"You realize how silly that is? Things have changed. Nobody cares who sleeps with me or anyone else these days."

"I care. It would be...unseemly."

"So we're just going to skulk around, continuing this illicit romance behind everyone's back forever?"

He pulled her into his arms, still strong from a lifetime of manual labor. "It makes it even hotter, don't you think?" He flashed a smile revealing white teeth within in the gray beard. "Now about that shrubbery..."

She laughed. "You're incorrigible. We just did it last night, and you already want more?"

When he kissed her cheek, she saw their reflection in the hallway mirror. His dark skin against her alabaster was so striking that it made her smile. Who would have thought the priggish, puritanical, mildly racist Ingrid would be carrying on like this with an illegal immigrant laborer? No one who used to know her, that was certain. It was never too late to become a better human being. She worked on it every day.

"We need to give your back a rest," she said, with some regret. "How is the arthritis today?"

"It is a little better. Amelia came by with a soothing balm. That is what the smell is, in case you were wondering."

"Amelia, hmmm?"

Hector laughed. "My dear, you have nothing to worry about from her. She is at least twenty years younger than us, and she has a boyfriend already. Trust me, she is not interested in this old Mexican."

"She doesn't know what she's missing."

"I think Fergus keeps her happy."

"He's an odd duck. There's something very strange about that man. And I don't just mean his hair."

"Never judge a book by its cover, *mi alma*."

"You're right. I shouldn't have said anything. But you have to admit, he's rather mysterious. One day, I'd like to get him alone and pick his brain."

"Is it me who should be jealous now?" He gave her bottom a gentle squeeze. She had an impressive derriere for a seventy-year old.

"Absolutely not. I'm devoted to my sexy gardener."

"And I am devoted to my white boss lady."

"Perhaps your back doesn't need a rest..."

"Shall we test the mattress in the Lilac Room? I think it is the only one that has not been christened."

"Excellent idea. Ask me in French though. And then Italian. And then Mandarin. And then Swahili."

Hector's grasp of language was extraordinary. He spoke a dozen different ones, including several African dialects she had never even heard of. He had recently revealed this fascinating talent which, she realized soon after, worked on her like an aphrodisiac.

Chapter 5 — Tyler

Tyler agreed with Kenny. The female sitting on the sand with her hands behind her back and a pissed-off expression on her face did look like a grown-up, real-life version of the Little Mermaid.

"Zip ties? Is that necessary, Lucas?" Rosemary spoke to the man who was in charge of all things security-related in the Colony. Lucas also happened to be Rosemary's boyfriend.

Tyler liked Rosemary both as a person and as the leader of their small citizenry; she was fair, candid, and one of the smartest people he had ever known — next to Kenny. He had yet to decide how he felt about Lucas.

"Err on the side of caution," Lucas replied in a Cajun drawl. He wore his signature Ray-Bans; the perfect nose and chiseled jaw were smeared with zinc oxide. Lucas was a man who had beaten Chicxulub and seemed equally determined to beat skin cancer. The sunglasses and buzz cut evoked images of every highway patrolman in every television series since the seventies. He hadn't ridden a motorcycle in his previous life, although he might have begun his career on one. When the end came, he had been a rising star in the homicide division of the New Orleans PD.

"She doesn't look dangerous to me," Kenny said. "She looks like a beautiful drowned rat. *Banging bitch!*"

Tyler punched his arm.

"Let's hear your story," Rosemary said. "What the hell were you doing swimming across the channel today when the current is so strong?"

"Trying to find food." The low, dulcet voice seemed at odds with the youthful face. She was stunning under all that wet hair and gritty sand.

"What's your name?"

"Zoey."

"Where are you from?"

"From the mainland, obviously."

Rosemary arched a shapely eyebrow. "Smart-assery will get you nowhere."

"I'm originally from Tallahassee."

"And where have you been living the past two years?"

Tyler watched the face pull down in a frown and the chin begin to quiver. He resisted the urge to wrap the bedraggled mess in comforting arms. Kenny's smirk told him the compulsion must have registered on his face.

"I've been on the road since my sister died, just trying to stay alive and find food. Decided to cross the peninsula and see what was on the other side. I hooked up with some people in Tequesta, but they were a bunch of psychos. I had to leave."

Tyler saw the skeptical expression on the face of the Colony's leader. He knew what she was about to say next.

"What a load of bullshit. You tell us the truth or you swim right back across that water. You have three seconds, starting now."

"Fine." The chin-quiver vanished. Sapphire eyes regarded Rosemary like a science experiment that had taken an interesting turn. One corner of the full mouth turned up in a lopsided grin.

Rosemary had seen through the poor-pitiful-me act.

"I'm a spy. I was sent here to surveille the area and report on any indigenous people and their defenses. Most importantly, I'm to inventory any food and provisions which may be appropriated, whether by stealth or by force."

"That sounds about right."

"But since I don't intend to go back to that bat-shit crazy group, you have nothing to fear from me. I wasn't lying when I said they were psychos. I only lied about the rest of it."

"You don't intend to go back? Then where will you go? North, up the island? We've placed land mines in that direction," Rosemary lied, "so probably not the best choice. Perhaps out to sea, then? We can provide you with a kayak, a gallon of water, and some dried fish. Lucas, please escort this woman to the Atlantic. Take the circuitous route, not by the Love Shack." She turned and began to walk away.

"What? Wait! I want to stay here. I was honest! I told you everything, and I didn't have to."

Rosemary stopped, then pivoted at half-speed. "Of course you had to. I would have known otherwise, and I would have had you restrained and confined without food or water until I got the truth. We don't believe in torture here, but we do believe in honesty."

"I won't go back there. I can't."

"I'm not asking you to."

"I want to stay here, with you people. I can tell you're...kind and good. Not like what's out there." Wet tendrils tipped in the direction of the mainland.

"You're not invited to stay. You're a liar and a spy."

"I'm neither. At least not under normal circumstances. I had to promise them I would do this mission so I could escape. I jumped through hoops and promised all kinds of revolting sexual favors just to be considered."

"Then why not explain all that in the beginning instead of the drivel you first gave me?"

The sodden red hair tilted to one side. "For one very good reason — you may have another spy already here."

Tyler watched skepticism mingle with alarm on Rosemary's face; watched her think furiously for a few moments before speaking. "Lucas, take her to our house, restrain and confine her."

Chapter 6 — Rosemary

"So much for staying under the radar," Rosemary said, plopping down on a bench next to one of five picnic tables positioned outside the Love Shack. The shaded area had become an informal meeting place for anyone feeling social at the end of the day. At the moment it served as an outdoor conference room for an impromptu gathering of the Colony's leaders.

She studied each of the half-dozen faces while Zoey's words echoed in her mind: *You may have another spy already here.*

"I can conduct a one-on-one interrogation of everyone," Lucas said. "I bet I can find out who the spy is pretty damn quick." He had removed the sunglasses, revealing unusual golden-colored irises. Those eyes were what had initially attracted Rosemary to the former New Orleans police detective, and there was no denying the confident "predator" vibe the man exuded — another turn-on. She had known where she would place him after a cursory interview soon after his arrival; she had also known he would be a handful.

So she slept with him.

There was no more effective method for controlling a man than through his penis. Once they were lovers, he settled into his role as head of security, and thus far he was doing an excellent job. It was a bonus that he was also generous in the sack.

She glared at him. "We're not going down that path, Lucas. We don't torture people."

"We do if they have bad intentions."

"Right. But we'd be torturing innocent folks in the process. I won't do that."

Tyler spoke up from his seat at the back of one of the tables. "Maybe this Zoey person knows more than she's saying. I think we should start with her." As a marine biologist, he was in charge of anything that involved the Atlantic Ocean and the Intracoastal Waterway, and since it was a position of some authority, he was also a key member of Rosemary's advisory board.

"Yes, we'll do that, and soon. But I wanted to get everyone's thoughts on the situation before we proceed." Rosemary took pains to at least give the appearance of a democracy. After winning the popular vote in a landslide a year ago, she had the final say in all matters. But involving others in her decisions fomented good will. Making sure people were happy was an easy way of extending her stint as Colony leader for years to come. It was a job she had grown to love, and she had no intention of relinquishing it. Just as she had been addicted to the adrenaline rush of separating rich people from their money, she was now addicted to the admiration and respect she received from her constituents. She would not fail them.

"She said 'maybe,' correct? That could mean 'maybe not' too, yes?" Hector said from the other side of the picnic table, where he sat next to Ingrid.

Hector and his horticultural knowledge were arguably the Colony's most vital resource. It didn't hurt that he was also a charming gentleman. Rosemary noticed he and Ingrid had become cozy, but she kept the observation to herself. Who cared if the two oldest citizens of the community were sleeping together? If it made Ingrid happy, it was beneficial to everyone. That cantankerous old broad could be exhausting.

"Yes, but we have to assume it's true, for our own sake, and we have to take steps to identify the person. Think about what would happen if the spy returns to the fold and relays every detail of our operation here to a bunch of hungry, desperate people. They would want to launch an immediate invasion. This," Rosemary gestured to the Love Shack and the hundreds of solar panels generating electricity on the sunny day, "is enviable. Who wouldn't want what we have? Fruit and vegetables and clean water, thanks to you, Hector. And Ingrid too, of course." The old woman narrowed her eyes at the hasty placation. "And the aquaponics facility, courtesy of Tyler, gives us a buffer when the wild fish aren't biting. We have created not just quality of life, but genuine sustainability. And we've done it in paradise. Good grief, if I wasn't already here, I'd want to invade."

"Who all knows about this alleged infiltrator?" Amelia asked. The tiny Native American woman was the closest thing to a doctor they had, and her wisdom extended beyond dealing with sick and injured humans. Rosemary often found herself asking for the woman's advice.

Rosemary said, "Lucas, Tyler, Kenny, and me. Lucas spotted her from the watchtower before she tripped the wire."

Amelia nodded. "It's my opinion that we keep this under wraps. The last thing we want is neighbor distrusting neighbor after we've all worked so hard to forge this community through cooperation, symbiosis, and harmony. It is quite a remarkable place, and if others knew about it, they would want it for themselves. There are evil, lazy, opportunistic people who would rather steal than build."

The last comment met with a round of nodded heads. Most of the Colony's citizens had come from somewhere else. After surviving the plague, they had lived through the collapse of modern civilization and its brightly-lit, law-abiding, well-fed world.

Starving people are capable of the worst atrocities.

"Exactly my point," Lucas said. "People will want what we have if they know about it. At any time, the spy could decide to go back to the mainland and report. Most of our security measures are for keeping people out, not for keeping folks in. We have to know, Rose. I know you don't like it, but there's no other way."

"Who's going to interrogate you, Lucas?" Ingrid said. It was no secret that the two disliked each other. "You've only been here a few months. You yourself could very well be the spy."

Lucas flashed the old woman a smile that would have melted most females under the age of eighty. "I'm no spy. And even if I had been at one point, I would have switched sides. I love it here."

"You have a point," Rosemary said. "If there is a spy, he or she could have made that same decision. Why would they choose to leave? Unless, perhaps, the Tequesta group had some kind of leverage."

"And that's why we have to assume the worst," Lucas replied. "The spy is here and intends to return with critical information about us. Maybe they're holding a loved one hostage. If I were in charge over there, that's what I would do."

Ingrid made a snorting sound of disgust.

Lucas ignored it and continued. "We have to interrogate the swimmer, at the very least. There's no point in waiting."

Rosemary nodded. "Yes, you're right. We don't all need to be present for the...questioning. Let's get on with our jobs. Hector and Ingrid, you two have a lot on your plate with the well upgrade. Please keep me posted. Tyler, the sea is perfect today. I assume you'll be taking out a small crew?"

The young man nodded. "Yes. I have a good feeling about tuna. I'll take Kenny and a couple of guys out on the *Celestial Seas*. We'll drop a few lures and see what happens."

They would likely be eating fresh yellow fin for dinner. When Tyler said he had a good or bad feeling about fish, weather, or anything relating to the sea, she always paid attention. He was young, but his education in marine biology and a lifetime of fishing with his father off the Florida coast made him priceless.

"I'll go with you, Tyler. If you don't mind," Fergus said.

It was the first time the red-haired man had spoken during the impromptu meeting. As with Amelia, Rosemary found herself going to him for advice more and more frequently. He knew a lot of things about a diverse variety of subjects, and she could count on him for a laugh during every conversation.

Amelia turned to Rosemary. "I'll go with you, dear. I'd like to be on hand if the young woman needs any kind of medical assistance." She darted a glance at Lucas.

Lucas rolled his eyes but remained silent.

"Very well. Tyler, remind Kenny that the spy business is top secret. Can we trust our little genius to keep his mouth shut?"

"Yeah. No problem there. But I'll talk to him again, to put your mind at ease." Tyler grinned. "Come on, Fergus. Have you ever gone deep-sea fishing? It'll ruin you for any other sport."

"As a consummate lover of women, I find that highly unlikely. However, it sounds vastly more entertaining than shuffleboard or Scrabble. I'm right behind you, captain."

Hector and Ingrid left too, heading back to Ingrid's house and the overseeing of the reverse osmosis system.

"Amelia, we need to let Lucas do his thing," Rosemary said after everyone else was gone. "He's a professional. He conducted countless interrogations during his career."

The petite woman scrutinized the former police detective with eyes that, like Rosemary's, didn't miss anything.

"Of course, dear. I'll just stay in the background in case I'm needed."

Amelia would not be brushed off so easily.

"Fine by me," Lucas said. "It's not like I'm going to waterboard this chick. Keep quiet, though. Please," he added after seeing a flash of anger in the keen brown eyes.

"All right then. Let's get this over with," Rosemary said, feeling a wave of fatigue. The morning had started out so nicely: she had perched on a piece of driftwood with a cup of instant coffee while watching a glorious pink-blush sunrise bloom above the Atlantic. Now, though it wasn't even lunchtime, she had three new problems to worry about: a spy in their midst, an untrustworthy would-be immigrant, and the threat of an invasion from the mainland.

Her day had gone to hell faster than usual.

***

Rosemary scrutinized every nuance of the scene before her. Lucas had positioned the female across the breakfast table from himself, just as she imagined he would have done in the bowels of the New Orleans police headquarters. Sunlight streamed through an open window of the modest bungalow they shared, near-blinding to the woman seated in its path. The interrogator's trick didn't seem to bother the suspect, though. Even with zip-tied wrists resting on the table, she seemed composed and relaxed.

Was the body language insouciance, bravado, or genuine lack of concern for her own well-being? Rosemary couldn't read her, which in itself was cause for concern. In her old life, she could have written a person's resume after spending ten minutes with them. This ability ensured success in whatever challenge she undertook, whether it was extorting gullible millionaires or leading a colony of post-pandemic survivors. The suspect sat within an invisible psychic fortress, impervious to Rosemary's talent. As a result, another demerit was added to the expanding 'Zoey' list.

"You're telling me the Tequesta people — the 'psychos' — don't have any kind of leverage on you? Sounds sloppy," Lucas said, then took a casual sip of tepid coffee.

"That's just what I call them. They have an official name, actually, like a freaking motorcycle gang. They call themselves the Tequesta Terminators. How lame is that?" Zoey gave him the disarming, lopsided smile from earlier. "I think the idea was that a scary name would intimidate outsiders. Maybe that works on some people, but not me. I was in the inner circle within a month after I blew into town. Easy peasy."

Rosemary noticed a pinky finger twitch on the wooden surface. She hid her own smile. The female had just revealed a 'tell.' She wondered if Lucas had seen it too.

"These people aren't the sharpest tools in the shed, but they're damn good at being bad-asses. They've managed to terrify everyone in a hundred-mile radius, stealing their stuff and demanding weekly tributes. The plan is flawed though, thus my decision to get the hell out."

"How is it flawed?"

"Because residents took off. It's not like there's a shortage of real estate now. People living in the area who were barely scraping by decided to haul ass, relocating in the next state over, or wherever else that wasn't close to the

Terminators. So the dumbasses ran off their indentured servants. They got greedy...classic blunder."

Lucas gave a slow nod. Suddenly, a blur of tanned skin streaked across the table, ensnaring the twitching finger. He bent it backward, then watched the expression on the face transition from smug to pained.

"How about the truth now?"

Rosemary stood by the front door with arms crossed, witnessing the interrogation. She glanced back at Amelia sitting on the sofa, noting the dark eyebrows drawn together.

"Okay, okay. Damn it, let go."

"We may be nice people, but we're not idiots. Don't make me hurt you, Zoey, because I will. I won't hesitate either. I'll do it before anyone can stop me. You get it?" Lucas lowered his face, leaning forward so he was a handbreadth from the young woman. He pressed the delicate finger another few millimeters.

Rosemary saw something pass between them. Understanding, perhaps — an unspoken warning sent and received. She didn't like the situation, but she had to let it play out. The safety of her people depended on getting to the bottom of this.

"Yes, I get it." The bravado had vanished. Rosemary saw candor now, perhaps even a willingness to cooperate. So she was surprised by the defiant words that came the next moment. "Now go fuck yourself."

The next sound she heard might have been the snapping of a chicken bone.

Chapter 7 — Tyler

"You don't look like someone who has spent a lot of time on a fishing boat," Tyler said.

"What, because I have this damn plastic string all in knots?" Fergus replied.

Tyler could see the man was getting frustrated. It was common for a novice fisherman to be overconfident. Fishing didn't seem difficult, and in truth, it wasn't. But he believed you either possessed the gene or you didn't. The rock stars of the deep-sea fishing world had been born near the ocean and spent every spare moment on the open water. Sun-bleached hair and bronzed skin were hallmark cards for the pros, but there was more to it than just time and experience. The exceptional ones, like Tyler himself, felt a profound connection to the sea and all the creatures gliding beneath her surface.

"Anyway," Fergus continued, "this isn't a fishing boat. Fishing boats look like the one on *Forrest Grump*."

"That was a shrimp boat."

"Oh, right. Well, this isn't anything like what I expected. She's a real beauty. If she were a woman, I'd call her Michelle Pfeiffer, the most beautiful woman that ever lived."

"She is magnificent, isn't she? I mean, for an older vessel. She's a 37-foot Tartan *Jocale* with a self-tacking jib and a 150 percent reacher on the forward fuller. That gives you maximum sail area off the wind...easy to manage short-handed."

Tyler laughed at the bewilderment on the small man's sunburned face.

"Meaningless sailboat stuff. Dad got her for a wing and a prayer after the stock market crash in '08. Before her, we had an 18-foot Hobie cat. I still have the cat. I take it out when I'm by myself. I've been sailing my whole life. I think that makes me the luckiest person in the world."

Fergus smiled at him; or rather, small even teeth abruptly appeared within the wiry crimson beard, and the blue eyes twinkled. Tyler smiled back.

"Brokeback Mountain!"

"Shut up, Kenny," Tyler said, with a laugh. "Remember our little talk earlier? About the outbursts?"

"Yeah, yeah. I have a disability, man. I can't help it," Kenny said, using his own voice for once. The quick mind was focused on the task at hand: catching more fish than anyone else on the boat. The mimicking stopped when the kid was distracted, and glimpses of the former innocence were visible instead of the usual sardonic expression. Seeing those glimpses made Tyler happy and sad at the same time.

No child should have to go through what Kenny had.

Tyler noticed Fergus eyeballing the youngster, and realized what was about to happen. The little fellow wouldn't be the first one to try to one-up the Colony's resident genius.

The weather was perfect; winds streamed out of the south at ten knots and the sky was cloudless. He breathed in the salt air and waited for the inevitable entertainment.

"*Brokeback Mountain,* eh? What the heck do you know about movies like that? You're what, eleven? I bet your acorns haven't even dropped."

Kenny snorted, working the 150-pound test line like a professional angler. "I'm fourteen, and I bet you're an expert on hairy gonads. Does the carpet match the drapes, Fergus? I'm asking for a friend. The color of your hair does not fall into the visible light spectrum. I'm guessing L'Oreal's Scarlet Harlot No. P67."

Fergus's beard twitched furiously. "I'll have you know the magnificence before you is one hundred percent natural from head to toe. I've had no enhancements of any kind...no hair color, no Botox injections, and no penis enlargements. That last one would be superfluous. I didn't even wear braces on my pearly whites as an adolescent."

"Hmmm...your adolescence. When was that? The Mesozoic Era?"

Tyler saw a flash of something on the older man's face, then it was gone. Had Kenny gotten a rise out of him?

"You're an interesting little crayon gobbler, Kenny. I think I'll let you live. For now." Fergus's tone was convivial, and the beard still twitched.

Kenny snorted again, but was too distracted with the fish on his line to respond.

Tyler felt relieved. He very much wanted these two to get along. In a short time, they had become some of his favorite people in the colony. He wanted them to be friends.

"Looks like you got a mack, little dude. Maybe a fifteen-pounder by the look of your line."

"A mack?" Fergus asked.

"Yeah. Mackeral tuna. Decent eating, although a yellow fin would be better. We'd have to go farther out for that monster."

"Then what are we waiting for?" Fergus said. "Can the *Celestial Seas* aka the *Michelle Pfeifer* handle going farther out?"

"Oh yeah. We could sail around the world in this baby. And the weather is perfect. You guys up for going out to the dark blue?"

Kenny replied with a "Whoop!" The other two deck hands, newcomers to the colony but experienced sailors who were also identical twins, gave the same response.

"Okay, boys. Let's bring home a few hundred pounds of sushi!"

At that moment, Tyler felt a modicum of genuine happiness for the first time since the plague. Memories of the loved ones he had lost and other, more recent problems were banished from thought. He felt the normal exhilaration he always felt when sailing, and also something else — a tentative sense of well-being.

He knew it wouldn't last, though. It never did.

Chapter 8 — Amelia

"Rosemary, can you run to my condo and grab my other medical bag? It's the one with the finger splints. I didn't think I'd be needing them," Amelia said with a venomous glance at Lucas.

"Sure. Lucas, come with me. The suspect is secure, and I think you need to take a breather."

She watched them leave then directed her attention back to the young woman who was tied to a La-Z-Boy in the small living room of Rosemary's bungalow. Zoey studied her in return. If she were in pain, as she should be, she didn't show it.

"That didn't go well," Amelia said.

"What would you expect from a Neanderthal? Such crude tactics. I doubt he was any good at detective work." The auburn hair was dry now and it framed a heart-shaped face that could have graced the cover of a romance novel. She might have been one of the loveliest women Amelia had ever seen, and she had seen many in her very long life.

"How did you know he was a police detective?"

Zoey gave her an indulgent smile. "Come now. We both know it's obvious. I'm sure Rosemary knew it too the first time she laid eyes on him. We three are members of a rather exclusive club, yes?"

"What club would that be?"

"You know. I can tell you're a highly advanced creature, just like me. Just like Rosemary, and a few others I've run into since the end of the world."

She nodded. "Yes, I believe you're right. Although Lucas isn't the simple brute you've decided he is. Don't underestimate him."

Zoey continued, eyes narrowed now, "There are a lot of exceptionally intelligent people these days. More on average than there were before. Don't you agree? But there are others too that, despite their intriguing talents, are bat-shit crazy. I find the situation fascinating. How fortunate to be alive during this most exciting phase of human evolution. If there are any anthropologists still kicking, I bet they're having a field day."

Amelia only blinked in response.

"So what's to be done with me?"

"I'm not sure. It'll probably be put to a vote."

"I'm not buying the business of sending me off in a kayak with some dried fish. That was a pretty good bluff, though. I think she meant it on some level."

"How do you know she didn't?"

"Because I'm a threat, and she's smart. She can't allow me to leave. There would be no stopping me from paddling south of the island, then right back up the Intracoastal to Tequesta. It would be difficult, but not impossible. No, she has to either kill me, keep me a prisoner indefinitely, or become convinced that I will stay of my own volition. For that last part to happen, she must believe that those psychos don't have any leverage on me."

"But they do."

"It's not what anybody thinks."

"Why not just tell all this to Lucas before he broke your finger? Here, let me see it. I imagine it's quite painful by now."

A shrug of the slender shoulders. "Because I hate macho douchebags like that guy. Rosemary would have been smarter to question me herself, but she's following her own protocols, put into place for the purpose of making people feel important...that their opinion matters. You and I both know Rosemary is queen bee. She can pretend it's a democracy — and probably everyone believes it — but nothing happens here that she doesn't orchestrate or manipulate in some way, including any would-be votes."

Amelia didn't respond. Instead, she gently grasped the injured hand, leaning in to get a closer look. When her fingers touched the pale skin, she felt an electrical jolt. The images picked up by her *scythen* through the physical contact were confusing and disorienting, unlike any she had experienced with other survivors. Surprise escalated further when she saw that the broken pinky was neither swollen nor bruised, and the slightly askew angle was straightening of its own accord right before her eyes.

***

"We can't let them hurt her or banish her," Amelia said to Fergus the moment he walked through the front door of their condo. He was more sunburned than when he had left, and he wore a huge grin.

"And we can't let her go back to Tequesta," she added.

"Hello, darling. I had the most fabulous afternoon. Sailing is thrilling! And who would have thought I could enjoy the company of men so much? It's not as delightful as being with women, of course, or you specifically, although today came close."

He tried to pull her into his arms, but she gave him a gentle push.

"Not now, love. We have a situation."

"What is it? Colony politics?"

"There's always that, but this is different. Zoey, the swimming intruder from this morning, is gifted."

"Everyone is gifted these days," he replied, serious now after her *scythen* had telegraphed a deep unease.

"She has *langthal*."

As with *scythen*, there was no translation for the word. It conveyed an ability to self-heal, or in extraordinarily rare cases, the ability to heal others. The dynamic force of *langthal* abided in the DNA of a handful of humans, inert, until it was stirred to life by injury, disease, or the touch of an afflicted person.

"Indeed? Strong, is it?"

"Yes, from what I can tell. I watched her broken finger mend itself before my eyes."

Fergus plopped down on a sofa that had been upholstered with sunny yellow fabric. It made his sunburn and hair appear even redder by contrast.

"You're right about keeping her safe, then. We'll have to conduct the tests covertly. It won't be easy if she's a captive."

Amelia nodded, distracted, and then noticed his appearance. "I should see if she can alleviate your sunburn. You do realize that skin cancer isn't a myth."

"The *Cthor* can fix me up if it comes to that."

She made a clucking sound with her tongue. "Perhaps as a test, I could see if Zoey can heal Kenny's Tourette's."

Fergus chuckled. "That wouldn't be an effective test. He's faking it, you know."

"I should have known. During one of his outbursts he called me a salacious squaw."

"I assume you touched the female? What did your *scythen* reveal?"

Amelia shook her head. "That's the other thing. Her output is so imprecise and confusing, I couldn't get a clear picture of what's going on inside that exceptional brain."

"So she's brilliant in addition to the *langthal*?"

"Yes. We have much to discover about this one. It very well may be that we have a recruit on our hands. In which case, you'll have to be the one to harvest her. I know that's not your usual objective while above ground, but it can't be avoided. There are no others like us in the vicinity, and I'm no longer welcome back home. No, no, I don't want to hear it. I'm quite happy here. Which raises another point: this is my home now — will likely remain my home for the rest of my life. If that young woman has nefarious intentions toward this Colony and its people, we have to put a stop to them."

"Right, and protect her as well. I feel like a plate-juggler."

"Your face does look rather clownish at the moment."

"You are a hard woman, Amelia, my love. Fortunately for you, I am a hard man at the moment." Crimson eyebrows waggled.

She laughed. "Very well, just a quickie, as the people call it these days. Then we have to strategize. I'm sure we're not the only ones doing that at the moment."

"Rosemary?"

"Yes. She's remarkable too, though not in the way recruits must be, as you know. Still, it will be fascinating to watch those two interact."

"Mmmmm...I'm picturing it now. Rosemary's creamy café au lait skin and ebony ringlets lying on a pillow next to Zoey's tantalizing tendrils and pale Irish deliciousness."

"Your fantasy sounds like a Maxwell House commercial."

"So you admit you watched television before the plague."

"Not as much as you, love. Now let's get down to business," she said, then shed her clothes in the sunlit room without a hint of self-consciousness.

Chapter 9 — *Cthor-Vangt* and Jessie

Hundreds of feet below what was once a thriving wheat farm in rural Kansas lies the home of the *Cthor*, the highly-evolved, virtually immortal ancient race of humans responsible for bioengineering the current one and all those before it. They had been creating and destroying people for millennia in their never-ending quest to perfect them. The survivors of their most recently orchestrated plague were barely meeting the minimal standards to allow their continuation. People were smarter, taller, and more physically attractive than the last population, but there had been unexpected and unwanted psychological pathologies present in a significant percentage.

Defects were never part of the plan, but they did happen.

The *Cthor* created ever-evolving human populations by utilizing the harvested DNA of gifted recruits. But sometimes the process backfired. In an effort to cultivate a stronger mental and emotional constitution, they had introduced a genetic molecule that had mutated in some, resulting in the opposite of the desired outcome. Many current survivors suffered from some form of personality disorder or psychosis. The conditions ranged from mild Asperger's and low-spectrum autism to malignant narcissism and full-blown schizophrenia. Some exhibited characteristics of sociopaths and psychopaths. But because there were also shining examples of desirable traits — Jessie's *langthal*, for instance — as well as a marked increase in overall intelligence, the *Cthor* had decided to let it play out. For now.

There was always the possibility, however, that they would bring about another earth-cleansing event and start over.

***

Jessie understood what she was now, but it didn't make living below ground any easier. She missed seeing the sky full of puffy sheep-like clouds; missed feeling the soft desert breeze on her skin; missed smelling flowers, and rain, and campfire smoke, and all the other smells that made her smile. Nothing down here smelled like anything. It was just plain old air. Most of all, she missed Amelia and Gandalf the Grey, the kitten she'd had to leave behind in Liberty, Kansas. Animals were not allowed in *Cthor-Vangt*.

So she was excited at the prospect of her first mission with Tung. He had taken Amelia's place as her mentor, and he would be the one to escort her the first time back up. Nobody got older while in *Cthor-Vangt*, but once above ground, the clock started ticking. Tung would be sacrificing himself to aging so that Jessie could also get older. Others would have to take turns, of course; she needed to add seven years to her current nine, and her new mentor was unwilling to age that much.

Children had been non-existent here until Jessie's arrival, so there had been much discussion among the *Cthor* and the other residents both ancient and young — gifted ones like Jessie herself — about what to do with her. The solution was to send her up once per year and stay for six months each time. While doing so, she would be involved in the mission objective of the adult who escorted her. It would mostly be observing people, but she had been told to expect an occasional 'harvesting' too, just as she had been harvested. The notion was very exciting.

Harold wanted to come with them, but he was already old, so his request had been denied. He wasn't happy about it, but rules were rules. The biggest rule in *Cthor-Vangt* was you had to do what the *Cthor* told you. If you didn't, you would get kicked out. That's what had happened to Amelia when she meddled in matters she wasn't supposed to by using Jessie's *langthal* to cure Maddie of the poisoned medicine she had been given. It had been a big no-no, but she had done it anyway. That's how much Amelia had loved her adopted family: she had sacrificed immortality to save Maddie, which in turn had saved Maddie's baby, and Pablo's sanity; he would have lost his mind if Maddie hadn't survived the poisoning. The sacrifice made Jessie love Amelia even more. She missed her so much and hoped someday to travel to Florida for a reunion.

"We're not going to Florida," Tung said in the archaic language Jessie was still learning. She was a fast learner but it was pretty hard. It was much more complicated than English. He had picked up her thoughts with his *scythen*, which was better than everyone's except for the *Cthor* themselves.

"I still don't understand why I can't go up just for a month or two," Harold said.

She liked Harold. He had been harvested in London around the time she had been harvested in Kansas. He was a doctor but not the medical kind, and he was an expert in languages, so he didn't have a hard time learning this new one. She was a little jealous of that, but he didn't have some of her gifts, so it balanced out. He was very smart though, and sometimes they would sit and talk about their former homes. As the two newest recruits, they had much in common, even if he did come from across the ocean and spoke with a funny accent.

"Why can't we go to Florida?" she said.

"Because we need to go to a location that is as safe as possible," Tung replied. "We don't want to put you at risk while you're up there. At the same time, I hope to get some work done too. There's a community in Tennessee that I'm considering. I'm still collecting data on the area. Once it's been approved, we'll leave."

"Why isn't Florida safe?"

"Hurricanes, floods, tornadoes, wildfires, alligators. And people. There's a group of undesirables we're keeping an eye on."

"I've never been to Tennessee. It doesn't sound nearly as fun as Florida."

Tung smiled and his eyes twinkled. That meant he was amused, and it was always a good thing when Tung was amused.

"I could be quite useful, you know," Harold said.

"I realize that, but there's not much I can do."

The three sat in one of the small conversation rooms. All the furniture in *Cthor-Vangt* contained material that conformed to the body of the person sitting in it at the time. Jessie didn't understand how that worked, but it was pretty cool. Sometimes she would sit in strange positions just to put it to the test. No matter how weirdly she sat — one time she even did a headstand — the furniture adjusted to her body and made her comfortable. Those chairs and sofas would have been a big hit in her old world; they were something right out of a science fiction movie, the kind her father used to watch on television.

"You could ask them again. Or let me ask them. I'm the superior advocate since I'm invested in their decision. My *scythen* is exceptional, you know. They'll hear me."

That was another thing she liked about Harold. He always said exactly what he thought and you were never unclear on where he stood about things.

"Very well. I wouldn't get your hopes up, though."

Jessie wasn't surprised when, thirty minutes later, happy noises came from one of the many corridors. Sound traveled well here, although she might have heard it with her *scythen,* which improved every day.

Chapter 10 — Ingrid

"I don't trust him," Ingrid said. "Not one bit. There's something...reptilian about that man."

She spoke to Hector over an elegant candlelit table. They had enjoyed a delicious dinner of grouper cooked on the backyard fire pit and prepared Spanish-style with stewed tomatoes from Ingrid's secret canned-goods stash. The bell peppers and onions came from her own garden. She was able to grow a few vegetables herself, but the variety available from the community farm was far superior. Still, there was much to be said for self-reliance.

"Is this something from your dreams?" Hector asked, dabbing at his mouth with a cloth napkin, another tradition from her old life that she insisted on carrying forward into this one.

"No, it's just a feeling. You don't sense it? That nagging sensation in your belly? The bristling of the hairs on the back of your neck?"

"No, I do not. Clairvoyance is your talent not mine. I will stick with languages and gardening and leave the mumbo jumbo to you."

Ingrid regretted telling him about her sixth sense. She had done so in a weak moment soon after they became romantically involved. Because of his love of learning and his open-minded nature, she assumed he would believe her; she had cited many examples of when she had known or seen something simply by touching a person or an object. So she was surprised when she saw a cloak of disbelief, perhaps even disdain, unfurl on his face. His reaction was the reason she had told so few people about it in her former life. She had been considered Jupiter Inlet Colony's resident curmudgeon, and she had not wanted the title of 'nut-job' added to her resume.

She sighed. "Very well. I'll keep my mumbo jumbo to myself then."

"Perhaps you should talk about this with Tyler. Birds of a feather, they say."

She nodded. She suspected Tyler possessed a similar gift — another of her gut instincts — but they had yet to discuss it. Now might be the time. "I think I will. Do you mind cleaning up?"

"Not at all. It is my pleasure, and also a way of partially compensating for my meal. Consider it a down payment. I shall pay the outstanding balance later tonight, through a different form of manual labor."

Ingrid giggled, then kissed the swarthy cheek. "I won't be long. *Hasta luego, mi amor.*"

"Excellent! Those Spanish lessons are coming along nicely. *Después, mi pollita.*"

"Did you just call me a little chicken?"

"Indeed I did. It is a Mexican term of endearment."

"If you say so."

She grabbed a few items from the butler pantry, stuffed them into a fabric bag, and then navigated the uneven flagstone sidewalk with care — a broken hip at this stage would likely be a death sentence. When she reached the level blacktop of the residential street, she turned east toward the small house that Tyler shared with Kenny. The sun was setting and the air was beginning to cool, although she didn't feel discomfort from the hot summer temperatures like most — it was one of the few benefits of getting old.

The door opened just as she had raised her fist to knock. Tyler greeted her with a warm smile.

"What a nice surprise. Come in. We just finished dinner and are sitting out back. The breeze is best there. Would you like to join us?"

"Yes, that would be lovely. Do you have any stemware? I brought a Bordeaux." She withdrew the bottle from her bag and showed him the label with a coy smile.

"I think I just fell in love with you. How do you feel about younger men?"

"No offense, but I doubt you could keep up with me in the sack."

"My loss then. Head on out while I finish inside. I'll bring the glasses in a few."

Tyler had picked one of her favorites in the neighborhood — a modest Key West design in pale butter-yellow. Unlike some of the new McMansions that had sprung up on the million-dollar lots during the final years before the plague, his house was understated elegance and pure Floridian. She stepped through French doors and into a landscaped yard. Kenny sat in a patio chair, fiddling with an ancient Rubik's Cube.

"Good evening, Kenny," she said with genuine warmth. Ingrid liked the boy, despite his embarrassing outbursts — or perhaps because of them. They could be quite entertaining.

"Hey, Ingrid. What's shaking?" He didn't take his eyes off the toy. She remembered those things from the eighties and wondered where he had found it. His fingers were a blur as they clicked the colored boxes. She realized the next moment that he was completing the puzzle by making all sides a solid color, scrambling them up again, and then — in what was probably record time — returning them to the 'solved' state.

"At seventy, everything shakes in one way or another."

Kenny snorted, then said, "What's in the bag, girly? Chocolate to seduce me? I can be bought, just so you know. And I'm cheap."

She chuckled, then withdraw a Hershey's bar from the satchel and handed it to him. The teenager wasn't psychic; he was observant and intelligent. He could assemble pieces of information in a situation then deduce the outcome with lightning speed. She thought of him as an African-American Sherlock Holmes in miniature.

"Well done. That chocolate should still be edible, although I can't say it will be as delicious as it would have two years ago when I bought it."

"No worries. There's no such thing as bad chocolate, just like there's no such thing as bad sex," Kenny replied taking a bite.

"And how would you know that? You're only fourteen, young man. I hope you haven't been picking up hookers on the docks again."

"Only ones that are missing all their teeth," he said with an exaggerated wink.

Ingrid laughed. "You're incorrigible. I think that's why I like you so much. Listen, I need to talk to Tyler in private. Can you skedaddle somewhere for a half hour or so?"

"No problem. Just be gentle with him. He may look like Brad Pitt on the outside, but on the inside, he's Angelina Jolie...all fragile and spooky."

"What does that mean? Is something wrong with Tyler?"

"I'm just being a smartass. It's what I do. Catch you later, Ingrid."

He was gone the next moment. She took a seat at a wrought-iron table thinking about the comment. Tyler emerged from the house soon after.

"Will these do?" He waved two Baccarat cut-crystal glasses as he walked toward her.

"Perfect. The former occupants of this house had excellent taste."

"I agree. There's something to be said for having nice things, but only if acquiring them doesn't become an obsession."

Ingrid smiled. She had committed that very transgression in her old life. In hindsight, she realized how lonely she had been as a result of her priorities. But that was the old Ingrid. The new, improved version was determined to live out her days as a kinder, gentler human being. It wasn't always easy.

"I assume there's a reason for this unexpected visit?" Tyler prompted, taking a sip of the wine. "Oh, man. That is heavenly."

She nodded, studying the handsome young man; frank, emerald-green eyes gazed back at her. She could imagine the tanned face with the sparse golden facial hair on a billboard or a movie screen. He must have had many girlfriends before the end, but he didn't exude the typical conceit that went along with being a womanizer.

Fragile and spooky on the inside. She hoped she hadn't misjudged the young man.

"I'll be blunt. I have some...talents...that I don't share with just anyone. I want to talk about them with you, though, because I sense a kindred spirit." She paused, gauging his reaction.

"You mean your ESP?"

"How do you know about that? Did Hector tell you?"

"Of course not. Hector's the man. He would never betray a confidence."

"You're right. I know that."

"It's like you said. Kindred spirits."

"So you have them too? Psychometry? Precognition?"

"I wouldn't go that far. I just get feelings about things and about people. I don't read too much into it, though."

"You don't seem especially interested."

"It's not that I don't find parapsychology interesting, but it's not hard science. I'm a marine biologist. I'm a facts guy. I believe in what I can see and touch."

"But you admit you get feelings, which brings up my reason for coming here tonight. Lucas."

It was Tyler's turn to frown, then she saw a façade of neutrality unfold on his face. "What about Lucas?"

"My gut is telling me not to trust him. And now that we know there could be a spy in our midst, I'm even less inclined to do so."

"Are you aware of any questionable behavior? Witnessed him doing anything unethical or immoral?"

"No, of course not," she said, irritated now. "If I had, I would have gone to Rosemary. But there's the crux — she's sleeping with the man. Makes it tricky to have a discussion with her about him."

"I understand. But until you have tangible evidence of some kind of wrongdoing, I think it's best to keep your thoughts about Lucas to yourself. He's good at what he does, which makes us all safer."

"What does your gut instinct say about him?"

"Not much. I think what I'm picking up is residual cop vibes, you know? An authoritarian thing. That's all I'm comfortable saying at the moment. I hate to speculate, and I hate to gossip."

She nodded. "Very well."

"You're a sweetheart, Ingrid. No matter what anyone says."

She laughed, breaking the tension that had crept into the conversation.

"Tell me more about your sixth sense. That's what you call it, right?" he said.

"Yes, that's what I call it." She smiled. "It began in my late teens after a minor head injury. I had been riding a scooter in Munich without a helmet. Crashed somehow — that part is a complete blank — and woke up in the hospital with a concussion. The dreams and the feelings started soon after. I tried discussing it with my parents, but they were staunch Roman Catholics. That kind of talk came straight from the devil."

"Dreams? Like precognitive dreams?"

"Yes. I began having a recurring dream that I have yet to interpret, and also dreams of events before they happened. Small things, big things. I dreamt of Black Monday — one of the more significant stock market crashes — a couple of months before it happened. Prior to the event, I was able to position myself financially to make a killing. That's how I came to live here."

"So you're a self-made gazillionaire?"

"Yes. Well, was. An impressive portfolio doesn't carry the weight it once did." She laughed. "My father was a professor at Ludwig-Maximilians, a university in the heart of Munich, and my mother was a housewife. I never married. I had always known I wanted to live in this part of the world...felt drawn here. So I moved to Florida in my thirties. Not here, of course — I couldn't afford the real estate even back then when it was much cheaper. So when I had the dream about the stock market crash, I borrowed some money to invest. Thankfully, it worked."

She remembered the thrill and terror of borrowing two-hundred-thousand dollars at an exorbitant interest rate, then risking it all to buy high-quality stocks that had bottomed out. Her gamble paid off. With additional future savvy investments, she became one of the wealthiest women in the state.

"That's a huge risk to take based on a dream."

"Crazy, I know, but by then I trusted them. Knew that what I had seen would come to pass."

"What's your recurring dream about?"

She gave him a mysterious smile. "That I will not discuss. It is of a romantic nature."

"Did you dream about Chicxulub?"

She hesitated, considering how to frame her response. "Yes and no. I knew something terrible was going to happen. I dreamt of it in metaphorical terms...dreams that were nebulous and confusing. It was as if my sixth sense couldn't dial in the manner in which the end would come, but knew that it was imminent."

"Did you tell anyone?"

"Who would I tell? What would I say?"

Tyler nodded.

"Since I couldn't warn people, I decided to take steps to assure my own survival. That foresight is the reason you're enjoying a fine Bordeaux this evening."

"My palate thanks you. This is the best wine I've ever had, but that's not saying much. I'm more of a Corona and lime guy."

"As a German, I can't begin to express my horror at the thought of drinking Mexican beer with fruit. I'd love to hear about your life, Tyler. Before. What was your family like? Was there a special lady?"

The young man's facial responses were immediate: first sorrow followed by a quick mask of indifference. The juxtaposition would have been fascinating to watch if not for the genuine fondness she felt for him.

"I'm sorry. I shouldn't have asked such personal questions. It was inappropriate of me."

The mask was still in place when he answered. "I just don't want to talk about that stuff."

"I understand. Just know that if you ever do want to talk, I'm here for you. I'm an old crab who doesn't make that offer to many folks, so don't take it lightly."

"Are you two finished with your May-December belly bumping?" Kenny said, stepping around the corner of the house.

"Oh my god, dude. Don't be so disrespectful."

"Kenny, don't listen to him. You can say anything you want to me. I find you refreshing. The world could use more people like you, even if you are a handful sometimes."

"You got that right, sister," the teenager said, squeezing his crotch.

Tyler closed his eyes in embarrassment.

Ingrid chuckled. "I've overstayed my welcome. I better be getting home before full dark when all the ghosts and goblins come out."

"Thanks for the wine. Would you like me to walk you home?"

"No, I don't need an escort, thank you. I'm old but not decrepit."

When she stepped through the French doors, she heard Kenny whisper, "She's hurrying back to her geriatric Valentino."

"Shut up, Kenny."

She smiled, then headed home to Hector.

Later that night, she dreamt of a hurricane spinning in the Atlantic Ocean — a malignant, colossal beast of swirling salt water and dreadful, unrelenting winds. It was unquestioningly one of her precognitive dreams. When she awoke from the nightmare, her heart pounding, she had much to think about. And since sleep would elude her until daybreak anyway, she had hours to ponder what she would do.

Chapter 11 — Anonymous

Dear Diary,

Today was arduous. It is a test of my patience to be in the presence of imbeciles. Still, there are fewer idiots now than there were before. So there's that. Which brings up some tantalizing questions: Why are people these days so intelligent? So attractive, their facial symmetry near-perfect? Why does no one talk about it? Do their powers of observation not mirror their intellects?

Genetics was a field of study in which I self-educated, as I have done in many areas, but nothing explains how a global plague that occurred virtually overnight could have produced survivors that are above average in intelligence, beauty, talent, and perhaps in other ways too. I'm only now beginning to suspect this goes deeper than I thought, but I'm not ready to speculate on that yet. There's more thinking to do before I commit ink to your hallowed pages.

On other matters, I managed to refrain from killing anyone today. It wasn't easy. The desire lurks always just below the surface, niggling and scratching at my thoughts. Soon I'll give it free rein, but the longer I hold off, the better. I would prefer my nature not be discovered until I'm ready to leave on my own terms.

Until then, I'll continue to play the benign person they all believe me to be. It's fun, yet challenging, pretending to be something so antithetical to my true self. Perhaps because of that, I'm able to stave off my impulses. I'm not self-deluded though. I know I can't last much longer.

Perhaps an animal to tide me over for a bit. It's midnight and the moon is waxing gibbous — perfect conditions for a night hunt.

Yes, I think that's an excellent idea.

Farewell, Diary. I shall report on my nocturnal activities tomorrow…

Chapter 12 — Rosemary

Rosemary rarely found herself in a quandary about anything. Between her honed instincts and quick mind, she could produce a solution within seconds of analyzing a problem. So the issue of what to do about Zoey vexed her. It didn't help that the female was imprisoned in the spare bedroom. She hated the thought of her lovely little bungalow being used as a jail.

As she lay in bed listening to the sound of Lucas breathing, she pictured a flow chart of the issues. Next, using imaginary lines, she connected them to viable solutions, then below each solution more lines linking them to potential negative and positive outcomes. Most people would have to sketch all that out on paper or plug it into a spreadsheet, but she could picture it as if it were a chalkboard filled with data.

In terms of the Zoey conundrum, however, there were no good scenarios.

Rosemary did not trust her. Nor would she send her off in a kayak just to paddle back home and report in. Even though the would-be immigrant had been denied access to the Love Shack, the community garden, and the aquaponics facility, there was still plenty of information an intelligent person would have observed: the Colonists were well-fed and healthy; they were organized; they had devised a clever system to protect their island, which meant they may have assets worth protecting.

If the roles were reversed, these pieces of information alone would have been enough for Rosemary to launch an invasion. And if the situation in Tequesta were as dire as Zoey claimed, the 'Terminators' had nothing to lose.

She took a deep cleansing breath and began her nightly, sleep-coaxing exercises. She focused on the sporadic breeze wafting through the open window and the balmy ghost fingers fondling her skin. She noticed a shaft of moonlight illuminating the white face of the wind-up alarm clock on the bedside table: two minutes past midnight. She breathed in the scent of Lucas — sweat and sunblock lotion — and found it comforting. She had never been in a long-term relationship before, and even though she had no delusions about the longevity of this one, she would enjoy it while it lasted. From two blocks away, she could hear the music of the sea — waves ebbing and flowing, pulled and pushed by the moon. The calls of night birds; the croak of frogs; the chirps of crickets; the rustle of lizards scuttling through the shrubs outside her window.

Then, piercing the tranquility, she heard the sudden screech of an animal in agony, abruptly ending the next moment. She wondered if one of the feral cats had just become dinner for an enterprising coyote.

The circle of life.

She had just begun to get sleepy when movement at the door sent a shot of adrenaline through her body. Her hand was already clutching a seven-inch hunting knife before her mind registered that she had removed it from its drawer.

Zoey stood in the doorway, shrouded in shadow and holding a finger to her lips. Then she lifted empty, open palms: *I mean you no harm.* Then the crook of a second finger: *Come with me.*

When Rosemary rolled off the bed onto the floor, Lucas didn't stir. Her bare feet made no sound on the ceramic tile. She pressed the knife to Zoey's throat the next second, ushered her back out the door, and then closed it behind her with a soft thud.

Zoey whispered, "Can we talk? Just us girls? If I wanted to hurt you, I would have done it by now."

Rosemary studied the female. The cocky smile was back. The sapphire eyes, illuminated by ambient starlight, were frank and compelling.

"Outside."

A minute later the two women stood in the backyard. Like Tyler's, it had been elegantly landscaped before the end of the world, and when Rosemary took ownership, she continued to maintain the gardens. She hauled waste water from the fishery for the plants during the July drought. The extra work was worth it; this place was her sanctuary. Even washed in the sepia tones of night, the foliage was enchanting...her shadow flowers.

"How did you get out of that room?" she whispered.

Zoey gave a derisive snort. "Please. Zip ties? Deadbolt locks? Hardly a challenge."

"What do you want?"

"I want you to see that I'm on the level. I could have surveilled your operation and then headed back to report before you even knew I was gone, if that had been my goal."

"So I'm to assume this little stunt proves you're harmless?"

"Of course not. I'm no more harmless than you. But it does prove that my motives are not to spy on the Colony then spill my guts to the Terminators. I want to stay here, like I said before."

"It's that simple?"

The lopsided grin. "Is anything simple these days?"

Rosemary didn't respond. She was plugging this new development into her mental flow chart. Zoey had just proven she could escape confinement, that she didn't want to return to Tequesta, and that she didn't plan to murder the leader of the Colony, nor the head of security who had injured her earlier. All this tipped the scales in her favor.

"What do you have to offer?"

The grin broadened. "I majored in meteorology in college and minored in environmental science. The end came before I finished my degree, but I learned more than any of you people know."

"We don't need a weather girl to tell us it's hot in Florida in July."

"It's not about stating the obvious; it's about predicting the future so we can prepare for it. I can do a hell of a lot with a Farmer's Almanac and a barometer, and I have tons of data stored up here in my noggin." She tapped a temple. "Resource conservation, clean energy, effective composting techniques."

As with the hibiscus and oleander blooms, darkness had drained the vivid color from Zoey's long hair, but its splendor pervaded the gloom. The woman was gorgeous, an asset that had doubtlessly been exploited for years.

"I can be useful here. And I can be a team player."

"Funny. You strike me as a prima donna."

"Just like you."

She did see much of herself in this young woman. Unlike Zoey, though, Rosemary concealed her disdain for vapid and stupid people. It served no purpose to make others feel inferior.

"Oh my god! I thought you looked familiar. You're that broad that scammed those old rich people out of millions several years ago. I remember seeing your photo on TV. They never caught you! You were lighter back then. Now you look less like Halle Berry and more like Angela Bassett."

Rosemary's worst fear had just materialized. She did not want to kill Zoey, but she could not allow the Colonists to know about her past.

"Don't worry. I won't tell a soul. Just let me stay and I swear on my mother's grave I won't breathe a word about it."

Rosemary felt the weight of the pivotal moment; felt time slow down; felt herself teetering at the crossroads of two paths: morality and self-preservation. She could dispose of this woman and be done with multiple problems at once.

Seconds ticked by as she considered her options. A hushed silence had invaded her sanctuary, as if Mother Nature herself held her breath in anticipation of a decision.

"If you cause one iota of trouble here, I will have Lucas bury you alive. And I mean that literally. Are we clear?"

A slender hand reached out, grasping Rosemary's.

"Deal. I promise, Rose, you and I are going to get along famously."

Perfect, white teeth gleamed in the moonlight. The young woman's hand felt warm — almost feverish — in her own. The fine bones were delicate, but there was strength in them, and no apparent discomfort from the broken finger. Perhaps the young woman had a high tolerance for pain. These days, that could be a helpful commodity.

"We'll see about that," Rosemary said.

Chapter 13 — The Love Shack

"Quiet down, please. We have a long list of topics to discuss." Rosemary stood at the head of one of the picnic tables.

Firelight from a half-dozen tiki torches reflected off the faces of more than fifty people. The Atlantic Ocean, indigo this time of night, lay behind them. Upon its placid surface was painted a glistening snail trail, extending from the shoreline to the luminous celestial body that had created it — a mystical avenue used by otherworldly folk for traveling from earth to heaven and back again. It was an appropriate backdrop for a gathering that somehow radiated an eerie, preternatural undercurrent.

Everyone felt it. Something was different tonight. Something was off-kilter or askew. Something was either missing, or a new something, and not necessarily a good something, had been introduced into their community. Those who were tuned in to their 'gut instincts' or their 'sixth senses' felt it. Others fidgeted on the wooden benches or shifted from foot to foot on the sandy grass.

Life in the Colony had been clicking along smoothly for months. They were due for some bad news.

"I'm sure you all have heard about the intruder from yesterday morning. Zoey, please stand up." All eyes turned to the young woman, who was not wearing her usual cocky grin. She appeared serene and compelling while doing a slow, graceful pivot so everyone could get the full measure of her beauty. Several of the men, and perhaps some of the women, fell in love at that moment.

"Zoey swam here to escape an unsavory group in Tequesta. After a thorough vetting by myself and Lucas, we have decided to accept her into the Colony, if she can garner a majority vote. She has some skills, including a knowledge of meteorology and environmental science that could benefit us. She's also young, healthy, and strong. A show of hands, then. All in favor of her staying?"

Rosemary counted more than thirty upraised arms. The next part was superfluous.

"All in favor of her leaving?"

Ingrid and a handful of others raised their hands.

"Thirty-seven for staying, fifteen for leaving. Congratulations, Zoey. You're in. Now on to other business." Rosemary glanced down at her legal notepad. It was only for show; all the bullet points had been stored in her brain. "A feral cat was found dead on the beach this morning."

"Nobody brung it to me!" Charlotte said, emerging from the Love Shack. She carried a tray of cookies and began passing them out. Her comment evoked a round of laughter.

Rosemary smiled. "I don't think cat would taste very good."

"That's what most folks think about possum or squirrel. Them folks would be wrong." She finished serving the cookies and sat down in an empty seat next to Zoey. The contrast was striking.

"A dead cat isn't the problem. We know there are predators here on the island, but it wasn't killed by a fox or a coyote. It was eviscerated and skinned with surgical precision, then left to be nibbled on by scavengers."

A murmur went through the crowd.

"Surgical precision? How can you tell?" Hector asked from his seat next to Ingrid.

Lucas replied, "Because I've seen it before. I investigated a serial killer case a few years back where the suspect was a doctor. He used a scalpel to remove the skin and organs. The cat we found was just like it."

Louder voices now.

"Are you saying we have a serial killer here?"

"Of course not." A hint of annoyance flirted with Rosemary's normal composure. "There could be any number of explanations. Does anyone have any information about this event? Not conjecture. I mean have you seen anything out of the ordinary, specifically in regard to animals?"

"I saw Amelia luring one of those cats into her condo," an older man said. "And she's our doctor, so she would have the know-how and equipment to do something like this."

Amelia sat next to Fergus on one of the benches. She turned slowly to face the man who spoke. "I'm an animal lover, Howard. I thought I would adopt one of the wild creatures and give it a home. I don't own any scalpels, and I don't know how to conduct surgery. However, I'm quite skilled at setting broken bones and stitching up wounds, as I did on that nasty gash you sustained tripping over barbed wire. I believe I could manage a skinning and an evisceration if I wanted to, though. I'm contemplating it even now."

"Barbed wire? What were you doing at the northern perimeter, Howard?" Lucas said. "You know that area is off limits."

"It's none of your business what I was doing there," the man snapped.

"Wrong. It is our business," Rosemary said. "We have rules for a reason. They keep people safe. You pull something like that again and you're out."

Her statement evoked a wave of head nodding. There were few restrictions on personal freedoms in the Colony, but staying away from the northern perimeter was an imperative. They had cordoned off the uppermost part of the island from their small southern Colony as a means of managing less area. It was rumored Rosemary had used some of the leftover explosives from the bridge demolition for land mines placed on the northern side of the barbed wire; the Colony leader would neither confirm nor deny it.

Rosemary had evicted people for less than an unapproved perimeter breach.

"The new girl arrived yesterday morning and last night we have a mutilated cat?" It was Ingrid who spoke this time.

"She was restrained and in my house last night."

"Hmmmph. Well, it's rather suspicious, if you ask me. We've never had anything like this happen before, and within a day of her appearance, bizarre events begin occurring."

"There was just the cat, Ingrid. Please, people, let's not start pointing fingers. I only bring this up because you have the right to know what happens here. Let's stay calm and keep our eyes open. Report any curious behavior to me or Lucas ASAP. Got it? Okay, next business."

For an hour, the minutiae of survival on the island was discussed.

The henhouse was doing well; egg production was at an all-time high, thus the cookies everyone enjoyed that evening. Charlotte said they would soon have enough chickens to sustain their egg requirements and still have some left for slaughtering. People were delighted at the prospect of chicken instead of fish for a change.

The reverse osmosis system and the new wind turbine had been installed on Ingrid's well and should be up and running the next day, according to Chin, the Colony's engineer. The strange little man rarely spoke, and when he did his accent was so heavy that few people could understand him. He avoided eye contact with everyone and lived alone in a house set off by itself. If not for his skill in assembling the solar farm that provided electricity to the Love Shack,

Rosemary might not have allowed him to stay. He was a weirdo and a loner, but he was a genius with anything mechanical or electrical. You could put up with a lot of weird for someone that knowledgeable.

Tyler's aquaponics were thriving. The tilapia were breeding well, and there were plans to add watercress and arugula to the kale and spinach being cultivated. With Chin's help, Tyler had built an impressive system utilizing PVC pipe and plastic troughs. The power necessary to run the pump was supplied by a few of the precious solar panels. The set-up was ingenious, low maintenance, and sustainable in Florida, unlike other parts of the country where the temperatures were too frigid in the winter months.

Hector had some bad news to relate about the community garden. "We have a beetle problem. A Mexican bean beetle problem."

"Border bandit bean beetle!"

Tyler punched Kenny in the bicep. "Sorry."

"Anyway," Hector continued, unperturbed — everyone was eventually a target for the teenager, "they can be very destructive. As you know, we have some pesticides, but they are not as effective as they were two years ago. And they are not safe for our food. So we must look to natural solutions. First, we will replace the pole beans after the harvest with bush beans, which are less susceptible. I have some seeds in my collection. Second, we will move the lemongrass plants next to the crop that is infected. Their fragrance is a deterrent. Marigolds are also said to be useful in this way, but I do not have those seeds. If anyone has seen marigolds, please let me know so that we may transplant them. Third, we must pluck every one of those nasty creatures from the plants and squish them. This is labor intensive and I will need a few extra hands to get the job done. The last thing we want is for the infestation to spread. The soybeans are at risk, as are the squash and tomatoes. Do not be fooled by the cute appearance of this tiny monster which looks like a yellow ladybug. If you see one anywhere, destroy it immediately. On a more pleasant topic, I would like to cultivate a new area for an additional grain crop. I am considering oats. Does everyone agree with my choice?"

"It doesn't matter if everyone agrees," Rosemary said. "You're the expert. If you think oats would be best, that's all I need to know. Your seed collection must be extensive."

Hector nodded, squeezing Ingrid's hand under the wooden table. "I am grateful to have access to a variety of other seeds which we will introduce at a later date...perhaps avocados and pintos. This border bandit has a hankering for guacamole and refried frijoles." Hector winked in Kenny's direction.

"Very well. We'll send some people for the bug-squishing tomorrow. Next order of business..." she began, then was cut off mid-sentence by a flash of lightning, followed by the rumble of distant thunder.

It had been five weeks since the last measureable rain event. A steady soaking would be welcome — a thunderstorm with damaging winds or hail would not be.

All eyes were riveted to the burgeoning of night-gray clouds on the horizon.

"Chin, do we need to cover the older solar panels? I know only the newer ones are weatherproofed."

The small man lifted his nose up to the sudden breeze. Everyone waited. Chin dispensed words like a poor kid spending his hard-earned allowance.

He shrugged, and in his heavily accented voice, said, "How I know? I not a goddamn weather man." Then he clucked his tongue and gave a dramatic roll of his eyes.

Kenny snickered.

Ingrid snorted.

"Fortunately for you all," Zoey said, standing, "I am a goddamn weather woman. Well, almost. I only lacked a few credits to get my degree." She withdrew something from the pocket of her oversized jeans. She had brought no clothing on the swim over from the mainland, but she had sealed a few items in a Ziploc bag and tucked them into a backpack. Rosemary had gone through her possessions, of course, so knew what the young woman now held in her hand.

"What's that? A barometer?" someone asked.

"Yes, an aneroid barometer. Cool, huh? Now stand back, folks, and let me work my magic."

The device looked archaic — a sentimental artifact decorating the mahogany desk of a retired naval commander. The young woman fiddled with the gadget's two hands for the next few moments. She licked her finger and held it to the gusting wind.

The delicate brows frowned. More fidgeting with the instrument. Finally, she glanced up to a sea of anxious faces.

"The barometric pressure is at 29.80 and falling rapidly. The wind is out of the south and heading east. That's pretty much the perfect combination for severe storms."

"Like a hurricane?"

"No, duh. We'd have different conditions in advance of a hurricane...rain bands, etc. I predict this will an ass-kicking thunderstorm. High winds and hail are likely. Possibly a tornado."

"Chin?" Rosemary said to the small man.

"Yeah, yeah. All hands on deck. Plywood ready, next to Love Shack. I show what needs covered."

As everyone began to leave, Rosemary stopped Fergus from behind with a light tap to his shoulder. He spun, taking his time shifting focus from the eye-level breasts up to her face. By the time his attention was where it should be, his bright blue eyes were glazed and he wore a happy smile deep within the rusty beard.

She sighed. "Have you ever considered covert ogling? It's all the rage these days."

"Yes, yes. I've been meaning to work on that. Can't have jealous boyfriends knocking out these flawless teeth. How may I be of service to you? Just know that there is nothing — absolutely nothing — of a sexual nature that I would deny you. I just want to make that clear. Amelia and I have an open relationship, you know."

She blinked slowly.

"Sorry. There is very little of anything I would deny you, even if it is not of a sexual nature. What may I do for you?"

Rosemary scanned the picnic area. They had the place to themselves.

"I'm taking a chance on you, Fergus. I assume you're not the spy sent from Tequesta."

"You have assumed correctly. Of course, I would say the same thing if you had assumed incorrectly. Spies are notorious liars."

"I don't think you're a spy, and we need to know more about those Terminators. God, that's such a stupid name. I want to send someone...a trusted someone...over there to infiltrate their operation. Something tells me you fit in wherever you go. I think you could pull it off. You're quick on your feet, and you're smart. And you're a man. According to Zoey, that group is testosterone-driven. Think you could fake being a misogynistic jerk?"

"A few women from my past would suggest those traits come naturally to me."

"It would be dangerous."

"My dear, I don't merely laugh in the face of danger. I whip out my impressive wanker and piss on it until it drowns a lingering, ammonia-scented death."

"I'm serious."

"Then I slice it up into chunks, throw it on the grill, and feed it to lesser men for lunch. *Then* I laugh. And not just an amused chuckle, but a full-throttle, deep-chested guffaw."

Another slow blink.

"Very well. I accept your assignment. I've always wondered how it would feel to be a double agent. When shall I depart?"

"Tomorrow morning before dawn. You know how to avoid the trip wire. Take a kayak from the beach. Don't let anyone see where you're going."

"Except Amelia, of course."

A pause. "Yes, I guess that can't be helped. The fewer people who know about this mission, the better. I'll tell everyone that you're on a quest for replacement filters for the reverse osmosis system. That will make Ingrid happy."

"A kiss for luck then? You may be sending me to my death."

Rosemary kissed the wiry cheek with genuine affection.

"Fergus, do not get yourself killed. I've grown rather fond of you."

"I shall do my best." He was gone the next moment.

The Colony leader stood next to the picnic tables, watching the night sky. An electrified fork appeared suddenly, followed by an ear-splitting boom. The storm was almost upon them.

***

"Get out of here, now! I don't want you getting hit by hailstones!" Lucas yelled to Rosemary.

They were the final two Colonists standing in the solar panel field, exposed to the storm's ferocity. Everyone else had sought cover. Blustery gusts and a torrential downpour weren't as concerning as the frozen precipitation that had joined the party moments ago. With every passing second, the hail was growing larger, heavier, and more deadly. Pea-sized ice pebbles smacked against tender flesh with a malevolence that seemed intentional. Even worse, it was transitioning to the size of walnuts, capable of fracturing a skull. If it got much bigger, the plywood shields covering the precious solar panels could be compromised.

"We're almost finished!" she yelled back.

The gusts, coming every few seconds now, felt purposeful and determined — the focused energy of a spiteful god.

They struggled to haul the final piece of plywood to the farthest corner of the field. As they situated it on top of the panel, stretching the bungee cords around its girth, a frigid ping pong ball smacked against Rosemary's shoulder.

"Shit, that hurt!"

Lucas's feral grin didn't improve the situation.

"I told you. Now, let's get the hell out of this."

They ran together back to the porch overhang of the Love Shack. The remaining Colonists who hadn't fled to their homes stood huddled and miserable. Initially, when the deluge began, it was met with euphoria; rain water in a drought is a gift from the heavens. When the hail began, the elation vanished. Nothing good ever came from a hail storm.

"This is bad, Rosemary," Hector said in a quiet voice. She barely heard him through the din of the screaming-banshee wind and the hailstones crashing against the ceramic tile roof. "I know you are concerned about our electricity, but I am worried about the crops."

"I know, Hector. I am too."

There was nothing else to be said.

Chapter 14 — Tyler

"Most of the tilapia are fine," Tyler said to the small group that had gathered next to the aquaponics facility the next morning. It was located in the backyard of the empty house next to his. The hail and wind from the previous night had destroyed the kale and spinach. Leafy greens were fast growers, but it would still be weeks before the Colonists would enjoy a salad. Or fresh vegetables. The group had already inspected the community garden, where a similar tableau told a story of devastating loss. The lovely morning and achingly blue sky were at odds with the grim mood.

They faced a food shortage similar to that which had immediately followed Chicxulub almost two years ago.

"Next time we should install some kind of netting to cover everything. A sheer, protective fabric of some sort that would allow sun to reach the plants," Rosemary said.

Tyler noticed she spoke in the tone that meant she was dismayed but would not let it to show. He had heard her use that voice many times in the process of establishing their utopia. Looking at the destruction was gut-wrenching — so much hard work wiped out by a fifteen-minute hailstorm.

"Where would we get such fabric?" Ingrid asked. She was subdued this morning. Thoughtful, even, unlike everyone else, who looked shell-shocked. "The nearest Hobby Lobby is in Tequesta. I don't see us braving those ruffians for a bit of cheesecloth."

Hector said, "Not cheesecloth. Cotton rots. We would want polypropylene that allows sunlight to penetrate but is tear and puncture-resistant. It is quite expensive...well, it was. But we should be able to find rolls of it in any well-stocked garden center. I know of several on the mainland. We would need much yardage to cover everything."

"All that's fine and good for the future, but it does nothing to help our current situation." Ingrid's voice was gentler when she spoke to Hector.

"People are going to be hungry," Rosemary said. "We still have fish and eggs and some frozen vegetables at the Love Shack, but they won't last long. We'll have to initiate a rationing system. We've been spoiled, and now we have to tighten our belts."

There was resolve on the attractive face. Tyler did not envy Rosemary her position as Colony leader. Hungry people could be total assholes.

"Tyler, bring your bicycle trailer and come with me, please." Ingrid's abrupt directive interrupted his dismal musings.

"What are you planning?" Hector's smile indicated he knew what was about to happen.

"Don't worry your pretty head. Tyler? Chop, chop."

Five minutes later, he stood gawking at a treasure trove of non-perishable food. He had been in Ingrid's house many times and had never noticed the secret door that led to a butler's pantry. The doorway had been disguised before the end came, she explained. The room was spacious, its four walls obscured by Ingrid's foresight: shelf after shelf of canned goods; stacks of plastic buckets labeled 'emergency food'; columns of bagged rice, dried beans, rolled oats, salt, and sugar. Intricate metal scaffolding scaled the fourth wall, built for the purpose of holding wine bottles at the correct angle to keep the corks moist. He counted more than a hundred.

"Holy crap, Ingrid."

"I know. Impressive, isn't it? Now, here's the deal. You can't tell anyone. About the extent of it, I mean. I want to help, but I don't want people to become dependent. Do you understand? This would all be consumed very quickly if we got lazy and didn't grow and catch and raise our food."

"I understand, and I agree. Nobody else needs to know about this. Hector knows though, right?"

She nodded.

"Okay, this stays between the three of us. Allowing others to know would put you in danger. I'm not saying I don't trust everyone here, but..."

"Yes, I know what you mean. So we shall say that I just had the things that we'll load on the trailer today."

Tyler looked at the still-lovely face, noting the delicate wrinkles around keen blue eyes and parchment skin taut on the jawline. Ingrid was a force of nature — especially for a seventy-year-old. And she was doing a Goliathan kindness, sacrificing for the greater good. As with her well, which was producing an abundance of water, she would again save their collective asses.

"You don't have to do this."

"I don't. But it is the right thing to do. I have always put myself before others. You should know that about me. But it's never too late to improve oneself. This old leopard is changing her spots. I've decided to go with Madras plaid instead. It's perfect for summer." She winked. "Now let's get some food loaded. I imagine Charlotte can create some culinary wonders with this stuff. God knows I can't."

Soon after, Kenny helped Tyler unload the food at the Love Shack under Charlotte's supervision.

"There are fifty-three residents, right?" the teenager said, standing idle now with arms crossed. He had been unusually quiet while carrying all the cans, buckets, and bags inside the building.

"Yes. Zoey makes fifty-three."

"All that food we just unloaded will last two months, by my calculations."

"You have a computer for a brain?"

"Pretty much."

"Seriously, how did you come up with that?"

"I kept a running tally as we unloaded it, then factored in portion sizes, caloric content, and the Colony's population. Elementary, my dear Watson."

"Is that an accurate assessment? Or are you just pulling a number out of your butt?"

"The pearls dispensed by my butt are superior to the vocalized so-called wisdom of some."

Tyler laughed. "I believe you, little dude."

"It's accurate. Trust me."

"I hope it's enough."

"It has to be." Charlotte stood in the kitchen doing prep work for the evening meal.

"I'm guessing no more cookies for a while."

"Yep. They was a luxury. We was all gettin' a little spoilt anyway. We'll be fine. I ain't gonna let anyone go hungry."

She turned her back and began gathering pots and pans and placing them on the commercial stove.

"Come on, Kenny, let's take the *Celestial Seas* out and see if we can't haul in a marlin."

"Is that the creature with the pointy nose that could murder a little black dude who's trying to hook it?"

"Yes. Try not to get stabbed by a fish today."

"I should bring my poison darts in case we encounter pirates."

"No, leave those at home. I mean it. You're going to hurt yourself with those someday."

"What's this?" Charlotte said, using a manual opener on one of the #10 cans.

"Kenny is an evil genius. He found fentanyl tranquilizer darts and a gun for shooting them at some vet clinic in North Carolina. Then he collected wolfsbane on his way down here from Brooklyn. Now the little monster has a poisonous tincture for his delivery system."

Everyone carried knives or other weapons now — it had become common practice after the plague when survivors would kill you for a protein bar. Of course, someone with Kenny's intellect wouldn't be satisfied with just a switchblade or baseball bat. The kid could hit a target the size of a dessert plate from eighty feet away.

"That don't sound like a good idea to me," Charlotte said. "Seems like a boy could get some of that poison on hisself."

"Or a boy could be mighty careful with it, meanin' folks don't need to fret about it." Kenny's impression of Charlotte's Kentucky accent was flawless.

"Keep it up. When there's cookies again, I reckon there might not be enough for smarty-pants boys."

"Oh, gorgeous," Kenny said, switching to Tyler's voice, "You know you can deny me nothing."

A chuckle emanated from the vicinity of the stove.

"Come on. Let's go catch some fish," Tyler said.

"Should we see if Fergus wants to go?"

"He's gone on some secret mission for Rosemary. I think he's looking for extra filters for the well. That should make Ingrid happy. We owe her now more than ever."

"Yeah. Ingrid's a keeper. *Smokin' hot grandma!*"

"Gross, Kenny."

"What can I say? I'm not an age discriminator."

As the door to the Love Shack slammed shut behind them, Tyler heard the opening notes of one of Charlotte's gospels. She might not be much to look at, but she had the voice of an angel. It made him smile.

Chapter 15 — Fergus

"Whoa there, Arnold. I come in peace. No need to get fresh with me," Fergus said to the enormous, muscle-bound man frisking him.

"My name isn't Arnold. Why did you call me that?" replied the giant.

Rather than with cognitive thought, the majority of the man's neurons were likely preoccupied with body movements, the human equivalence of a blue whale whose brain is large enough only to orchestrate its biological processes.

"Arnold Schwarzenegger. Get it? You're a big muscly guy."

The man stared at him with emotionless eyes. "Very funny." There was no smile to support the remark.

Fergus sighed. "May I go in?"

The giant nodded. "No tricky stuff or we'll kill you."

"Of that, I have no doubt. Give my regards to the missus."

The next moment he stepped through the open door of the Tequesta Costco Warehouse, located just south of the exclusive Jupiter Hills Golf Club, where prior to Chicxulub, one might rub elbows with Tiger Woods or Rory McIlroy. The former homeowners in this part of the world would have sent their housekeepers here to buy groceries, toilet paper, and light bulbs in bulk.

It was where the Terminators had set up shop.

During the pat-down, Fergus had noticed the sound of generators coming from the back of the building. Now inside, he scanned what was visible, making a mental note of the plywood walls, perhaps erected for the purpose of keeping the warehouse's interior hidden from view. He smelled the overpowering aroma of bleach, and a slight lingering stench of rotted meat. It wasn't as hot inside the building as it should have been, and some of the ceiling lights functioned. They had gotten the power back on. Two armed men stood in front of what would have been the customer service desk before the plague. They might have been Arnold's younger, smaller brothers.

"Good afternoon, gentlemen. I would like to have a word with your boss, if I may. I have some information I think he might find useful."

"You got an appointment?"

"Sadly, no. For some reason my phone calls wouldn't go through."

"Being a smartass ain't gonna get you nowhere." The young man's torso was covered with crisscrossing bandoliers glutted with cartridges, ostensibly for the M16 he held in his hands. The other man was his twin, not only because of the matching weaponry, but because their faces were carbon copies of each other.

Lots of twins these days, he thought, then tucked away the observation for later contemplation.

"Please allow me to retract my statement. I would like to speak to your boss, though. I guarantee that what I have to tell him will be worth his time, and you two shall be rewarded for your excellent decision in allowing the meeting."

"It better be good or we'll kill you."

"Yes, it's been made clear to me the dire consequences I face with any sort of misstep."

The first man hesitated, then seemed to make up his mind. He knocked twice, then three more times on an office door behind the customer service desk.

"What the hell is it?" Despite the muffling effect of the closed door, the voice was discernibly female.

Fergus had been expecting a man to respond. Caterpillar eyebrows lifted in surprise.

"Got a guy out here says he has information. Says you'll want to hear it."

"Send him in."

The last thing Fergus expected in this alleged misogynist mecca was a woman in charge.

The sentry tipped his shorn head, indicating Fergus should go in.

The temperature of the room was comfortable due to the cool air blowing through a ceiling vent. Light cast by a banker's desk lamp created a cozy ambience. The scent of lavender pervaded the space.

Fergus stood in the small office, mouth agape with dawning comprehension. He realized he had been wrong in his previous assessment: a female in a position of authority would have been the next to last thing he might have expected. The very last thing was a young woman sitting behind a desk overlaid in neat stacks of paper and who looked like a real-life grownup version of the Little Mermaid.

He was looking at Zoey's identical twin.

"It better be good or we'll kill you." She repeated the mantra, glancing up from her notepad scribbles.

Fergus didn't miss a beat. Rosemary was correct — he was quick on his feet.

"I know where there is an extensive supply of propane that you've missed."

Eyes as blue as his own revealed no interest.

"What makes you think we want propane?" The voice was low and musical; the subharmonics were tempered with steel.

"It's powering your operation. You have lighting and air conditioning, but I'm guessing the majority of your electricity is used for refrigeration. Most of the gasoline these days is no longer viable. I didn't see any wind turbines, solar panels, nor waterfalls for hydroelectricity. What's left? Propane generators."

"You heard the motors."

"I did. But I managed to piece the rest of it together using the impressive gray matter between these handsome ears."

"I don't see handsome ears. All I see is some alarming hair. How do you get it to do that?"

Fergus sighed.

"Never mind, I don't care. Where's the propane?"

"Well, about that. I would like to enlist. I've been lonesome and bored wandering this desiccated continent alone. It's time for me to become part of something bigger than myself. That's what all the cool kids are doing."

"Bigger than yourself? That's not saying much. We let you join in exchange for the location of the propane? Why don't we just torture you to get the information?"

"Because I also offer other services. I would be your most capable sycophant."

A sniff and a half-grin. "I'm already surrounded by capable sycophants."

"I've met the intellectually-challenged Incredible Hulk out front, as well as Lennie Small and his twin brother on the other side of your office door."

"Am I supposed to be impressed that you've read Steinbeck?"

"Only if it helps my cause. My point is that you have plenty of brawn, but perhaps you need more brains. Some help with your workload." He indicated the stacks of paper on the desk.

"I'm Fergus, by the way." He extended his hand above the paperwork. It was ignored. "May I ask to whom I have the pleasure of speaking?" he said, retrieving the hand.

"Where's the propane?"

"What an unusual name for such a stunning lass. Is it Native American? Like Stands With Fists?"

He saw amusement in the blue eyes; his own crinkled in response.

"Andy," the woman yelled at the door, "Come get this joker and kill him."

"No, no, no," Fergus said, crinkles vanishing. "My death is unnecessary. I'll share with the class now. I surmise you've tapped out the local commercial distributors. The hospitals as well, because you're smart and would know they store it for their backup generators. It doesn't do to have the lights go out during open-heart surgery."

One of the twins opened the door and grabbed Fergus by the arm.

"Give us another minute," the woman said to her hired muscle, who promptly exited, closing the door behind him.

"I wager you've sent scouts out looking for tankers abandoned in parking lots or on the highways and have drained those as well."

"Get to the point."

"I wonder if you know that in addition to hospitals, landline telephone utility companies utilized backup propane generators during power outages."

He saw that he had scored.

"The AT&T complex is in Vero Beach. I passed it on my way here."

The half grin became a full one.

"But wait, there's more. All those cell phone towers you barely notice because they're so prolific these days? They often utilize propane generators as well. So for every one of those intrusive blights on the American landscape, there may be a nearby tank to feed its generator."

He watched the lovely face as she processed the information and, most likely, deliberated on his fate. If she had shaken his hand, his *scythen* would have given him a better read on her, so he had to rely on gut instinct alone.

"I'm just getting started, my dear. I'm a fount of useful knowledge on a variety of topics, both broad and esoteric. I served in the military, so my weaponry know-how is more extensive than that of your young thugs outside. I owned a private security company before the end came, so I'm intimately familiar with the ins and outs of keeping the beautiful people of the world, such as yourself, safe from would-be assailants. I can make chocolate soufflé, juggle chainsaws, and pick any lock this side of a state prison. I'm your huckleberry."

"You're a movie buff as well."

"Indeed. Val Kilmer as Doc Holliday is perhaps the most sublime piece of cinema ever filmed."

"Disagree. The fava bean scene from *Silence of the Lambs*."

"That's a little before your time, isn't it? And such dark subject matter...serial killers and cannibals?"

"I find psychopaths fascinating."

"I see. Well, perhaps I should be going. I don't want to waste any more of your time." He took a step toward the door.

"Not so fast, Lucky Charms."

The moniker struck a chord — it was the name Dani used on the occasions that she wanted to goad him, which had been most of the time. It brought back wonderful memories as well as a few unpleasant ones. This female reminded him of Dani in many ways: beautiful, clever, and predatory. However, despite some off-putting personality traits, Dani was good-hearted. He wasn't convinced this girl nor her sister could make that claim.

"Prove yourself. Take Lester and show him where the propane is. If he returns with a glowing report, you'll not only be allowed to live, you'll become part of our operation."

"And how will we travel there?"

"Scouts ride bicycles. We don't use gasoline until we know we've found something worth using it for."

"Oh dear."

"What's the problem?"

"My ass has an aversion to bicycle seats. Don't you have horses or donkeys or camels anywhere? Perhaps a Great Dane?"

"You'll do this my way or you'll die."

"Very well. When do we leave? I need to prepare my backside."

The smile broadened into something shark-like. "No time like the present."

***

Lester was the giant from earlier. Fergus could not imagine a more reticent companion.

"We're traveling the entire sixty miles to Vero Beach in one day?"

The two men pedaled north along the Florida Turnpike. The sun was a malicious, fiery orb of torture in the cloudless sky. The only positive aspect of this excursion was the inherent flatness of the state. Hills would have made it unbearable rather than just miserable.

"Yes." The man was barely breaking a sweat. He wasn't even breathing hard.

Fergus hated him for that, if for no other reason.

"You're not much of a talker, are you?"

"Talking will only make this harder for you, weakling."

That was the longest sentence he'd gotten from the man all day.

"True enough. I'll save my pithy chatter for later. We are camping out tonight, I assume? Share some cowboy songs and tall tales over a campfire? Listen to the coyotes howling in the distance while eating beans from dented metal plates?"

The behemoth glanced at him, then turned his focus back to the blacktop stretching before them. Fergus thought he detected a ghost of a grin.

There might be hope for the giant.

Hours later, they were doing an eerily similar version of Fergus's earlier projection. Lester decided they would make camp for the night and inspect the AT&T facility in the morning. The sun was setting, not optimal conditions for an inspection of a complex of buildings that may or may not contain hostile people.

Lester had a small fire going in record time. A rectangular stainless steel grid with long, fold-out legs hovered above the flames. Canned beef stew simmered in an aluminum skillet. It smelled heavenly after a long, exhausting day with few breaks to drink water, let alone eat anything.

"This is quite a set-up."

"I like to be prepared."

"For what? Unexpected cattle rustlers asking for a dinner invitation?"

"Cattle rustlers would be sorry they asked to dine with me."

"No doubt. We have not officially been introduced. I am Fergus. It's a pleasure to meet you, Lester."

He offered his hand over the fire, then watched the man ponder whether or not to grant this courtesy. It was a relief when an elephantine hand reached out, dwarfing his own.

The physical contact, as short-lived as it was, provided a wealth of information.

Fergus smiled.

The two sat for a few minutes in companionable silence.

"Lester, I think I might have misjudged you."

A shrug of the massive shoulders. "Most do."

"Sorry about that. Why all the gear? Why not just eat something out of a can or a box or a package? People these days don't take the time to heat food that's already cooked."

"I like camping, and I like campfires."

"Do you often go on these scouting missions?"

"I do what my boss tells me to do. And I like to camp."

"But you like the missions, yes?"

"Yes."

Fergus hid a smile at the brevity which was simply a character trait, not an indication of intelligence. This man was no blue whale.

"You like to lie on the ground and gaze up at a trillion stars in the sky, yes?"

"That's part of it."

"What else?"

"I love nature. I like to be outside as much as possible. I prefer to be by myself, but that's not always an option, in which case I favor people who don't ask too many questions."

"A bit of an introvert, then?"

A nod of the prodigious head. "Classic high-functioning introvert."

"What did you do? Before?"

"Guess."

"Hmmm. Clearly you spent a lot of time at the gym...fitness trainer? Lumberjack? Porn star?"

"I wrote books."

"Really? What about?"

Another shrug. Fergus could imagine small worlds being jostled about on those colossal shoulders.

"Everything. Travel guides, short story anthologies, suspense thrillers, a few historical romances, some poetry."

At that moment, Fergus was closer to being at a complete loss for words than he had ever been in his exceptionally long life.

"I have to admit, I did not see that coming. Who was your publisher? I might have read some of your work."

"I didn't have a publisher."

"Ah. Self-published?"

"No. I never published anything I wrote. I didn't write books for others. Just for myself."

"That seems a bit selfish. Why not share your words with the world?"

"My words are for me only."

"I see. Does your boss know this about you? What is her name, by the way? She never bothered to tell me."

"That one is Aubrey."

"Is she an effective leader? Do you like working for her?"

"She's okay."

"I didn't see anyone else besides you and the other two guards. How extensive is your operation? I have no idea what I'm getting myself into here, but I'm tired of being on the road. Thought I'd join a group...break the monotony of my sojourn thus far."

The man studied him over the flames. It was full dark now, and firelight reflected in the dilated pupils.

"You ask a lot of questions."

"True. I have an inquisitive nature."

"I'm finished talking now. Don't try anything tricky or I'll kill you. I'm a light sleeper."

With that, the man stretched out on top of his sleeping bag and closed his eyes.

Fergus sighed, then did the same. Soon after, he sent out his *scythen* to Amelia.

~~~

Fergus: Lots of goings-on in Club Terminator.
Amelia: Do tell.
Fergus: Zoey has been less than truthful in her description of the Terminators. Currently in charge here is her twin sister.
Amelia: Oh my.
Fergus: I'm trying to get to the bottom of this. Keep an eye on her, my dear.

Amelia: That should be easy to do. Rosemary has assigned the young woman to me. I am to teach her all my medical knowledge.

Fergus: That's perfect. You'll be able to perform the tests on her, discover the extent of her langthal and any other talents she may have.

Amelia: Yes. Are you safe there?

Fergus: I'm bunking next to a giant at the moment. As long as I don't piss him off, I'll be fine. I will not be scaling any beanstalks, I can tell you that.

Amelia: Very well. Good night, my love.

Fergus: Good night, my darling. When I return, I intend to thoroughly ravish you.

Amelia: I would expect nothing less.

Chapter 16 — Anonymous

Dear Diary,

Oh, my. What a fuss my feral feline incident caused. Who would have thought anyone would be bothered by a skinned and disemboweled pussycat? Tee hee! Well, I couldn't help myself. SomeONE or someTHING had to die. That should last me a few days, then I will have to add another trophy to my collection. I took one of the front fangs. What an enchanting object! So sharp and white and filled with memories of all its kills. Lucky kitty. He doesn't get a bad rap for committing murder.

I don't mind though. It makes the game even more interesting. I am an excellent killer but also a discreet one. How sad for all the people who don't want to play! How boring must their lives be? Being an Angel of Death is the most fun there is to be had. It is such a pity that it took me so long to discover my purpose. There I was, miserable and misunderstood in my old life, shunned by a society that was so unremarkable. It took the end of the world to reveal my true nature. Billions of people are dead, a few million are scratching about on the surface of the earth trying to survive horrific conditions, and yet I am thriving and happier than I have ever been. I was born from the apocalypse — not a phoenix rising from the ashes, but a cloaked, sickle-wielding monster clawing its way out of a dying womb.

And oh, Diary, I am magnificent!

In other news, we suffered a hailstorm that decimated most of our crops. People will become hungry, and that will make them testy. When people get testy, they will start picking at things they might not otherwise pick at. I envision our adorable little Colony as a tapestry...a work in progress...not nearly finished, nor will it ever be. Like a jagged fingernail, the hailstorm's destruction will soon snag on a few crucial threads in our woven saga. It may be that the whole thing unravels over the next few weeks, and it will be fascinating to watch. I will bide my time, as I always do — I am nothing if not patient! — and let the epic tale continue. Will this charming community populated with so many Polly Anna do-gooders prevail, or will it implode? I cannot wait to find out.

Speaking of, I had a brilliant idea today. When it is time to leave this place, I shall go out with a bang. Not a literal bang; I would never resort to crude tools such as guns or bombs. No, by 'bang' I mean a massacre. How delightful to exterminate dozens of people at once! I doubt all those terrorists before

Chicxulub acted because of some silly religious war; I imagine some were Death Angels, like me, and were drawn to extremist ideologies for the opportunity to slaughter people for the pleasure of it. But oh, such barbaric techniques! There's no skill or finesse in driving a van into a throng of people or shooting off a gun in a crowded nightclub.

Sledgehammer versus scalpel. Get it?

Perhaps not every person in the Colony will die, but most will. The timing is critical. It all must unfold on schedule to succeed. Just thinking about it is thrilling! I shan't sleep much tonight. There are so many details to work out. Fortunately, my superb brain doesn't require more than a few hours of slumber at a time. I might embark on another hunt. Nothing as overt as the pussycat; rather a light appetizer before the main course, which I'm planning even now.

I know, I know. I thought I would wait a week or two, but the mass murder epiphany has whetted my appetite...

Chapter 17 — Ingrid

"Giving away so much of your food was a generous act. Don't try to pooh-pooh what you did," Hector said, spooning peat moss and vermiculite into segmented plastic containers. Morning sunlight filtered in through the kitchen windows, highlighting the strands of silver in his dark hair.

"Pooh-pooh? What is the Spanish translation for that?" Ingrid followed behind him, pressing seeds into the rich mixture. It was July in Florida, which meant the best environment for seedlings to germinate and grow was indoors, away from the fierce sun and occasional hail.

Much depended on the success of the new crop. She would have to decide later if she would be willing to part with more of her secret cache of food if it failed. It wasn't a matter of being selfish; it was about sustainability and self-reliance. If her rice and beans always came to the rescue, what would happen when it all run out?

"Caca-caca?"

She laughed. "I doubt that."

Seedling trays and peat moss were littered all about her granite countertops and marble floors. A scene such as this would never have happened before Chixculub. In some ways, she wished a few of her snooty neighbors had survived to see it. She smiled when she imagined sharing details of her illicit affair with the gardener.

"You were moaning in your sleep last night," he said, noticing the smile.

"I was? Interesting. I must have been dreaming about my boyfriend."

He chuckled. "Now you're being disingenuous. Was it one of...those?"

Ingrid hadn't decided what to do about the hurricane dream. Like the precognitive dreams she'd had before the plague, it was frightening but murky. Was it a metaphor for something? Or was a monstrous storm literally going to destroy their home in the near future? She knew something dreadful was coming but could not identify what form it would take, just as she had not known in what guise the apocalypse would appear. Should she say something to Hector? To Rosemary? If she did, would the Colony leader think less of her? Most people didn't accept the notion of precognition and thought little of those who claimed to have the ability. Poor Cassandra in Ancient Greece had the gift but had been cursed so no one would believe her warnings. Ingrid could relate. Her own lover looked at her askance when she spoke of such things.

She sighed. "I dreamt of a hurricane."

"And you are worried it will come to pass?"

"Yes."

"This place has endured hurricanes in the past. Your own house was built to withstand the most intense storms."

"Winds, yes. We don't know how it would handle the surge from an immense, slow-moving storm. Since I've been living here, the worst we've experienced was 120-mph winds from Hurricane Jeanne back in 2004. Jeanne was a category three. There was significant flooding that time, and it wasn't even a direct hit. Jupiter Inlet Colony resides on a narrow strip of sand that barely rises above sea level. As a barrier island, we're even more at risk than most. What happens if we're in the center bullseye of a category five?"

"I've lived here only a decade, my dear. In landlocked Torreón, I witnessed no hurricanes. I have no idea what to expect."

Hector's hometown was in central Mexico. After crossing the border into the United States, he had soon found his way to Florida. He told her that even as a boy, it had always been his desire to live near the ocean, just as it was hers as a young woman in Munich. They had so much in common, but it had taken a catastrophe of epic proportion to bring together a wealthy white woman of German descent and an illegal immigrant from Mexico. How sad that she would never have given such a man the time of day in her previous life.

"You remember I told you about my dreams of the apocalypse?"

"Yes. You said when you awoke from them, you felt an impending sense of doom on a monumental scale."

"Exactly. I knew the end of the world was imminent, but I did not know what it would look like."

"Compared to your dreams of Chixculub, how bad is this one?"

"You can't compare a pandemic that killed eight billion people to a hurricane, but our tiny populace here on the island would be decimated. So they are similar in that regard."

"Yes, I understand."

Ingrid's eyes narrowed. "You don't believe me."

"I am trying, my dear, but it is not my nature to accept what I cannot see with my own eyes or touch with my own fingers. I am a skeptic. That has always been my way."

"Precisely the reason I share this type of information with so few people."

"Would you prefer that I lie to you? Pretend to be a believer when I am not?"

"Of course not." She blew out a measured breath. "I'm sorry, Hector. It's just that I've dealt with skepticism and ridicule my entire life. I can give many examples of how my precognitive dreams came to pass, but still people don't want to believe."

"Do they always come true? Every single time?"

"Not always."

"Well, then. Perhaps this will be one that does not."

"Unlikely. This is a 'for sure' one."

Hector laughed, then abruptly stopped when he saw her frown.

"Perhaps you should talk to Rosemary? Will that make you feel better? Or Tyler, whom you believe shares this talent with you?"

"Tyler doesn't like to discuss his talents. He's a scientist and a skeptic like you. And talking to Rosemary is a gamble. She is already one step away from usurping any authority I have here. She could use this as a way to discredit me."

"I doubt that."

"At the very least, she might think less of me."

"Ah, I see now."

"Damn it, Hector, don't give me that look. I know what I'll do. I'll talk to Amelia. She seems like a person who would be open to such things."

"Excellent idea. I like her, and Fergus too. They're rather odd folks, but odd in a good way. Now that I think about it, there are many odd folks these days."

"True."

"I'll finish up here. You go on over to Amelia's house. I think it will make you feel better to discuss the dreams with someone besides an old Mexican Doubting Thomas like myself."

Fifteen minutes later, she tapped on the front door of Amelia's beachfront condo. Ingrid had always despised this building; thought of it as an eyesore during her daily beach walks. But at least there were fewer monstrosities like it here than in other parts of Florida, and for that she was thankful.

When Amelia opened the door, there were furrows between her brows which smoothed when she saw her visitor. Something about this woman made Ingrid feel as if they were connected somehow — kindred spirits. She knew Amelia had lived in Arizona and served as a midwife for her Native American tribe, the Hualapai. Her medical and anatomical knowledge was extensive for someone who was self-educated, and she always exuded patience and kindness. So there was very little commonality between the two women on the surface, but on a deeper level, she sensed a bond. She would test its limits now.

"Come in, my friend. I was just going over basic reproductive anatomy with our newest resident."

Seeing Zoey sitting on a bright yellow sofa evoked a frisson of disdain; whether for the young woman or the garish furniture was unclear even to her. Perhaps both.

"Please, sit," Amelia said. "Would you like some water? Or is this more of a tequila visit?"

Ingrid laughed. "Water would be lovely for now, thank you."

She sat down in a chair opposite Zoey, trying to ignore the parrot-covered fabric on the armrests.

"To what do I owe this honor?" Amelia asked, setting three glasses of water on the coffee table. Next to the water, she placed a small bottle of Jose Cuervo.

"Can the girl go away? I need to talk to you in private." Ingrid knew she was being rude and didn't care. This young female was nothing to her.

Zoey smirked. "We haven't been formally introduced." She offered her hand across the coffee table.

Ingrid hesitated, then acquiesced. The hand felt warm; almost hot. Young people were always so hot-blooded.

The smirk blossomed into a full-blown smile.

"I hear you're the oldest resident here." There was a subtle emphasis on the adjective.

"That is correct. Now run along, *child*. I have business with Amelia." Two could play that game.

"You're worried about a hurricane."

Ingrid's jaw dropped in a most undignified manner.

"I'm clairvoyant," Zoey said with a blinding smile. "Just like you."

Chapter 18 — Rosemary

"Come on, Rose. The old broad had a nightmare. Why are you so worked up about it?" Lucas was sprawled out naked on the bed. A smile played about the corners of his mouth. He knew how sexy he looked.

"She was credible. Gave me examples of dreams she'd had before that came to pass."

"How do you know she was telling the truth?"

Rosemary had pondered Ingrid's veracity. The two had been butting heads since the beginning, but despite the occasionally contrary disposition, Ingrid was honest. Besides, there was no benefit for her to lie about being clairvoyant. Or none that came to mind.

"She's being truthful. I feel it. Amelia agrees with me."

The two women had left an hour ago after a lengthy discussion about the hurricane dream. Lucas had come home just as they were leaving, evoking identical expressions of distaste on both women's faces. Ingrid didn't even try to hide it.

What should that tell her? These women whose intellect she respected couldn't stand her boyfriend. Did it matter? Should it matter?

"I didn't realize Amelia was a human lie detector."

"I like her, and I think she's trustworthy."

"And why is that? She's only been here a few months. You vetted her less thoroughly than anyone else so far, myself included."

He had a point. There was something about the petite Native American woman that had resonated with Rosemary. Her gut instincts about people had served her well her entire life, so why second guess them now?

"I can't explain it. You'll have to trust me."

"You're the only person here I do trust," he said, his handsome face open and candid.

"That's because you assume everyone is lying to you."

"That's because they usually are."

"Says the former police officer."

"Former homicide detective. There's a difference, you know. And I was damn good at it because I could sniff out deception, just like you. Chicxulub didn't change the nature of people in general, you know. There are just few liars left in the world now."

She tilted her head. "I'm not so sure about that."

"Most people are shitty. The end. Some of them try to come across as goody-two-shoes, like they give a rat's ass about others, but when the chips are down, they're going to look out for number one."

"You're so jaded."

"Not jaded. Realistic. When you don't expect much from people, they can't disappoint you. So what are you going to do?" he said, pulling her down onto the bed. He began kissing her neck while unbuttoning her cotton sundress.

"I have no idea. I have to think about it. Even if it's nonsense, there is always the possibility of destructive storms...even worse than what we just had. We have to come up with contingency plans. These people depend on me, and I don't intend to let them down. I've never been in a situation like this before, making critical life-and-death decisions for others. We need an evacuation plan. Hurricane season has begun."

"Yes, I know. I lived in New Orleans, remember? I was there during Katrina."

"I bet that was horrible," she said, closing her eyes as his tongue flicked first the right nipple, then the left. He was making it harder to think.

"It was bad," he murmured against her belly. When his tongue found its way between her legs, she put aside worrisome thoughts and gave in to the fleeting diversion of sexual pleasure.

An hour later when he was snoring beside her, she booted up her mental hard drive.

A wave of guilt washed over her. Of all the people in the Colony, Lucas trusted only her. There was some irony. Before the plague, it had been her job to deceive people so she could steal from them. Yet so many people here liked and admired her while barely tolerating him. Maybe it was the cop thing; because he exuded distrust, people distrusted him in return. Both his old job and his current one were about protecting people...keeping them safe. Why didn't the Colonists appreciate that?

It wasn't fair, and it bothered her even more because she felt unworthy of the esteem in which people held her. This post-apocalyptic world provided the perfect environment to make restitutions for her past, to make amends for transgressions that went well beyond ripping off a few old farts who had more money than they knew what to do with. Leading these people — assuring their safety, happiness, and well-being — was how she would pave the path to redemption. It was the only way she could live with what she had done.

She felt the familiar white-hot fingers clutch at her stomach as memories flooded in.

"You're so beautiful," the short man said, his voice trembling with emotion.

From her vantage a foot above — courtesy of her height and the five-inch stilettos she wore — she could see her reflection on the shiny bald pate. The little man was correct: she was beautiful. Gilbert, a paunchy middle-aged accountant, was neither handsome nor interesting, but he had skills. In particular, he excelled at finding tax loopholes for the wealthy. His clientele were some of the richest residents of Palm Beach; Rosemary had been cultivating his friendship for months. He would be her entree to those gilded circles in which she would make her fortune. It would be easy for a cultured, articulate black woman to breech the walls of their privileged world because all those white people wanted everyone else to believe they weren't racist. 'Look...I have a black friend!' She would be less vetted than a white woman in a similar position. She just needed Gilbert's help to open a few doors.

That had been the plan, at least. He complicated things when he fell in love with her. He was no longer content with just sex, which she offered in exchange for introductions. The silly man wanted to marry her, so she ended the relationship soon after his proposal. She had gotten what she needed.

A week later he hung himself from the chandelier in his dining room using one of her silk scarves as a noose.

She was the one who found his body: dead eyes bulging, petechial blossoms on the pasty cheeks, blackened tongue poking out one side of the mouth. The tongue was the worst part — it made him look cartoonish.

She sighed in the darkness, willing the memories to recede and the knots in her stomach to relax. Gilbert hadn't deserved that end. He had been dignified, compassionate, and kind. And she had killed him. It didn't matter that she hadn't been the one to kick away the step ladder under his dangling feet. His death was on her hands, and it always would be.

Impatient fingertips brushed away tears; she forced herself to shift gears. Wallowing in guilt wouldn't help anyone.

She began making a list of all that needed to be done the following day. Once that was complete, she conducted the nightly analysis of the physical world around her — her version of counting sheep. There was a strong breeze tonight, so the darkened bedroom wasn't as warm as usual. How lovely it would be in the fall, she thought. Cooler temperatures in paradise would be welcome. She could hear the riotous crashing of waves and imagined how the ocean looked at that moment. She was tempted to slip on a robe and go for a beach walk, but she needed sleep more than she needed to gaze upon whitecaps painted pewter by the gloom of night. She caught the ambrosial scent of jasmine wafting through the window. The frogs and crickets performed their evening concerto.

She pondered the animal screech she had heard the other night. Had it been the mewling of the mutilated cat in its death throes? With so many other pressing concerns, the incident had been delegated to a mental back burner. She vowed to address it the next day.

A spy living in their midst was one thing. A serial killer in the making, quite another.

Chapter 19 — Amelia and Fergus

Amelia lay in bed listening to the ocean waves crashing just outside her window. She was emotionally drained. In the span of an hour, she had learned that not only was there someone in the Colony who had precognitive dreams — just as Maddie had back in Kansas — those dreams told of a tempest that may obliterate their home in the near future.

She didn't for one second doubt Ingrid's story. She knew psychic abilities had manifested in the current human populace, and it was no accident; those talents had been cultivated by the *Cthor* through genetic engineering. Despite her age, Ingrid would need to be tested as a potential recruit if it turned out that her intellect was also exceptional. If she possessed healing *langthal*, as Zoey did, she and Fergus may have two new recruits for *Cthor-Vangt* on their hands.

But the Ingrid matter would have to wait for now. Amelia needed to focus on more pressing issues.

~~~

Amelia: Are you there, my love?

Fergus: Yes, but my attention is required elsewhere at the moment. May we chat later?

Amelia: (frowning) Is everything okay? Are you safe?

Fergus: Safe as a pit bull puppy suckling at its mother's teat.

Amelia: Very well. Contact me as soon as possible then. It seems we have a hurricane to prepare for.

Fergus: How unfortunate. I shall, my darling. I promise.

***

Fergus severed the mental connection with Amelia so he could focus his attention on the man who pressed a blade against his throat. A woman with biceps that looked like flesh-covered baseballs did the same to his new friend Lester. The sky was beginning to lighten in the east. Fergus could think of a million different ways to wake up in the morning that would be more pleasant than the current scenario.

"I thought you were a light sleeper," Fergus said, keeping his attention focused on the man who held him at knife-point while picturing the annoyed expression on the face of his companion.

"These two must be quite stealthy," Lester replied. Was there a hint of amusement in the deep voice?

"If I were you, I'd keep my mouth shut and not make any sudden moves," Knife Man said.

"Yeah," Muscle Woman said. "We'll cut your throats if you give us any shit."

"Very well. No shit shall henceforth be given."

A low snort came from Lester's vicinity. Fergus realized he had just heard him laugh for the first time. The thought made him smile, despite the circumstances.

"I didn't catch your name, sir. I'm Fergus and this is my new best friend Lester. Whom do I have the pleasure of addressing?"

"Fuck you. Why do you talk like that?" Muscle Woman said.

Fergus's banter diverted her attention just enough to give Lester an opening. For such a large human, he moved with feline speed. The next moment, the wrist of the knife-wielding hand was in Lester's vice grip; the long, powerful fingers of the other hand encircled her neck, python-like. Knife Man's eyes flicked toward his partner, giving Fergus the opening he needed.

Fergus whipped his elbow up and into his captor's Adam's apple, causing the man to drop the weapon. It wasn't a death blow, but not being able to breathe would disable a person for a few minutes.

"Nicely done." Lester smiled.

Two more firsts: the smile, which revealed flawless teeth, and a compliment.

"Not bad for a weakling, ay? Now, what to do with these two?"

"We'll tie them up and leave them in the shade somewhere."

"We're not going to kill them?"

"I don't believe in killing except in self-defense. These two are pesky horseflies. They bite at my ass but can do no real damage."

Knife Man writhed on the ground, struggling for air.

Muscle Woman moved her mouth in such a way that Fergus knew what was about to happen. Before he could give warning, she spat a glob of mucus onto Lester's cheek.

The amused grin vanished. The python hand tightened on a neck which looked scrawny in comparison, an overgrown farmer throttling his dinner chicken.

The woman's eyeballs bulged. Her tongue protruded.

"Lester..." Fergus said.

The giant gazed at his captive. Her saliva snailed down his jawline, then dripped onto the ground.

"Lester."

"Yes?"

"You're killing her."

"No. I'm teaching her a lesson. It is impolite to spit on someone."

The python constricted further. The female's face turned crimson.

"I agree. There are few actions as rude as spitting, unless it's taking a piss in someone's beer or wiping a booger on a child."

"That's disgusting."

"I know, but the child had it coming."

Another bass chuckle.

"I think that will do," Lester said finally, releasing the woman. She fell to the ground, gasping for oxygen, as her accomplice had done moments earlier.

Side by side with arms crossed, they watched their would-be assailants writhe on the grass.

"You have tie-wraps?" Fergus said.

"Of course. I like to be prepared, remember?"

"Turns out we did have a couple of cattle rustlers show up uninvited."

"And you see how they regret it now." Lester patted Fergus on the back, almost knocking him to the ground.

Soon after their attackers had been dealt with, the two stood inside the AT&T industrial complex next to a nondescript one-story building. Printed on the door was 'GENERATOR FACILITIES.' Next to it was a fenced area containing six sausage-shaped white tanks lined up in a neat row.

"What's their capacity?" Fergus asked.

"A thousand gallons each. If they're not tapped out, we've hit the jackpot."

Lester climbed the eight-foot chain link fence as easily as a spider monkey navigating a rainforest canopy. Next, he took a handkerchief from a pocket and wiped at the glass-covered gauge on one of the tanks.

"Looks like you're in the Terminators," Lester said over his shoulder.

"So this was my initiation?"

"Of course. Everyone has to prove himself. Or herself. You just did. This tank is seventy percent full, which means there are seven hundred gallons of liquid propane inside."

After a quick inspection of the remaining tanks, Lester returned to stand beside Fergus. "You've earned your paycheck for the week."

"I won't spend it all in one place. What now?"

"We return to headquarters and report our findings. They'll send one of the tanker trucks to get the propane."

"I suppose you'll be wanting to leave posthaste?" Fergus said, rubbing his backside with a frown.

Lester tilted his head, studying the man who stood almost two feet below him.

"Would you like to take the day off? You've earned that too. You'll be a hero when we get back."

"You mean with Aubrey?"

"I mean with everyone."

"Has it earned me the right to know more about the Terminators? I would like to have a clearer picture of what I'm getting myself into. I'm like you, Lester. I don't believe in killing people."

"Understood. I'll answer five questions, no more. Consider them carefully."

He gave Fergus another vigorous back pat, added a shoulder squeeze, and then took off at a brisk pace back toward the complex entrance. Fergus rubbed the shoulder, which felt like it had been struck by a Winnebago.

"Just how tall are you, anyway?"

"I'm seven foot two inches. Now you have four questions."

Fergus chuckled, then took his new friend's advice and contemplated, carefully, the wording of his remaining questions.

***

An hour later, the two men sat on the edge of a manmade pond. The nearby tropical foliage was unkempt and overgrown, since there were no longer greenskeepers to maintain it. Soon all these golf courses would become jungles or forests or prairies again, and maybe that wasn't such a bad thing.

Two pairs of feet, size seven and size fourteen, dipped in the water, creating tiny circular tsunamis for the insects that skidded and hovered on the surface. The din of the cicadas was so clamorous the men had to raise their voices to hear their own conversation. The Florida shoreline was delightful with its cooling breeze coming off the ocean and its picturesque views. A half mile inland, where they were now, was a different story: flat, humid, and insect-ridden. Fergus couldn't imagine why anyone would live here.

"I've formulated my next question," he said.

"Did you consider it carefully?"

"I did, after you tricked me with that height thing."

"There was no trickery. Merely a lack of focus on your part."

"I should have known better. I've seen *Monty Python and the Holy Grail*."

"The Bridge of Death scene."

"What is your favorite color? Blue...no! Aaaahhhh!"

A trio of deep chuckles emanated from the man. Fergus thought of green giants wearing leafy togas standing in verdant, hilly farmland.

"What's your second question?"

"How many people are there in your organization?"

"Forty-seven...living...at this time."

"What do you...? Wait. Never mind."

Fergus mulled the answer. Did that mean they'd had more at some point? What had happened to them, if so? Forty-seven was not an intimidating number. The Colonists could handle that many invaders as long as they didn't all look like Lester.

"Next."

"Would you consider the majority of your people to be moral or immoral?" The question had come to mind when Fergus considered the residents of both Hays and Liberty, Kansas. While the people in Liberty weren't without flaws, they were generally good, whereas the people in Hays were generally very bad.

The large head tilted to one side. "Interesting question, although too subjective. You're assuming that my definition of moral and immoral are similar to yours."

"Yes. I've decided you are a good person, Lester. My spidey sense tells me so."

"Much is riding on your spidey sense. For your sake, I hope it's accurate."

"So what's the verdict? Are the Terminators mostly moral or immoral people?"

"Before I can answer that, we should have a philosophical side discussion. I wrote a book on philosophy."

"That no one ever got to read?"

"Correct. My philosophies are for me, no one else."

"Right. This side discussion doesn't count against my remaining three questions?"

"It does not."

"Very well. Philosophize away, sir."

Lester paused, then said, "Is a man justified in killing another man for the purpose of defending his wife and children?"

"Of course, assuming the victim was intent on doing harm to the wife and children."

"Is that same man justified in killing another man for the purpose of defending his property? His livestock? His beloved pet?"

Fergus hesitated, then said, "Property, no. Livestock, no, unless it results in the family starving. Beloved pet, yes."

"So a man who kills another man to protect a beloved pet is still a good man? The life of a human is less than the life of an animal?"

"It's not about which life form is more worthy. It's about the justification of the act itself which springs from love. Then there's the secondary issue: a human who would want to kill a beloved pet is evil, unless of course the pet bit the guy in the ball sack. Then all bets are off."

Another deep chuckle. "Is a man justified in killing another man because he knows with certainty that at some point in the future that man will cause great harm?"

"How can he know that with certainty?"

"This is hypothetical. Let's assume he does."

"So this is your version of whether to kill baby Hitler?"

"Not really. We're not killing a baby here. We're killing an adult."

"Then I say the man is justified. He's probably a hero, even."

"What if the man who will cause great harm in the future is currently popular with his people? What if he is considered a good man himself, practically a saint? What if he has saved the lives of others by providing food and shelter for those in need? Should he be killed now despite all the good he has done and will continue to do for a time because he will someday do great harm?

"I would have to think about that for a minute." Fergus rubbed his beard, then smiled when Lester continued without waiting for a response.

"On the subject of baby-killing, why is it acceptable to eat baby cows and baby sheep but not baby dogs or baby cats? And on the subject of eating flesh in general, why not utilize that of dead humans? I'm not suggesting we knowingly eat Uncle George for Sunday dinner, but why shouldn't every scintilla of our dead bodies be used to benefit the living rather than taking up precious real estate in cemeteries? We could ship human sirloin steaks over to feed the starving people in Africa."

"That is some weird shit, Lester."

"Truly. But you see now why moral and immoral are so subjective. There are countless justifications for our actions. Rarely is anything black or white."

Fergus sighed. "Duly noted. May I retract my question?"

"No, and I will answer now, although I don't think my response will enlighten you. Morality is subjective in ways you may never have considered.

There are more good people than evil within our organization, but you might not see them as such. Next question."

Fergus never expected to be enjoying himself on a propane-scouting mission with the largest man he had ever met. Yet he was, and immensely so. Situations such as this were one of the reasons he loved being above ground. Yes, he was aging and therefore shortening his lifespan, in addition to putting himself in danger on a regular basis, but it was worth it to have such fascinating interactions with the newest incarnation of humans. Despite the few bad seeds, Fergus decided this new crop was spectacular on almost every level. And it didn't hurt that the women were more attractive now than during any other time on earth.

"Perhaps I should switch back to more straightforward subject matter? That's not one of my questions...don't answer. All right, then, Lester, where do you get your food?"

"You chose well because the answer is multi-pronged. You'll get more bang for your buck."

Fergus chuckled. Lester smiled. The droning of the cicadas pervaded all other sounds of nature until it was pierced by the sharp report of a rifle shot. Fergus watched a crimson flower blossom on the khaki fabric covering Lester's chest. He pulled his new friend to the ground.

A second bullet zipped above their heads, taking a half inch of flaming red hair with it.

"There are many ways I've envisioned my death," Fergus said, "But shot in the head on an overgrown golf course in Florida while in the company of a philosophizing giant is not one of them. How bad is it?"

"Not bad. I believe it missed my heart and lungs. I'm breathing without trouble and the blood escaping isn't arterial."

"You're a combat medic too? Let me guess. You wrote a book about it."

Lester responded with a grimace. The big man might not have sustained a life-threatening injury, but it surely hurt like hell. He was right though. The blood oozing through the hole in the khaki shirt was seeping, not pulsing.

Another bullet zinged overhead.

"The shooter is in that copse of oak trees in our eleven o-clock position," Lester said in a calm voice.

"Yes. I agree. Do you think it's those two we left tied up this morning?"

"There's no way of knowing at this point, but I suspect as much."

Fergus reached into the side pocket of his cargo shorts, extracting a cylindrical item covered in a pink plastic wrapper.

"I prefer Tampax," Lester said.

"The generic brand was on sale." Fergus unwrapped the sterile cotton tampon and plugged it into the bullet hole.

"What does it say about a man who carries feminine hygiene products in his pockets?"

"It says I'm a man in touch with my inner goddess."

"I need my backpack. You're a smaller target. Do you think you can bring it to me without getting your tiny self shot?"

Fergus army-crawled the ten feet to where the backpack lay on the ground. There was a slight dip in the topography at the water line, so a few inches of grassy elevation protected most of his body from the shooter fifty yards away. That didn't stop the gunman from continuing to take shots, though. Amelia would be furious if he managed to get himself mortally wounded again. Jessie was not available to save him this time.

"Excellent," Lester said when Fergus flung the pack his direction.

The two men lay flat on the ground next to the pond. Fergus imagined what the scene would look like from above. If anyone happened by in a hot air balloon, they would puzzle over what the paltry human and the titanic human could be up to all splayed out like gingerbread men next to a water hazard on a golf course.

"What's the plan?" Fergus asked, watching Lester unzip the backpack's front pocket by touch.

"I'm going to retrieve my .357 revolver. It is fully chambered. I'll give you the Glock. It's smaller and will fit your hand better. You said you were in the military, so I assume you know your way around firearms."

"Sadly, I do. This is a symbolic act, you know, Lester. It means you trust me. Perhaps you've fallen in love with me a little."

"I have spidey sense too. I know whom I can trust and whom I cannot. We'll wait until our assailant stops shooting, at which point they will assume we're injured or dead and will then approach. When they get close enough, we will spring up and shoot them."

Fergus was on shaky ground. *Cthor* protocol demanded no humans be harmed or killed by his hand except through self-defense. Escaping a dangerous situation and allowing the participants to work things out themselves was always the preferred action. He may be able to escape on his own, thus avoiding a shoot-out and a potential violation. However, he would not abandon the man lying next to him. Fergus had decided Lester was remarkable. More importantly, he liked the stoic man, and wouldn't allow harm to come to him if he could stop it.

"Sounds like a reasonable plan. How will we know when they're in range?" Fergus said.

"My hearing is exceptional. I'll know. Just follow my lead and have patience."

"Very well."

The minutes ticked by. The drone of the cicadas came in waves, a chittering tide of noise that ebbed and flowed in the air like water. Mosquitos bit them. Flies bit them. Ants bit them. At any moment, Fergus thought, an alligator would emerge from the pond and bite them too. Everything in this state wanted to bite you.

"Get ready," Lester whispered finally.

Fergus gripped the Glock with the proficiency of someone who did, in fact, know his way around firearms.

"On the count of three. One...two...three!"

The two men popped up from the ground like pilots ejected from a crashing fighter jet. He would only shoot if he or his friend were in imminent danger. He had confidence in his ability to make the correct split-second decision even under duress.

Lester's reflexes were similarly adept. Neither fired a shot at the child approaching through the tall grass. Her movements were predatory, a diminutive lioness stalking prey in the Serengeti.

She saw them at the same moment they saw her, but her instinct was different. She fired the rifle which was already in position to do business.

This time the shot went wide, hitting the water with a robust splat, perhaps killing the imaginary alligator. Before the child could get off another round, Lester was on her.

He grabbed the barrel of the rifle and tossed it behind him into the water as if it were a plastic toy and not an authentic Remington bolt-action. The child's hand moved to her leg where a hunting knife, almost as long as the tiny femur, was strapped. Before she could strike at him with it, he caught her wrist and squeezed until the knife fell to the ground.

"Ouch," the miniature would-be murderess said, while her second hand snaked over a scrawny shoulder. The next moment, a gleaming machete came close to slicing off Lester's ear.

He released the slight wrist and took a step backward, grinning as he studied the machete-wielding child in front of him.

Fergus looked at the china doll face so at odds with the weapon in the grubby, dimpled hand. His heart sank. This is what the *Cthor* had wrought with their manipulation of humankind and the world. Such beauty and innocence...

"Bring it, asshole!" the cherub taunted, brandishing the machete.

"Little girl, we mean you no harm."

"Fuck you," the moppet replied, then launched herself at the giant. She was whipsnake fast, but Lester was nearly as quick and he possessed mass and muscle to compensate for the minor speed deficit.

Fergus stood back and observed, his blue eyes bright with unveiled fascination. Movies were delightful, but the real-life scene playing out before him was more compelling than any cinematic experience.

Lester soon separated the formidable weapon from the child and held her in a restraining bear hug. He might have been a doting father, but the squirming female Chucky Doll was no adoring daughter. The golden eyes framed by blond corkscrew curls exuded venom. A lesser man would have found them daunting. Lester laughed, that bass-tone, barrel-chested chortle that sounded like it came from some benevolent god on a distant mountain.

"What is your name, child?"

"Let me go," the urchin said, her voice deadly calm.

"What if I don't?"

"I will get loose somehow, capture you, and torture you until you are dead."

"Goodness. How can such a sweet little girl say such terrible things?"

A shrug of the restrained shoulders. "Because that's life. You have to be a killer to survive."

"Not true. Who told you this?"

"My mother. Now let me go, dickhead."

"Tsk tsk. Children shouldn't use such offensive language. Rule number one: no more naughty words. Are we clear? Say yes with sincerity and I'll let you go."

"Yes," the child said quickly.

"Not sincere."

A dramatic sigh came from the rosebud mouth.

"I won't say any more naughty words."

"Also, I want your word of honor that you will not try to hurt or kill me or my friend over there."

"The leprechaun? I could take him down in two shakes of a lamb's tail."

Fergus's rusty beard twitched at the corners.

"Do you agree to the terms? No hurting and no killing?"

"Sure."

"More sincerity, please."

Another exasperated sigh. "I agree not to hurt or kill you or the leprechaun."

Lester released the child. She scampered ten feet away, then turned to face them, small hands on prepubescent hips. She wore an expression of frank curiosity.

"Are you guys a couple? There's nothing wrong with that, you know. My mom always said that all forms of love between people were good. Didn't matter what color they were or if they were two girls or two boys."

"Your mother sounds like an enlightened soul," Fergus said.

The amber eyes fringed with impossibly long eyelashes slid from Lester to him. He felt the weight of them — they had seen things no child's eyes should ever see.

"She's dead."

"I'm sorry for your loss," Lester said. There was a gentleness in his voice Fergus had not heard before. At that moment he realized they would be bringing a new applicant back to the Costco headquarters of the Tequesta Terminators.

"Hey, you got blood on me." The child looked down at her filthy cotton dress. It might have been pink at some point in its dubious past, but now it was a grimy brown festooned with giant's blood. "Did I do that?" she said, gazing wide-eyed at Lester's chest.

"You did. And it hurts like the dickens at the moment. The least you can do is tell us your name, seeing as how you shot me."

"It must not have been a kill shot. You're lucky. I'm really good at shooting."

Fergus froze. The memory of another golden-eyed sharpshooter came to mind. He hoped with every fiber of his being that this child would not reveal herself to be of the same ilk.

"I'm Annabelle. Like the lady in the poem. My mom loved Edgar Allen Poe. Read his stories to me at bedtime."

"Poe isn't suitable reading material for children," Lester said.

"My mom said Poe was a genius, and I wasn't interested in *One Fish, Two Fish, Red Fish, Blue Fish.*"

"That's too bad. Dr. Suess was also a genius."

"If you say so. I like the scary stuff. Always have."

"So Annabelle, how old are you and why did you shoot at us?"

"I'm nine and a half and I shot at you because you probably have food. I'm pretty hungry and there aren't as many squirrels as there used to be."

"We have food. What would you prefer, peanut butter or Campbell's Chicken and Stars?"

"Can I have both?"

"At the same time?"

"Yes. Like I said, I'm pretty hungry."

"Then the answer is yes. Remember you gave your word not to hurt us, so let's find a place to set up camp and I'll heat the soup for you."

"I don't mind if it's cold."

"We're not animals, Annabelle. We eat our soup warm. Unless it's gazpacho."

"What's gazpacho?"

"Oh child, you have much to learn. Fortunately, I'm a patient man and an excellent teacher."

"What about my weapons? Is my rifle ruined now that it's in the water?"

"Maybe not," Lester said, wading into the pond and reaching down into the possibly alligator-infested water. He brought forth the firearm like Excalibur emerging from a mystical lake. "We'll dismantle it and dry it out. Did your mother show you proper firearms maintenance?"

A shake of the blond curls. "No. There wasn't time for that before she died. She only showed me how to load it. I figured out on my own how to fire it. I think I have a knack for it. I can get a squirrel from really far away. There's not much meat on them, though. Takes three or four to fill me up. Can I get my machete and knife too?"

"Can I trust you not to use them on us?"

"Yes, I promise."

This time Fergus believed her.

"What are your names?" she said, sliding the knife under two pieces of string tied to her leg. The next moment the machete was secure in a sheath made of rags and secured to the tiny back with more of the string.

"I'm Fergus, and the big guy is Lester." He extended his hand which the child merely stared at.

"So are you a couple? You look like you both came out of a storybook. I've never seen hair that color. And I've never met anyone that tall before."

"No, we're not a couple. Just friends." Lester smiled. "Let's make camp and get that soup warming. Then I'd like to hear your story, Annabelle."

"Okay. It's safer this way. Follow me," she said, sprinting away in the direction of a house.

"What are we getting ourselves into here?" Fergus said. "She could be leading us into a trap. What if there are a dozen adolescent assassins holed up in there? A real-life *Lord of the Flies*?"

"I thought of that. I don't think so, though. I think this one has been alone. My spidey sense tells me so."

"Much is riding on your spidey sense, Lester. I hope you're right."

Chapter 20 — Tyler

"What's wrong with you?" Kenny said to Tyler.

It was late evening and they were taking advantage of the last vestige of sunlight to work on the hail-damaged aquaponics facility. Most of the tilapia survived, but all the vegetation had been ravaged. They would have to wait on Hector's seeds to sprout before they could transplant them here.

"Nothing. I'm fine," Tyler said, not meeting the laser gaze behind the Clark Kent glasses.

"Liar. I've been living with you for months. I know something is wrong. Normally you're just a sad puppy, but lately you've been a petulant teenager."

"That's hilarious coming from you, a smartass nerdy teenager."

"But not a petulant one."

"True. You're a lot of things — rude, sarcastic, belligerent — but not petulant."

"Are you sure you even know what that means, blondie? It's kind of a big word."

"Yeah, little dude. I'm not the wordsmith you are, but I'm not an idiot."

Kenny shrugged. "If you say so. So what's up with you?"

He would not be diverted.

"Nothing. I just have some things on my mind."

"Sharing is caring. Tell me all about your troubles, bro. I'm here for you."

"There's stuff I don't want to talk about. Just like you not wanting to talk about what happened on the way down here from Brooklyn."

Tyler saw the familiar mask slide over Kenny's face. He had yet to get him to open up about the months after Chicxulub before the teenager had arrived at the Colony, hungry and traumatized.

"Check and mate," Kenny said after a few seconds. "I guess some things are best left buried in the past."

"Yeah, I guess so."

"But something tells me your past isn't buried very deep. I think there's a skeleton hand clawing its way out of a shallow grave even now."

"You're delusional."

"No, I'm not. It's okay that you don't want to talk about it, but don't act like I'm making shit up."

"Language."

"Whatever. Just know that I know something is amiss. You can tell me or not tell me, but don't deny that the roller coaster in Tyler World is sliding off its tracks."

Tyler didn't answer.

Kenny sighed dramatically. "So that Zoey chick. There's some sexy vanilla, am I right?"

"She's very pretty, if that's what you mean."

"Very pretty? Please. That gina is country pie."

"Talk in English, little dude. I don't speak ghetto slang."

"She's about the prettiest girl I've ever seen in my life."

"Yes, she is." He could feel the intelligent eyes on him, but wouldn't look up from the work he was doing on one of the troughs. Fish glided inches below the water's surface; he never tired of watching them swim. When problems weighed him down, he would come to the aquaponics farm. It was almost as good as his old salt water tank filled with angelfish. The tilapia weren't as colorful, but in their own way they were lovely too.

"That's all you're gonna say?" Kenny said.

"What do you want me to say? Yes, she's pretty."

"You should hit that."

"Don't be vulgar."

"How does that make me vulgar? All I'm saying is the two best-looking people on the island should hook up. Maybe squirt out some glorious bambinos."

"Get your mind out of the gutter. We have stuff to deal with that's more important than hooking up."

"True dat. We'll all be starving to death before much longer."

"Not if Hector gets the new crop going. And there's an entire ocean of food out there, you know."

"Yeah, but I'm getting burned out on seafood."

"Beggars can't be choosers."

"At least Charlotte will be cooking tonight. She may be dentally-challenged, but that redneck is a goddamn culinary genius."

"Language," Tyler said again, distracted now.

The sun was beginning its daily descent into the turquoise water; the luminous half-orb floated at the edge of the horizon. It was time to head over to the Love Shack for the emergency meeting Rosemary had called. When Tyler thought about being in the company of Zoey, a tight knot of anxiety blossomed in the pit of his stomach.

***

"Yes, Howard, I realize a direct hit from a hurricane is rare, but we have to consider the possibility. After the hail storm, we can't dismiss the notion of an even more destructive weather event," Rosemary said.

Tyler sat at the back next to Kenny. Charlotte and her helpers had served a delicious meal of jambalaya made with rice, Spam, and some freshly-caught fish. Now it was time for Rosemary to get to the point of the meeting. He tried to keep his eyes from gravitating to the redhead sitting next to Amelia at the front. The warm, flickering light of the torches made her face even lovelier, if that were possible.

"An evacuation plan seems extreme," Howard said. "These houses are made to withstand hurricanes." He always sat up front near Rosemary, as if being close to the Colony leader would elevate his own status within the community.

Tyler liked almost everyone he encountered, but he could not warm up to Howard. The middle-aged man was an insufferable blowhard; there was a shiftiness about him too...a cagey cast to his eyes. He would always place his own interests above those of the colony, and he never volunteered for any extra work beyond his job of maintaining the boat engines. He had been a marine mechanic in his old life, which made him an asset, despite his disagreeable personality.

"How is creating a few protocols extreme?" Tension was evident in Rosemary's jawline.

"I imagine you'll want to do drills...practice your little evacuation procedures. That's a lot of effort for something that probably won't even be needed. It's not only a waste of fuel, but also a waste of our time and energy, which is better spent getting food and making sure we're safe."

The smug tone in the voice was more than Tyler could stand. He nudged Kenny with an elbow, giving him a look that said, *Do your thing.*

"Dick don't do drills or diddly squat!"

Laughter rippled through the crowd. Kenny's Tourette's was often a source of amusement for those who weren't the target. He smiled at the seething man who turned to face the fourteen-year old. Kenny shrugged his shoulders and tried to look sheepish.

Rosemary's mouth twitched at one corner, then a stern façade replaced the amusement.

"Kenny can't help the outbursts, Howard. You know that. About the drills, you're wrong. It is never a bad idea to be prepared for the worst. I think it's a prudent course of action, and we will take a vote now. All in favor of a full-participation evacuation plan, raise your hands." She counted, frowning. "All who oppose, raise your hands." She counted again, then sighed.

"Twenty-three for, twenty-eight against. Very well, then."

Tyler knew Rosemary. She would still put something together, even if the Colonists didn't participate. It was another quality he admired about their leader — Rosemary placed the safety and well-being of her people before everything.

"Next order of business," she started to say, but was interrupted by an outburst at the front table.

"He's choking!" someone yelled.

Everyone stood, trying to see what was happening. Through the melee, Tyler watched Amelia push aside people much taller than herself to get to the table where Howard sat. Tyler edged his way to the table as well. He had taken first aid classes during his academic career, and even though they had focused on drowning situations, his training might be useful to Amelia.

The tiny woman stood on a bench with her arms wrapped around the torso of the much larger man — a backward bear hug. She was giving him the Heimlich maneuver.

"I don't think he's choking," she said after several attempts.

The man's face had turned crimson. His eyes bulged.

"He's getting air. See his chest?"

Rosemary nodded.

Howard collapsed onto the sandy grass.

"If he can make sounds, he's not choking," Amelia said.

He was making sounds — horrible, gurgling, gagging sounds.

"Can't you do something?" Rosemary said.

"No," Amelia replied, tilting her head as she watched the man on the ground. "No, I can't because I believe he's been poisoned. I've seen it before."

"Poisoned?" someone shrieked. *"Oh my god!"*

As if to underscore her diagnosis, foam began streaming out of Howard's mouth, a bubbling rivulet of pink saliva. His eyes rolled back.

"A fast-acting poison. I'm afraid it's too late for ipecac syrup or charcoal, which I don't have at the moment anyway."

She kneeled beside the dying man, taking his hand in her small one; the gentle, wise expression was tinged with sadness now.

She said, "Go to the light, my brother. Your time here is done. It is not the end, but the beginning of your next adventure. Be at peace." She might have been speaking to a wounded animal.

Another stream of red-flecked saliva gushed out of the open mouth and pooled on the sand beside him. The Colonists watched in mute horror.

His chest rose and fell a final time, then didn't move again.

For several heartbeats, nobody spoke. Finally, an anguished sob pierced the night, breaking the collective reverie. Everyone started talking at once. Tyler took a few steps back, allowing his focus to shift from person to person.

Lucas stood next to Rosemary now. The two exchange pointed expressions.

Hector wrapped a protective arm around Ingrid's shoulders. She frowned, but was not distraught.

Kenny wormed through the crowd to get a look at the dead guy.

Chin, the Colony's oddball mechanical engineer, studied the crowd as did Tyler. The face was inscrutable as always.

An angelic voice began to sing the loveliest rendition of Amazing Grace he had ever heard. Charlotte stood off to the side, still wearing her apron. In the moonlight she appeared almost pretty, even with the missing teeth.

He felt something being slipped into his hand. He didn't turn; he knew who was behind him.

Amelia returned from the kitchen carrying a tablecloth. She draped it over the dead man's face and then his body.

After Charlotte's song ended, Rosemary said, "The meeting is adjourned, folks. Lucas and I will get to the bottom of this, I assure you. Do not panic. Be vigilant in locking your doors and windows. I recommend the buddy system. Try not to go anywhere by yourself."

"The buddy system isn't going to stop a poisoner," Ingrid said.

"Maybe our murderer will choose another method next time."

Ingrid pressed her lips into a tight line.

Tyler took a few steps farther away from the mass of anxious, horrified people, and turned his back. He sought the light of one of the tiki torches, then unfolded the note in his palm.

Midnight.

There was no written location for the rendezvous, but he didn't need an address. He knew where to find Zoey.

***

"Tell me you're not responsible for Howard's death," Tyler said to the woman who stood inches away.

Even in the gloom of night, her beauty was flawless. Achingly so. His stomach tightened into a painful clenched fist. He hated the effect she had on him — an effect she had evoked the first moment he laid eyes on her all those months ago. He could deny her nothing.

"What if I were? The guy was a douchebag."

"Were you or not?" Tyler demanded.

The full lips spread into a smile. "No. Feel better now?"

She reached up to him, winding her fingers into his hair then pulling his mouth down to hers.

He was lost in her kiss. Minutes, perhaps hours, passed. Finally, with strength he didn't know he possessed, he pulled away.

"What's up your ass?" she said, amusement in her voice, and also a hint of annoyance. She didn't like it when someone resisted her.

"I've become attached to these people, Zoey. I don't want to see them get hurt."

"Even the douchebags?"

"Even the douchebags."

"I wondered what the hell was going on here. You were supposed to report back weeks ago."

"And that's why you washed up on our shore."

"Of course. Do you think I would let you go so easily? Or allow these people to have a better life than we do? Have you forgotten your mission?"

He had not forgotten his mission. But he wrestled with whether he would complete it or spill his guts to Rosemary instead. If he chose the latter, it would allow the Colonists to prepare for the inevitable invasion from Tequesta...

...his home before he had traveled to the Colony as a spy.

Chapter 21 — Jessie

"I forgot how hot it can be up here," Jessie said. She wasn't complaining, but she admitted she might have become a bit spoiled in *Cthor-Vangt*, where you were always comfortable and always had enough to eat.

She walked on a cracked, weed-choked blacktop highway in Central Kansas. She supposed now that cars were no longer driving on the surface and there were no workers to fill in the cracks, the weeds would take over. She wondered how much time would pass before all evidence of people was gone.

Thousands of years? Millions?

"It doesn't get this hot in England," Harold said, removing his fisherman's hat and mopping his brow with a bandana.

Harold walked on the other side of Tung, who said he needed to be in between them all times. He said that was so he could keep them both safe. Jessie's *scythen* told her he felt a heavy burden. They were above ground now, and she and Harold were his responsibility. If anything happened to either of them, it would not go well for Tung with the *Cthor*. They could be kind of mean sometimes. Tung carried a weapon that he would use 'as a last resort.' She caught a glimpse of it when they had first emerged onto the Kansas prairie after the ride up on the special elevator. She would like to study the opening of that elevator when they returned. If you didn't know where it was, you would never see it. It was disguised to look like a grove of cottonwood trees, but if you squinted your eyes just right, those trees looked like something on an alien planet. Just like the weapon Tung carried in his pocket. Of course neither were alien at all, just 'futuristic.' That was the word he supplied when she had asked about their appearance. Maybe when she was older, she would be taught how all these futuristic things worked. At the moment, though, she was excited to be above ground. And if she were lucky, there might be an opportunity to go to Florida.

She missed Amelia so much sometimes it gave her a stomach ache.

"Are we walking all the way to Tennessee?"

It was funny to hear Harold's British accent while speaking in the ancient *Cthor* language. Harold had mastered it already, but Jessie still struggled with many of the words, so she was relieved when Tung replied.

"When we're up here, we speak in English. Or whatever is indigenous to our location. We don't want the locals to inadvertently hear a language that hasn't been spoken for millennia. Even if they won't recognize it."

"Very well. So that's a yes on the walking?"

Tung smiled. He seemed almost cheerful today. Jessie suspected he enjoyed being on the surface almost as much as her. Of course the world had changed since he called the above ground home. He had been recruited many thousands of years ago. Jessie herself could live to be very old, maybe even as old as Thoozy, who had been the oldest harvested human ever.

She missed Thoozy almost as much as Amelia, but because Logan had murdered him back in Liberty, she would never get a chance to see him again. The thought made her eyes water.

"What's wrong, Jessie?"

"I was just thinking about Thoozy."

"I miss him too." Tung paused, then said, "Harold, we'll try to find a vehicle or perhaps some horses along the way. The problem will be to find a car that will start and which contains gasoline that's still good. I expect most of it has turned by now."

Harold nodded. "Oxidation."

"Exactly. Batteries will no longer start on their own, so we'll need one with a manual transmission, which we can push start."

"Righto. We call that 'popping the clutch' back home."

Even though Harold's areas of expertise were old civilizations and old languages, he knew a lot of other stuff too. Like the word for what happens to gasoline when it goes bad.

Jessie had much to learn. In addition to a regular education such as any nine-year-old child would receive, she was also learning about the *Cthor* and *Cthor-Vangt*. She didn't mind, though. She loved to learn.

"Riding horses would be fun," she said. "I hope we find some."

"I don't," Harold said with a grin. "I'm quite spry for a sixty-seven year old, but sitting in a saddle all day wreaks havoc on one's bum."

Jessie laughed. She liked when he said that word.

Harold gave her a wink, then said to Tung, "I'm surprised you don't have some advanced chemical to put into the gas tanks of these vehicles."

"The *Cthor* protocol is 'When in Rome.' They want us to fit in, which means no magic elixir to make the cars run."

"Pity, that. Well, at least it's a lovely day, and we're getting plenty of exercise."

"There's a car up ahead." Jessie shielded her eyes from the sun with one hand and pointed with the other. "A Cadillac Seville. That's what it says on the trunk. It's white. Do you see it?"

"I can just make out a metallic shape. Goodness, child. Your vision may also be exceptional. That's something we hadn't considered." Tung looked at her like she had suddenly sprouted an extra eye in the middle of her forehead.

She shrugged. "I can see really well. My daddy always said so. Even at night."

"That may come in handy on this mission."

Jessie could tell her new mentor felt even more weighed down with responsibility now. Perhaps she shouldn't have let him know how well she could see. She liked him and didn't want him to be stressed out. That was a term she had learned from her daddy before the end came. He had been very stressed out when everyone started dying. It was an awful time and she had tried to block it from her mind, but sometimes the memories crept back in. The months she had spent at the Circle K convenience store in Arizona after he died had been lonely and terrifying. She didn't ever want to be alone like that again, so she always tried to make the people around her feel happy.

"What are the odds it will have a manual transmission?" Tung said, standing next to the Cadillac now.

It was getting hotter by the minute. The sound of the cicadas came in waves — *a chittering tide of noise that ebbed and flowed in the air like water.* The words streamed into her mind, unbidden. She knew now what it meant when that happened — her *scythen* had picked it up from someone. When she got better at managing the skill, she would be able to determine who had sent their thoughts and whether they were intended for her or had just randomly escaped from the sender. That's how Tung had explained it. When she was younger, she believed they had come from monsters. She was glad she understood them better now, but they could still be scary. The thoughts of some of the people these days were not very nice.

"Less than ten percent, I would say." Harold studied the car which was coated with a thick layer of dust and grime.

"Feeling lucky?" Tung said, then opened the car door with a metallic screech.

This was the part Jessie dreaded. There was a dead person in there. At least they were mostly dried out now, though. Two years had gone by since people had started dying. She figured all those human bodies would decay and go back into the dirt long before the things those people built did.

She pinched her nostrils as the stench wafted from the vehicle. Boxes, bags, suitcases, blankets, and water bottles surrounded the body, obscuring the part they needed to see. Together, Tung and Harold scooped up the body sitting in the driver's seat, and placed it on the side of the road as gently as her daddy did when putting her to bed. Neither of the men spoke, so she didn't either. They soon returned to the open car door. Jessie had no idea how a manual-shifting car looked different from a regular car, but Tung did.

"Here goes nothing," he said as he began clearing the debris covering the console.

She held her breath, not knowing whether the next moment would bring minor disappointment or giddy excitement. Before it was revealed, she felt a painful thump on the side of her head.

Everything went black.

***

Jessie felt like she was floating in a swimming pool. The water was warm. It must have been nighttime because everything was dark. Did people swim in their pools at night? She didn't know. They had gone to the YMCA community pool back in Arizona a few times in the summer, but it closed at eight o'clock every evening. She knew you weren't supposed to go swimming when it was raining, because if lightning struck the water, you would be electrocuted. Her daddy said water was an excellent conductor. She wasn't sure what a conductor was, but she knew about being electrocuted. She did not want that to happen to her. Swimming at night must be different, though. She couldn't imagine why it would be a bad thing, so she decided to keep floating in the darkness.

It would have been peaceful if not for the yelling.

It sounded like it was coming from miles away. It was a man's voice, and familiar. Was he saying her name? She couldn't tell. As she floated, she thought about whose voice it might be. It was definitely not her daddy's voice. With a stab of sadness, she remembered he was dead. She had buried him herself under some heavy rocks back at the Circle K two years ago. He was probably dried up now, just like the body they had pulled from the white Cadillac Seville...

Her eyes flew open when recent memories crashed into conscious thought.

"Oh, thank goodness." Tung stood over her with that stressed-out look on his face.

"What happened?" She rubbed the side of her head where it was hurting. When she pulled her hand away, her fingers felt wet. She stared at the bright red blood covering them, then squinted at her surroundings while trying to sit up.

"We were attacked by two assailants. I blame myself. I was distracted and wasn't keeping an eye on you and Harold."

"Where are they now?" she said, trying to sit up.

"Disposed of."

She laid back down. "Did you have to use your weapon?"

"Yes, regrettably. They were not nice people, though, which made the task somewhat easier. Stay still for now, Jessie. I need to check on Harold."

The next moment he was gone.

She lay on the hot asphalt looking up at the sky. There were no puffy-sheep clouds, so she soon lost interest. The meaning of Tung's words finally registered: *I need to check on Harold.*

She popped up like the jack-in-the-box she'd had when she was three-years-old.

Her head was spinning a little and her thoughts were a little fuzzy, but otherwise she felt okay. Sea-green eyes scanned the perimeter. She saw the Cadillac not far away. In the other direction, Tung was crouched down next to a lumpish something lying in the middle of the road on top of the double white lines, the ones that meant you could pass other cars if they were driving too slowly.

The lump was Harold. She was on her feet the next second, running toward her friends.

Please don't let him be dead...

"I told you not to move. You may have a head injury."

Tung had unbuttoned Harold's blue cotton shirt and was touching the chest with gentle fingers.

"I can help," Jessie said. She could barely get the words out; it felt like she had swallowed a ping pong ball. She realized how much she had come to love her newest friend, maybe even as much as she loved Pablo and Maddie.

"Please sit on the ground, be quiet, and stay still. Let me see what is happening inside of him."

Deft fingers continued to touch the older man, concentrating on the chest. Then they moved to Harold's head, covered in gray hair that looked darker now with sweat. The fisherman's hat lay next to him, like an anxious pet waiting to be reunited with its owner. Tung's eyes were half-closed as he sent his *scythen* into Harold's body. If anybody could find out if Harold was okay, it would be Tung and his *scythen*. He was the best at it.

After several minutes, he removed his hands. She knew the verdict was bad.

Panic washed over her. "Don't say it. He's not dead."

"I can't feel his heart beating, Jessie. Neurons are still firing in his brain, but I think it's too late. I'm sorry."

"I can help!"

He seemed to think about it, then shook his head.

"No. I think he's too far gone. It would be terribly risky."

"I helped, Fergus. I can help Harold."

"Fergus wasn't dead, just dying. This is different."

"He hasn't been dead for long, right?"

"No, just a couple of minutes, perhaps."

Jessie's mouth turned down in a frown. She was concentrating very hard on not being angry with Tung. She took a deep breath to calm herself.

"I'm going to save him. He's my friend, and I don't want to lose another person I love."

She watched the effect of her words on Tung's face. There was hope.

"We don't know what will happen, Jessie. We have no idea what *langthal* will do on someone who has clinically died."

"I don't care. I'm doing it anyway." She squatted next to Harold's body.

Tung didn't stop her.

She had memorized everything Amelia taught her when she healed Maddie and then Fergus. She closed her eyes and placed her hands on Harold's chest.

"It might be that Harold's brain has been deprived of oxygen for too long," Tung said in a soft voice.

She lifted her hands with a jerk. She remembered a news story her daddy had told her about a man who had been ice fishing and fell into a cold lake. He was rescued, but the rescuers figured he had been under water and not breathing for at least ten minutes. They brought him back to life, but he was never the same again — some parts of his brain didn't work very well. She thought about Tung's words. Would Harold be...different? Not as smart? Not as kind and friendly? That would be terrible, to bring her friend back to life only to realize he was no longer the same.

She shook her head. "I'm going to do this. I won't lose another person I love. Not if I can help it."

She closed her eyes again and went to work.

Chapter 22 — Anonymous

Dear Diary,

Someone was very naughty this evening! I bet you can guess who...

My heart is still racing from the adrenaline rush. I've never poisoned anyone before, and it just might be the most exciting method by which to fulfill my role as Angel of Death. Every part of the oleander is lethal, but it is also bitter-tasting, so I knew the dosage was critical. The very act of inserting the poison onto the targeted plate was a delicate maneuver which anyone might have observed. I didn't know how fast it would take effect. It was thrilling to watch the drama play out.

Did someone see me do it? What if I miscalculated the dosage and my victim experienced merely illness instead of death? Would Amelia have an anecdote in her adorable little black bag?

There's much about poison that I don't know. Sadly, it was not an area of self-study before the end came. There was so much to learn, and I hadn't realized yet what I was. However, my self-education did include horticulture, so I am familiar with the local flora. Florida hosts several varieties of indigenous poisonous plants besides the deadly oleander: foxglove, lantana, wild mushrooms, to name a few.

But the one I'm most excited to experiment with is ricinus communis. It is a lovely perennial with spiky leaves that look similar to those of the marijuana plant. It produces small seed pods that contain castor beans — not a true bean, but rather a seed from which oil is extracted. Castor oil has many beneficial applications.

But the seed has a dark twin: ricin, one of the deadliest poisons found in nature.

How delightful!

So while I haven't abandoned my plans for more straightforward killing, I do intend to have some fun traipsing down this new path.

On a side note, I doubt that many folks will grieve the loss of that insufferable man; he had no friends that I'm aware of. It's a mystery to me why anyone would choose to be obnoxious. Clever people — especially clever killers — put on a friendly façade. They appear compassionate and cooperative. They're always ready to lend a helping hand, unlike Howard who never volunteered for any extra work.

My seemingly beneficent personality is the perfect disguise for a killer who is moving up in the world.

Chapter 23 — Rosemary

"We need a fortified location several miles inland. That's the sticking point of our evacuation plan. We have the boat assignments worked out and the order in which the Colonists will be transported. People go first, then water, then food, then if there's time, these items." Rosemary held up a piece of notebook paper. Even in the dim lantern light, everyone at the table could see the details on the handwritten bulleted list.

Ingrid nodded after perusing it, then said in a kinder voice than she had ever used toward her, "Well done. I appreciate your taking this seriously. It wasn't easy for me to come forward. My entire life people have been skeptical of my dreams. I'm glad you weren't, and I'm relieved you didn't tell everyone else about them."

Rosemary smiled at the older woman. She felt they had overcome a barrier that existed between them. She saw respect — perhaps even admiration — in the keen eyes. Being on the receiving end of that, especially when it came from someone as imperious and reticent as Ingrid, felt like the old days when she had used recreational drugs. That high was addictive on several levels. It felt wonderful to be admired, but it also mitigated some of the guilt that she carried...would always carry, like a scarlet letter on her chest that only she could see.

"Tell me again why this chick is here," Lucas drawled from where he stood a few feet away, arms crossed, studying the faces at Rosemary's kitchen table.

"First, because she is a meteorologist...or close enough. Second, because she was present during the initial discussion of the hurricane dreams. She claims to be clairvoyant, like Ingrid. Also, Tyler believes her familiarity with Tequesta could be useful."

"I've already interrogated her about the Terminators," Lucas said, narrowed eyes glued to Zoey. "And Ingrid has lived here forever. She knows the lay of the land. Why the hell do we need her intel?"

"I'm referring to her detailed knowledge of the area as it applies to an evacuation plan. She has information gained from the group's raids."

The reasoning was a bit of a stretch, and she hoped no one would recognize it as such. She desperately wanted her dubious past to stay buried, which is why she had granted Zoey's request to be present at the meeting. The young woman had recognized her from a televised mug shot before the plague, and while there had been no direct threat of blackmail, the possibility was always there, nipping at her heels. The thought of living like this for the rest of her life weighed on her. Should she take extreme measures to rid herself of this subtle menace? Unlikely. The last thing she wanted to do was add to her lengthy list of existential transgressions.

"Zoey, what are your thoughts about where we should go? Storm shelters? High school gymnasiums? What's easy to get to, unoccupied, and can accommodate our people, preferably with adequate plumbing?" Rosemary said.

"The bigger question is how are you going to get past the Terminators on your way to safety? They have lookouts, you know. People watching for anyone coming into their territory."

"Perhaps we should go north or south of the town?" Ingrid said.

Rosemary shook her head. "Think about how rough the water will be and how strong the currents and winds during the onset of a hurricane. The shortest distance from here to the mainland is a half mile, which will be risky to navigate. We can't make that any longer. Zoey, do you know where these lookouts are positioned? We could send a team to disable them."

"Of course."

Lucas snorted in disgust. "You're kidding, right? You're going to trust this broad? That's almost as stupid as letting her come to this meeting."

"I think that's enough for tonight, folks," Rosemary said, ignoring the outburst. "We'll pick back up next time. Lucas and I still have a lot to discuss...about the other issue."

Ingrid, Zoey, and Tyler stood.

"Ingrid, I'll walk you home," Tyler said.

She waved him off. "No, I have a flashlight, and my house is only a block away. I'll be fine. Hector is waiting up for me."

Rosemary smiled. This was the first acknowledgment that they were a couple. It was a source of amusement for everyone in the Colony that the two thought their relationship was still secret.

Tyler turned to Zoey. "Do you need help getting home?" he asked, stiffly. She nodded and flashed him a smile.

His body language was peculiar tonight. She would question him about it later, alone. Lucas shut the front door after everyone had left, then turned to her.

"So Tyler and Zoey are banging?" he said.

"I don't know. Maybe," she said.

"You saw it, right?"

I know something was wrong with Tyler. Not what, though."

"I thought you knew everything about everyone. You're a people-reading wizard."

"Just like you."

"Yeah, I'm good too. You ready to talk about the murder investigation?"

"Yes. Please tell me you've come up with a strategy."

"Yep, but you're not going to like it."

She sighed. "Let me guess. You want to interrogate everyone?"

"Nope. I want to search their houses."

"That's a huge violation of privacy."

"Fuck that. We have a goddamn murderer here, Rose. Jesus Christ, the last thing you should be worried about is civil liberties."

She took a deep breath. "You're right. Is this to be a covert search or a public one?"

"Covert, of course, which will take some coordination with you. I'll need people out of their houses while I'm working. That's where you come in. You'll figure out how to make sure they're somewhere other than at home."

"How long do you think this will take?"

"At least two weeks. If it were just me going house to house openly, I could get it done in a couple of days, but I don't want anyone to have advance knowledge of when their house will be searched."

"Don't you think people will suspect you're doing exactly what you're doing?"

"Yes. That's why it will take so long. I want them to become complacent. The murder just happened. The killer will be most careful now. Give him a few days to let his guard down. Or hers," he added.

"You hope to find the poison? It could be hidden anywhere. Doesn't have to be in the killer's house."

"It is. Trust me. But not just the poison. I'll get a vibe when I'm in the right house. It's a cop thing...kind of hard to explain. I'll know when I'm in the den of the killer."

Chapter 24 — Ingrid

"I was about to send out a rescue team," Hector said with a worried smile.

"I'm old but I'm not decrepit. And I was extra careful on the path."

Charming cobblestone footpaths traversed the narrow island from the western edge to the eastern shoreline, providing the residents with easy walking access to the beach. They had been well-maintained before the end came. Now, with normal shifting of the sandy topography, their surface was no longer level. The occasional elevated brick sought to trip an old woman in the dark.

"Did you solve all the world's problems at the meeting?" Hector said, shutting and locking the door behind her.

"No, although Rosemary has the beginnings of a competent evacuation plan. She is rather impressive, I have to admit."

"Yes, she is, but...?"

"But what?"

"I hear that tone. There is something you are not happy about."

"Mmmmm...yes. I'm not happy about Zoey being at what should have been a private meeting of vetted Colonists when we are discussing serious matters regarding our safety. She's not trustworthy. My gut tells me so."

"But she was interrogated by Lucas, was she not?"

"Yes, yes. So what? She's a good liar, most likely."

"Lucas is skilled in the art of drawing information from people. Besides, tonight was about an evacuation plan, not the murder of Howard, yes?"

"Yes. I'm sure they were going to discuss that after the rest of us left."

"It is a strange coincidence that the killing occurred soon after the young woman's arrival."

Ingrid was surprised by the remark. Hector was not one to gossip. She studied him in the flickering candlelight of a beeswax candle, one of hundreds she had procured before the end. No other candle's burning properties could compare to that of beeswax, and the scent made her home smell heavenly. She would share her food with the Colonists, but not her precious candles. The golden light softened the sun-wrinkled skin of her lover and reflected in his dark irises, turning them into glowing, bottomless orbs.

"That's something I would say, not you."

"Perhaps I read your mind," he said with a grin.

"Perhaps my talents are rubbing off on you. It's true, though. Very suspicious, in my opinion. And it's damned inconvenient to keep the house all closed up. It feels like an oven in here."

"I have opened all the windows upstairs. It's cooler than down here. I agree, though. Knowing there is a murderer in our midst has brought a dark cloud to paradise. We can only hope the person is soon caught. I wonder what Lucas plans to do?"

"He'll probably want to torture everyone to force a confession."

"He is not so bad. I think you are harsh in your judgment of the man."

"I doubt that. He may be good at security but he is a heavy-handed brute. I have no idea what Rosemary sees in him. He's not a gentleman, like you."

Hector smiled. "Should we retire, my darling? There are things I would like to say to you that require soft sheets and cool night breezes."

"I do believe you're trying to seduce me." She wrapped her arm around the proffered elbow as they climbed the stairs.

"Do you blame me? I am in the presence of the most dazzling woman on the island. It is only natural to want to bed such a magnificent creature."

Ingrid snorted. "Perhaps I was thirty years ago. Now, say all that to me in French."

He spoke to her in several languages as they made their way to the bedroom.

***

Ingrid dreamed. She knew it wasn't reality, but her heart raced within the dream as well as in the darkened bedroom where she lay sleeping. Her legs pumped as she sprinted down the cobblestone path toward the beach. In the bedroom, still-shapely legs twitched between luxurious sheets — a greyhound chasing a rabbit. On the path, the killer was behind her. She heard muffled footfalls in time with her own. She knew she must get to the beach for some reason; safety was there rather than at home. It was baffling, but she didn't have time to analyze it. She must escape. She hazarded a quick glance back. The figure, cloaked in night gloom, was gaining on her. Starlight reflected off a curved metal blade. What was the English word for that object? In German, it was *eine sichel*. She struggled to remember the translation. Oh yes. A sickle, the weapon of choice for the Grim Reaper.

Hurry up, old woman!

She ran faster. Faster than she ever thought possible. Others now darted beside her, trying to escape as well. She couldn't see who they were, but she knew they were Colonists. If she could only see their faces, she might discover the identity of the killer through the process of elimination — everyone who ran with her was innocent.

The dream logic made perfect sense.

She vaulted from the cobblestones toward the sandy beach. She had made it!

The killer caught her heel in mid-leap. She felt a cold vice-like grip on her foot, then her ankle, then her calf. It pulled her back onto the path just as she was about to reach safety in the sand.

She sobbed, in the dream and in her bed, as she was sliced open from sternum to pelvis. She watched her organs — intestines and kidneys and liver — spill onto the stones in a stream of blood painted inky black by the moonlight. There was so much of it; a river gushed from her body. As she lay dying, she reached up to push aside the hood covering the face of the killer...

***

"Darling, wake up," Hector was saying. He squeezed her shoulder, brushing her hair off her forehead.

She awoke. Pulling herself back into reality felt like dragging herself out of a tar pit. She was tangled up in the bed linens, panting as if she had just run a mile.

"Was it the hurricane?"

A shudder went through her body. She took a deep, ragged breath, trying to slow her racing heart.

These dreams may kill me one day.

"No. Not the hurricane."

"Then what was it?" he asked, his voice full of concern.

"I don't remember," she lied.

Chapter 25 — Fergus

"Would you like to come back with us?" Lester said to the precocious child. "You'll be safe there."

They sat in overstuffed leather chairs next to a fireplace in what was once the spacious home library of someone who could afford such extravagances. It was dank and dusty and smelled of rodents, dead and living, as well as their urine and feces, stale and fresh. Embers still glowed from the small fire they had made to heat Annabelle's Chicken and Stars soup.

Lester was right; civilized people heated their soup. The viscous, salty concoction was less revolting that way.

Fergus sat in a third chair and watched the two. The juxtaposition of the large, muscular man and the diminutive, cherubic child was visually entertaining, and their banter even more so. Annabelle had learned much in her nine and a half years on earth.

"What do you have to offer me? I'm doing pretty well here on my own," she said.

"Earlier you said you were hungry." Lester's sweat-soaked face gleamed in the dying firelight. It was hot in the room, but the stoic man was also in pain from his gunshot wound, inflicted by the child before him. There was not a trace of animosity, though; in fact the opposite was true. Fergus could sense that Lester felt a fatherly protectiveness for the girl and hoped to bring her with them when they returned to Tequesta the next day.

"That was just to trick you out of food. It's easier to get it from nice people — when you can find them — than it is to hunt squirrels. I've gotten deer, too. They're a cinch to shoot but harder to gut and clean. Mom never showed me how to do that part before she died, but I figured it out myself."

"A child can't grow up healthy on squirrel and deer meat alone. You need fruits and vegetables and milk and vitamins."

She gave him a slow blink. "It's the end of the world. That kind of stuff isn't around any longer."

"Ah, but you're wrong, child. Back home we have a large vegetable garden, several fields of grain crops, and five Holsteins...those are the cute black-and-white cows. Do you remember what milk tastes like?" He leaned in close to the little girl and said in an even deeper voice, "When was the last time you ate fresh cheese?"

"You never mentioned you had dairy, you magnificent bastard," Fergus said. Saliva flooded his mouth at the thought of cheese that had not been dehydrated or powdered, or worse, canned and labeled as something called 'nacho' and which smelled vaguely of vomit.

"Mind the naughty words," Lester replied without looking at him. He was focused on his mission to convince the child to come with them.

"We have butter, too. And bread to smear it on."

The golden eyes opened wide. "I don't believe you. Nobody has those things anymore. There's no electricity to make the ovens hot. You can't cook bread if you don't have hot ovens."

"Tsk, tsk. First, yes we do have electricity. Second, how do you think ancient people, and people from even a hundred years ago who lived in the country, baked their bread?"

Annabelle thought about that for a few seconds, then nodded. "Yes, you're right. I guess they would have used those old ovens that you build a fire in. Is that right?" She might have been a third-grade student eager to please her teacher.

"Yes, but there are many other methods that people have utilized for thousands of years. Do you like to learn? Did you enjoy school?"

A vigorous nod of the blond curls. "I loved school. I only got to first grade before everyone got sick and died. I wish I had gotten to go longer. I've been reading, though. There are lots of books here." She gestured to a wood-paneled wall lined with bookshelves. "But I have to look up a lot of the words in the dictionary. They're grown-up books. Not kid books."

"If you come with us, I will be your teacher. I will teach you anything you want to learn about...mathematics, science, history."

"Will you teach me Taekwondo and how to use other kinds of guns besides mine? I think killers need to know that stuff."

Lester's eyes glistened in the firelight. Fergus watched, waiting for him to answer.

A deep sigh came from the broad chest. "I will teach you Krav Maga — even better for killing than Taekwondo — under one condition: you must spend an equal amount of time studying subjects that don't involve killing people."

Annabelle didn't hesitate. "I'm in. When do we leave?"

An hour later the child was curled up on a sofa sound asleep. It seemed he and Lester had passed muster; she felt safe enough to sleep in their presence. In light of the little girl's well-honed survival instincts, Fergus wondered if she sensed their true natures — their inherent goodness. Perhaps the child had a smidgen of *scythen*. He would put that to the test as soon as possible.

Lester lay on the floor, cushioning his shorn head with a pillow; no furniture in the room could accommodate his bulk.

Fergus had chosen a sofa near the window they had crawled through to enter Annabelle's sanctuary. It was still open, allowing an anemic breeze into the stifling, smelly room. A nearly full moon shone through the filmy glass, providing enough light to see the rhythmic rising and falling of the tiny chest and the large one. He closed his eyes and sent out his *scythen*.

~~~

Fergus: Are you awake, my love?

Amelia: About time I heard from you. I was getting worried.

Fergus: I have had the most interesting twenty-four hours. I am in the company of a philosophizing giant and a tiny, cheeky assassin.

Amelia: You're safe?

Fergus: I am.

Amelia: You're missing all the action here in the Colony. In addition to the prophesized hurricane, which many don't want to prepare for, our resident killer has advanced beyond felines and taken a human life. Howard, the obnoxious man nobody liked, was the victim.

Fergus: Oh, dear. By what method?

Amelia: Poison.

Fergus: Fascinating!

Amelia: I knew you would say that. I don't share your enthusiasm.

Fergus: What's to be done about it?

Amelia: I don't know. That's for Rosemary and Lucas to decide. I suspect Lucas will use some kind of barbaric interrogation technique.

Fergus: He may surprise you and catch our killer.

Amelia: Or he may be our killer. In the meantime, I will try to scythen everyone with whom I come into contact. I'll have to be subtle. The last thing I want is for people to think I'm some kind of touchy-feely weirdo.

Fergus: You're the best kind of touchy-feely weirdo. I can't wait to have you interrogate me when I get home.

Amelia: When do you think that might be?

Fergus: Unknown. We leave in the morning for the Terminator headquarters. They've taken over a Costco Warehouse in Tequesta. I didn't get to investigate their operation before the giant and I were sent on a quest for propane. Speaking of, I have a new best friend. Lester is spectacular, both physically and intellectually.

Amelia: A potential recruit?

Fergus: I don't sense any scythen or langthal, but I'm enjoying his company very much.

Amelia: So it's possible, then? You can enjoy yourself with people who aren't attractive women?

Fergus. It would seem so. I must be evolving!

Amelia: Don't evolve too much. I'm rather attached to the old Fergus.

Fergus: Very well, my love. I shall endeavor to remain lascivious, just for you.

Amelia: Remain alive. That's all I want.

***

"Do you see that open window on the second floor of the building over there?" Lester said. "There is a sentry stationed inside with an M24 sniper rifle weapons system. He's very good at killing people before they realize they're being targeted."

They had ridden their bicycles all day, Lester pulling Annabelle in a jury-rigged shopping cart behind him. They rolled into Tequesta just as the sun was about to sink below the horizon. Fergus was happy not to have been asked to relieve the huge man, who seemed content to take on the burden of the child alone. He had the muscle and stamina to play draft horse for a day, even with a gunshot wound.

"Why wasn't I shot when I wandered up to the building the other day?" Fergus asked.

"The guards follow a certain protocol. I'm not privy to the details because that's not my responsibility. Perhaps they deemed you harmless because of your size."

"I could have been an assassin."

"Are you an assassin?"

"No."

"See? Since you were not shot and subsequently discovered the motherlode of propane, you'll enjoy a hero's welcome tonight."

"I just want to know about the cheese."

"Patience, my diminutive friend. We have to go through the proper steps. First, we report in to Aubrey."

"Who's Aubrey?" Annabelle asked.

"She's one of our bosses." Lester rolled to a stop on the side of the warehouse building. He started to lift the little girl out of the makeshift wagon, but she waved him off.

"I'm not helpless, you know. Your boss is a girl?"

"A young woman, yes. Aubrey and her sister Zoey are the leaders of our group. They're very beautiful and very clever. That's why I know you will fit in here."

"I've never heard of girls being in charge."

"Oftentimes women make the best commanders and administrators. They think before they act, unlike foolhardy men who often want to demonstrate their masculinity through warring."

"On that we agree," Fergus said.

"This way. Be polite, Annabelle. Much is at stake."

"What do you mean?"

"Aubrey will want to analyze you and your usefulness. She will ask questions. You will answer honestly and politely. Do you understand?"

A nod of the curls and a furrowing of the blond brows. It was the first indication of uncertainty Fergus had witnessed in the child. Lester saw it too.

"You'll do fine. A recommendation from me goes a long way."

A few moments later the three travelers stood in the small air-conditioned office. It felt like a cool slice of heaven. Fergus hoped to investigate the Terminator's entire operation soon; dairy cows, grain crops, and air conditioning hinted at progress similar to what they had achieved on the island. Before then, however, they needed to ensure Annabelle's acceptance into the Tequesta community. He got the impression Lester was less confident than he was letting on.

"Damn it, Lester. Why the hell did you bring a kid here? Especially one this small. How much work can we get out of that body?" Aubrey gave Annabelle a cursory inspection, glanced at Lester, and then targeted Fergus. The sapphire eyes felt like glacial laser beams searing into his soul. If he were going to die, it would be fitting to do so at the hands of an exquisite woman such as this.

"Well? Did the propane pan out or was this character blowing smoke up my ass?"

The question was directed at Lester, but the lasers were still focused on Fergus. He resisted the urge to fidget under their intensity.

"Six mostly-full, thousand-gallon tanks."

Fergus noticed Lester had reverted to his former reserved, taciturn self; the loquacity demonstrated on their expedition had vanished. It was an intriguing development and one about which he would question his new friend later, in private.

"No shit? Well, that's good news for you, Lucky Charms. Not only do you get to stay alive, you'll be allowed into our exclusive little club and enjoy elevated status as well. That's what happens when people prove themselves useful. Now, about this kid, Lester. What the hell were you thinking? You know the prerequisites for recruitment."

"She would have died out there by herself. Both parents are dead. She's been living on squirrels. Her name is Annabelle, by the way, named after the poem by one of your favorite writers." He gestured toward an overflowing bookshelf in the corner.

Fergus had already scanned Aubrey's collection, which included several Poe volumes as well as books on medicine and psychology. Two in particular caught his attention: *The Psychopath Inside: A Neuroscientist's Personal Journey into the Dark Side of the Brain* and *The Psychopath Whisperer: The Science of Those Without Conscience.*

"Cry me a river. I should be moved because she's an orphan named after a poem? You'll have to do better than that."

Rather than replying, Lester unbuttoned his shirt, revealing the angry, red bullet hole in his shoulder. The Neosporin they had applied the previous night was not staving off infection.

"She did this, from two hundred yards away," he lied smoothly.

"Really? With what?"

"Remington bolt-action. She's a natural. She's also interested in learning martial arts. She wants to be a more effective killer."

Aubrey barked a laugh. "You buried the lead. You should have told me this in the beginning. Very well, little girl. Today is your lucky day. Lester, give these two the tour. Where do you want the kid to bunk?"

"I'd prefer she stays with me, if that's okay. I'll put her in the top bed."

"That's kinda pervy."

Lester responded with a steely look.

"Sorry. I know you're not a pedophile. I guess you'll be taking her under your wing, then? She's your responsibility in every way. At least until she's old enough for sniper duty. Give the propane location to the tanker people. Tell them I want them on the road before sunrise. And get some antibiotics — that wound is infected. We have way too much invested for you to die at this point. Now everyone get the hell out of my office."

"Whew," Fergus said when they were on the other side of the door.

The three had moved away from the customer service desk where the bandolier-festooned brothers lounged, presumably protecting their leader from assassination attempts. Fergus could well imagine someone wanting to throttle the young woman in the air-conditioned office. She was as abrasive as Dani had been back in Texas, Oklahoma, and Kansas, but she lacked even a whiff of mercy or goodness. He knew this because his *scythen* had revealed the deficiency during their belated handshake.

He was dealing with a psychopath.

"She's rather intense," Lester said.

"She's the prettiest lady I've ever seen. She's very smart, too." Annabelle looked star-struck, which Fergus found distressing.

"You're in and that's all that matters. You'll be well taken care of here and get plenty to eat and any medications you might need. Vitamins too. Children need vitamins."

Fergus smiled at the big man fussing over the little girl as they walked through a doorway cut into the plywood barricade. The assembled panels created a cattle-chute type corridor leading from the front doors to Aubrey's office, and also provided a visual barrier to the stockpile of goods contained in the bulk of the building. Columns of rice extended halfway to the ceiling; hundreds of cases of canned vegetables towered next to them. Toilet paper, cleaning supplies, and dozens of other items filled the first two aisles they walked past. Then came cookware and dinnerware and all the other necessities of life former Costco shoppers demanded. The next aisle was packed with tidy stacks of clothing and outerwear, bins of white athletic socks, towers of towels and blankets, pyramids of rolled rugs, and additional merchandise Fergus couldn't identify in the seconds it took to walk past.

Before he could scrutinize the Terminators' vast resources further, they arrived at the pharmacy; a sign above the windowed opening identified it as such. A skinny man wearing a white lab coat slid open the glass.

"How's it hanging, Lester?" The man's voice was high-pitched; he reminded Fergus of all the rat-faced, sycophantic bad guys he had seen in a dozen gangster movies.

"Antibiotics." Terse Lester was back.

"What for? Gonorrhea? Bronchitis? Infected hangnail? You're gonna have to be more specific. They're specialized, you know."

"Gunshot wound."

"No shit? The legend got winged? I'd hate to see the other guy."

"You're looking at her." Lester patted Annabelle's blond curls.

"Hey, asshole, give the man the medicine before he rips your arm out of its socket. You got any Fintstone gummies back there?" Annabelle said, her voice deadpan and threatening.

The scrawny man's jaw dropped, but no pithy response was forthcoming. Instead, he turned and scurried through a door leading to the pharmacy stockroom; cool air wafted out. Before it swung shut, Fergus glimpsed shelves filled with bottles, tubes, and packages.

"Impressive. Most people are happy to find fungal cream for their jock itch these days."

"Most people aren't as organized as we are."

"When do we get to the cheese? I hope you weren't exaggerating. Tell me you weren't being a cheese tease. There's nothing I despise worse."

Lester's mouth twitched, but he didn't smile. He had reverted to the man Fergus had first met outside the Costco building two days ago. The stoicism was part of his Terminator persona. The gentle, kindly philosophizer must be hidden away so as to fit in here.

Rat Face soon returned. "Take two a day, twelve hours apart, for the next week. Cephalexin is like gold, you know. If it were anyone else, I'd have to see Aubrey's or Zoey's signature."

Lester took the proffered bottles without a thank-you.

"You're welcome, man!" Rat Face said.

"This way," Lester said, ignoring the remark and turning to his companions. "I'll give you a quick overview of the interior, then we'll head out back to Tent Town."

"Is that where the cheese is?"

Now that there were no Terminators present, Lester allowed a small grin. "You're all about the cheese, aren't you, little man?"

"There is nothing more important in this world than cheese. Everyone thinks it, but nobody will say it out loud. That makes me heroic."

Lester's face became sober as they approached the back of the building. Fergus had been inside a Costco prior to Chicxulub; he knew this area would have been the meat market in its former life. A frisson of dread surged through his body. Whether the sudden coldness came from his *scythen* or the cool air emanating from behind the empty cases, he could not discern.

"Remember our talk the other day?" Lester said.

"Which one? We had several."

"The one about sending sirloin steaks to starving people in Africa."

"Oh no."

"Don't judge and keep an open mind. I'd rather Annabelle not see this, but you both need to understand how things work here."

He motioned for them to follow as he walked behind the empty cases, which would have been crammed with pork chops and ground beef two years ago. An aroma of bleach permeated everything here but could not entirely banish the smell of rotted meat. Lester walked past stainless steel butcher tables, then opened a commercial freezer door in the back wall. He signaled again for them to follow him inside.

The frigid air in the walk-in freezer felt wonderful after the heat and humidity of Florida in the summer, but the pleasure soon faded as he studied the carcasses hanging on rows of hooks dangling from the ceiling. He felt bile rising in his throat.

"They died of natural causes or from injuries sustained during a raid. We do not kill people for the purpose of eating them, but we do make use of every resource. Meat is meat, whether it once walked on four legs or two."

"Are they easier to clean than deer?" Annabelle asked.

Fergus had hoped to see dismay, shock, or revulsion on the cherubic face. Instead there was only curiosity.

"First things first, child. You understand that it is not something we prefer to do. It is something we must do to incorporate adequate protein into our diets. The canned chicken and tuna fish ran out months ago. We have cows and some goats, but we utilize them for their milk, which provides the butter and cheese I mentioned. Soon we will build up sufficient livestock so we no longer have to do this." He gestured toward the human-shaped carcasses which — thankfully — were adult-sized. "But in the meantime, this is simply a matter of utilizing resources. When the people died and their souls flew home to the cosmos, they left something of value behind. Something that no longer was of any use to them. Do you understand?"

A nod of the blond curls.

"What the hell is wrong with seafood? The ocean is on your fucking doorstep."

"Watch the naughty words, please. We do some fishing too." He gestured to a case half-full of a variety of fish. "But too many of our assets are used, and even wasted, in the process. Precious gasoline is better utilized in our tanker trucks than in fishing boats. Our people's time and energy is better spent farming or raiding. Most significantly, fishing is not cost-effective for us because of the barrier island — Jupiter. Someone destroyed the bridges a while back and access to the Atlantic has been limited. We hope to establish an outpost there soon, which will make for easier access to the sea and all its bounty."

This kind of information was the reason he was here.

"Interesting," Fergus said. "What's your timeframe for the outpost?"

"Why do you ask?"

"The sooner I see fewer frozen people in here and more frozen fish, the better."

"We're making progress in that direction even now. Perhaps within the month. If you play your cards right, you might be considered for a position there. As I said, the propane you found bought you elevated status. Let's move on."

They backtracked through the meat market and out into the warehouse, which felt balmy now by comparison.

"So only certain areas of the building have electricity and air-conditioning? That must be some remarkable ductwork you have."

"Yes, it took weeks to accomplish. That's the kitchen over there." He pointed to a spacious well-lit room behind a wall of glass. Inside were commercial stoves and refrigerators being utilized by a staff of four Terminators. "I'll show you how the chow line works when it's dinner time. Now, here's what you've been waiting for." Lester wore a half-grin as they stopped in an aisle lined with refrigerated doors on both sides.

"Is this what I think it is?"

"It is."

Fergus perused the contents as they walked down the corridor. The shelves held Tupperware containers with neat handwritten labels on each side: mozzarella, ricotta, chevre, butter, and yogurt. On the other side were white plastic buckets filled with milk, according to the labels. Dates were also written on each one.

"Impressive. No hard cheese yet? No cheddar or parmesan?"

"They're in the works. Aged hard cheeses take many months." He sighed. "I know you're still thinking about the meat hooks. I tried to prepare you the other day during our philosophy discussion."

"You did. I realize that now. It's still rather dreadful, though."

He felt a gentle tug of his hand.

"They're not in there anymore," Annabelle said.

"What? What do you mean?"

He could see the child was struggling to find the correct words.

"What makes us people is what's in here," she tapped a ringlet. "When we die, that goes somewhere else. Daddy didn't believe in heaven, but mommy did. She said that's where our souls go when we die. So what's left here is just meat. Like a squirrel or a deer."

"Do you really believe that people are no more than animals, Annabelle? Would you eat someone you loved?"

"Yes," she said without hesitation. "If it meant I wouldn't starve. Because that's what they would want me to do."

Bile rose again in his throat. He would not ask this child if she had eaten her parents; it would be more than he could bear.

"You're getting caught up in hard-wired societal norms that no longer make sense," Lester said from almost two feet above. "Let's shift focus. On to Tent Town."

They had reached a metal door at the back of the building. A red EXIT sign hung above it, and a guard stood nearby holding an M16 rifle identical to the ones used by Aubrey's bodyguards.

"Hey, Big El." The woman wore a black tank top, cargo pants, and Doc Martens. She might have been the body double for Linda Hamilton in the second *Terminator* movie, which was fitting.

"Hey, Spaz. How are you?"

Lester was showing more respect to this woman than the pharmacist.

"Kicking ass and taking names. I finished that book you loaned me. Got any more?"

"Of course. I'll bring you something tonight after mess. Same genre?"

A curt nod of the brunette ponytailed head.

"Young adult fantasy romance, it is. We're heading out back. See you later."

The woman pushed on the crash bar, opening the door. It was full dark now, but torches provided sufficient lighting to reveal the tented civilization spanning several acres behind the warehouse building.

"Welcome to Tent Town. What do you think, Annabelle?"

"It looks like a carnival!"

"It only looks that way because of the tents. There are no rides and no cotton candy. This is where we eat and sleep and hang out when we're not working. The latrine is over there. See the port-a-potties? You'll get to do your business on a toilet seat instead of in the bushes. The men's shower is to the left of the potties, and the women's is to the right. You don't get a lot of privacy, but there's plenty of soap and shampoo. The towels are in the little building next to it. I think you're going to like it here."

"I know I'm going to like it here!" Annabelle reached for the enormous hand. Fergus stood behind them, watching. The figures of the muscle-bound giant and the curly-haired urchin silhouetted against the backdrop of flickering torchlight and rows of pointed-top tents begged to be memorialized in a photo. Since there no longer cameras or smart phones, he committed the scene to memory.

He liked these two humans, but he had not forgotten his mission, nor where his loyalties lay.

Chapter 26 — Tyler

"Dude, seriously. What the hell is up with you?" Kenny said. They were out on the *Celestial Seas* angling for grouper or perhaps dolphin fish. "And why the hell are we trying to catch a dolphin? They're smart, you know. Probably smarter than you, blondie."

"We're not trying to catch a dolphin," Tyler replied. "We're trying to catch a dolphin fish, known to landlubbers as mahi-mahi."

"Then why didn't you just say mahi-mahi? And why haven't answered my question. What is up your butt?"

It was another splendid day on the open water with just enough wind to propel the boat. Tyler had the fleeting thought of continuing to sail east forever. That would be one way to escape the impossible situation in which he found himself. He had to choose between Rosemary and Kenny and Hector and Ingrid and all the other Colonists he had grown to love, or a bewitching psychopath who had captivated his heart and soul.

Perhaps he should spill his guts to Kenny. That would shut up the little shit for once.

"Maybe I'm worried about having a killer in our midst. Weren't you even bothered by seeing Howard die right before your eyes?"

"I didn't like the guy. He was a pud wacker. Served no purpose in the Colony other than to give people a hard time. We're better off without him."

Tyler was not surprised to hear the teenager vocalize what everyone else probably thought. Still, the lack of empathy was worrisome. The thought triggered another.

"Poison. Now there's an interesting factoid. Who has access to poison?"

Kenny snorted. "You got me there, pardner. You think I'm the number one suspect? That could be fun."

"No, because I know you, but other people who don't know you are aware of your creepy little poison darts. I expect Lucas will come knocking on our door any day now."

"You may be right about that." He grinned while wielding an Abu Garcia rod and reel — Tyler's second best — and casting almost as expertly as Tyler did himself. There were few tasks the young genius couldn't master once he put his mind to them. The kid was exceptional.

"He probably will," Kenny continued, focusing on the water which had transitioned from turquoise to cobalt this far out. "He's the sheriff in these here parts, and he's not as obtuse as people think. So back to what's really up your butt..."

"Fine." Tyler adjusted the mainsail a fraction to utilize a sudden, cool breeze. "You open up to me about your past and I'll tell you what's been on my mind. Deal?"

Kenny didn't reply for at least a minute. Tyler decided he wasn't going to, until suddenly he spoke. His focus stayed on the rolling sea while he talked.

"I had two little sisters and a baby brother...half-sisters and brother, technically. Different baby daddies, not that it matters." This was Kenny's real voice, not an impression of anyone. "When the plague began, we were living with our mom in Brownsville...East Brooklyn. You ever been to the city?"

"Never in my life."

"That's what I figured. Brownsville is about as bad as it gets. Gangs. Violent crime. Public housing. All us poor folk need help from the guvment, ya know."

Kenny had slipped into what Tyler thought of as ghetto slang. He regretted using that term earlier. Because of the kid's intellect and eloquence, he had assumed his background was at least middle class.

"Gentrification had spread to almost everywhere else in Brooklyn, but not to our 'hood. You know what that word means, blondie?"

"Yes, I know what gentrification means."

"I made myself a small target...kept under the radar. I was two grades ahead of other kids my age and on the short side too, so of course the bullies and gangbangers wanted to pick on me. I had to be a step ahead of them at all times. Had to think five chess moves in advance to avoid being pummeled or recruited into the Wave Gang or the Hood Starz. Survival depended on being invisible. So that's what I became."

"Figuratively not literally, right?" Tyler teased, thinking to lighten the mood.

Kenny glanced up. The dark eyes exuded disdain behind the black-rimmed glasses.

"Sorry. I don't mean to make light of it. You're an impressive kid. I can imagine you actually having an invisibility super power."

"Your cracker-white ass ain't got a clue what us hood rats had to deal with back in the day."

"You're right. I'm sorry."

"Anyway, the plague was a game changer, for sure. Most folks in our neighborhood died within a couple of weeks. My mom was one of them." He swallowed hard, brushing at his cheek with the back of the hand that wasn't holding the fishing rod. "I think it got to her sooner than us kids because she was weak — she'd been saving what little food there was for us. We had been holed up in our apartment for days, with the sofa and a dresser pushed up against the door. Neighbors and strangers pounded on the door, but we didn't open it. I think that's why I'm still alive. People went fucking nuts. Then the electricity went out. I put my mom in one of the bedrooms and locked the door. Wouldn't let the little kids in there, no matter how much they cried for momma. No power, no air conditioning. The smell got real bad, real fast. Then both my sisters got sick at the same time. A few days after they were gone, my baby brother just faded away. I'm still not sure if he got the disease or if he missed his momma so much he couldn't bear it."

Tears streamed down Tyler's face. He didn't say a word, just allowed Kenny to continue. He could tell the boy needed to tell his story and would do it in his own way, on his own terms.

Kenny took a deep breath. "So then it was just me. I realized two things at that point: I wasn't going to get sick, and I had to get out of there. People had stopped pounding on the door, but I knew they were still out there. I watched them from the window at night. Fires burned all over the place. I could see shadow people darting back and forth in the firelight. I wrapped up my family in blankets and left them on their beds. I think that's better than being buried in the ground, don't you?"

Tyler nodded. The lump in his throat wouldn't let him speak, even if he could have thought of anything to say.

"And then I left. Took me two days to get out of the city. There were people blocking the bridges, taking your food or whatever you had on you. I made myself invisible to them, just like I had been doing for years. Finally got to Newark, which was a big relief. After that, I decided never to let myself get stuck on an island again. There's some irony, for you." He grinned. "That's when I began to formulate phase two of my plan. Phase one was getting the hell out of the city. Now that I was on the mainland, I needed a strategy...a goal. A destination. You ever read *Treasure Island*?"

"Of course," Tyler managed. "Doesn't every young boy?"

"Not in my neighborhood. So I decided to become Jim Hawkins. I would travel down to the Florida coast, pretend I was on Skeleton Island and search for buried treasure. In hindsight, I was half out of my mind, but at the time it made perfect sense.

"Lots of weird shit happened on the sojourn down here. Typical of what was going on everywhere, I assume. I did a lot of thinking, as I'm inclined to do, being a genius." He took a deep breath. The hard part was over. "And I realized the Jim Hawkins thing was pretty silly. Who the hell needs a treasure chest full of gold coins these days? Still, I liked the idea of living at the beach. It never gets cold there like in the city, and I figured I would learn how to fish. I was trying to decide about crossing the bridge when I ran into our culinary wizard from Kentucky. *Boy like you ain't got no bidness wandering around by hisself,* she'd said. So we decided together to take a chance on what lay on the other side of the bridge. Glad we got there before Chin blew them up."

Tyler laughed. Kenny must feel better now that his story was told. It felt cathartic just hearing it.

"Now it's your turn," the teenager said. "I want to hear everything that's going on under that gorgeous, sun-bleached mane. Don't leave out any sex parts either. I'm fourteen, you know. I'll be fifteen next month. That's practically an adult."

A full minute slipped by before Tyler answered. "I'm trusting you, Kenny. What I'm about to tell you can go no further. At least if you don't want me kicked out of the Colony."

"What the hell? Are you the killer?"

"No. Maybe worse. I'm the spy from Tequesta." Saying it out loud didn't feel as liberating as he imagined it would after months of harboring the shameful secret.

Kenny's mouth fell open. He almost dropped Tyler's second-best fishing rod into the Atlantic.

"Holy shit. Okay, start from the beginning." Kenny reeled in his lure and set the rod on the deck of the *Celestial Seas*. "And don't forget about the sex parts," he added, crossing his arms and wearing an expectant look.

Tyler told his story: losing his parents to the plague; sailing his Hobie Cat north from Fort Lauderdale; finding Zoey and her sister sunbathing in Palm Beach; falling in love with both of them a little, but with Zoey more as time went by. It wasn't until six months after the plague that he realized what they were. By then they were building a would-be empire from their headquarters in a Costco warehouse building.

"They have this magnetism...this ability to ensnare you and wrap their tentacles around you so you don't want to escape. That's how they got all these men, and women too, to do their bidding. People gravitate to them. It's partly because they're so beautiful, but there's more to it. You find yourself wanting to be what makes their eyes light up with happiness. You want to be the one who they kiss on the cheek and say, 'Good job!' to. I know that sounds crazy, but it's true."

"No, not crazy. I get it, Ty. I told you that Zoey chick was sexy vanilla. And now you're saying there's two of them? Double trouble, my friend."

"Oh, yeah. I fell hard for Zoey, though. They're not the same person. They look identical and neither have much of a conscience that I can tell. But they're smart — maybe as smart as you — they're gorgeous, and they're highly organized. You wouldn't believe what they've accomplished in Tequesta."

"Better than what we have?"

"Yes. Well, no. Not exactly. Better in a different way. We live on an island paradise. They live on the Florida mainland. They live in tents behind a warehouse building, we live in luxurious houses next to the beach. So we have those things going for us."

With the statements that had flown unthinking from his mouth, Tyler experienced an epiphany. He now identified himself as a Colonist rather than a Terminator. He realized that he had felt this way for some time, although he would be hard-pressed to identify the precise moment he had made the mental transition.

He smiled at Kenny.

"What? What the hell are you smiling about, Jason Bourne?"

"I just realized something. I came here as a spy for the Terminators because Zoey told me to. But something happened during my time here. I've become one of you guys. My subconscious realized this weeks ago, which is why I've felt so conflicted. That's it. I know what I'm going to do now."

"What? What will you do?"

"I'm going to have a talk with Zoey. Tell her to go back to Tequesta and leave us the hell alone. She'll threaten to expose me, but it won't matter because I'm going to come clean with Rosemary and Ingrid and everyone else as soon as we get back."

"Slow down there, Austin Powers. I don't know if that's such a good idea. People may decide you're not to be trusted. Banish you from the island."

"I don't think so. Unlike you, I'm a productive member of the Colony. I provide services that no one else can."

"True. Plus you have great hair."

Tyler laughed. He felt a lightness he hadn't felt in a long time.

"So you're going to take that chance?" Kenny continued, derision evident in the young voice. "You'll risk banishment just to feel a little better about yourself?"

"I think it's the right thing to do."

"I think it's the wrong thing to do. I don't care how perfect your hair is or how useful your education and your skill set. You. Are. A. Spy. Get it? People will never forget that, and they'll never trust you. You'll always have a fat black smudge floating in a word balloon above your head. People will forgive a theft. They'll forgive a lie. They may even forgive a murder if it was justified. But they won't forgive a betrayal."

Tyler sighed. "So what do you think I should do?"

"I think we have to kill Zoey."

"What? Are you crazy?"

Kenny laughed. "Just kidding, dude. Lighten up. I need more information before I can give you advice."

After an hour of fishing and strategizing, Tyler had a plan.

***

"Damn it, Tyler," Rosemary said.

He sat in the Colony leader's living room and waited for a flood of rebukes that never came. He had told her the entire story from the beginning, as well as the solution they had come up with out on the *Celestial Seas* that afternoon.

Kenny stood at the bungalow's front door, acting as scout. This conversation must go no further.

The intelligent chocolate-brown eyes bored into him. He squirmed under their judgment.

"It won't work."

"Why not? Kenny is an excellent liar. We know he'll be convincing. He admits to someone...maybe Charlotte...that he saw Zoey put the poison in Howard's food, but was afraid to come forward out of fear. Charlotte comes to you. We have a meeting, take a vote, and since we don't have the death penalty here, Zoey gets banished. Even if she reveals that I was the spy, I'll deny it. Who will people believe? Me or her?"

She closed her eyes and sunk into the sofa cushion.

"What? How will that not work?"

"Because she has dirt on me too."

"Oh my. The plot thickens, like the waist of a pregnant cheerleader," Kenny said from the open doorway.

"What? How can she have dirt on you?"

"Because she recognized me from a mug shot she saw on TV before the plague."

Tyler was stunned. Of all the people in the Colony, he would have bet his life that Rosemary was the most ethical, law-abiding person of them all. She didn't even allow crude language in their community.

She opened her eyes. "I used to be a con artist. I was wanted on several counts of fraud, racketeering, and embezzlement, as well as being a 'person of interest' in a suspicious suicide case. Apparently Zoey has a photographic memory. My appearance is different now than it was back then — I used to lighten my skin and I kept my hair short — but she still put it together. If we banish her or threaten her in any way, she'll tell everyone about me. I can't risk that. Not even Lucas knows about my past."

"I...I...don't know what to say."

"I know. You're shocked and disgusted. And you like me, so think how the people who don't like me will feel. I've made a few enemies here. Can you imagine how Ingrid the straight-arrow will judge me?"

"Yes. Yes, I can."

She leaned forward, earnest now. "I'm not the same person." She glanced up at Kenny who wore an expression of mild distaste. "Right there. That is the look I don't want to see on people's faces. I've worked my ass off to get us where we are. Would I do that if I were a horrible person?"

"No, I don't think you would. I believe you. People can change, if they want to."

"That's it exactly. I got a wake-up call. I swore to myself I would change, and I did. I work hard at being a good person every day. I have a lot to make up for."

"So what now?"

"We have to get rid of Zoey, but we can't let her go back to Tequesta, which is another reason banishment won't work. She'll report all the details of our operation to her sister."

"That's what I tried to tell him." The derision was back in Kenny's voice.

"And we have to get rid of her before she tells anyone about us."

"We're not going to kill her. I still love her, as crazy as that is."

"Of course we're not going to kill her. Weren't you paying attention just now? You think I want to make more bad karma for myself? I have an idea, but it would be asking a lot from you."

"I'm listening."

She gave him a thoughtful look. "Do you think Ingrid would be willing to part with more of that food cache that I'm not supposed to know about?"

***

"Ugh. My head is killing me," Zoey said, rubbing her eyes and trying to sit up on a v-shaped cushion in the forward berth of the *Celestial Seas.*

Tyler watched those lovely sapphire-blue eyes squint, then blink, then open wide in alarm.

"What the fuck? Where am I?"

He grinned. "You're at sea, my dear."

"What the hell is going on? Why am I on a fucking boat?"

She scrambled off the bed, lost her balance, and thwacked the Little Mermaid tendrils against a bulkhead.

"Careful. The water is rough today and you still have some of the sedative in your bloodstream."

"Sedative? What have you done?"

He recognized the menacing tone, but rather than being intimidated by it, he found it amusing. Maybe someday it would be adorable. That would depend on her, though.

"I've removed a dangerous person from the Colony and taken her to a place where she can only make trouble for me and herself. And since you don't know the first thing about sailing, you probably don't want to cause me too much grief."

He turned, gesturing for her to follow. A minute later she stumbled out onto the polished-wood deck. He took a moment to admire the aesthetics of the yacht's mainsail silhouetted against the 360-degree backdrop of a cloudless sky and cobalt water. The view was magnificent, unobstructed by land in any direction.

"I've always wanted to visit the Canary Islands," he said with a smile.

Chapter 27 — Jessie

Jessie watched her two friends through a thick fringe of lash. Her eyes were mostly closed, but not all the way. She was playing possum so she could listen to the grownups' conversation. They had set up camp for the night in a field of dead corn stalks. Tung had lead them through hundreds of the dried-up plants for what seemed like miles, until he reached a point that felt secure. Ever since they had been attacked by those people next to the Cadillac, he had been even more cautious. The weapon from *Cthor-Vangt* was no longer hidden in his pocket; he held it in his hand all the time now. It was a violation of *Cthor* protocol, but Tung didn't care. He said his prime directive was keeping them safe. Now that Harold was clairvoyant — her daddy would have used the word 'psychic' — he was even more precious to the *Cthor*. It was interesting that Maddie had acquired that talent after she had been shot in the head, and Harold got it after Jessie brought him back to life when he died two days ago.

In all other ways, he was the exact same person: funny, smart, patient when she asked a million questions. But sometimes his eyes would get a faraway look in them and he would start talking in a dreamy voice, just like Maddie had done. It had happened three times so far, and the things Harold saw when he was having one of his visions were a bit scary.

"I think you worry too much about us." Harold sat cross-legged on his sleeping bag, poking the remnants of their small campfire with a stick. Dinner had been something called MREs, which Tung explained were developed by the army years ago and were easy to carry. Other than Tung's futuristic weapon, they weren't allowed to bring anything, including food, from *Cthor-Vangt*. But Tung and the other traveling observers and mentors had access to several secret aboveground stockpiles of MREs. She liked macaroni and cheese the best.

"It's my job to worry. There are some dangerous people up here. Those two assailants I had to dispose of underscores the threat. I'm tempted to turn around and go home."

"I think that would be a mistake. We haven't accomplished anything yet."

"Except getting you killed."

Harold chuckled. "True. But look how well that turned out. I'm Edgar Cayce now."

"Letting Jessie bring you back was a risky and irresponsible move."

"From my understanding, there wasn't much you could have done to stop her."

"True. She was determined. I admit I didn't fight her, but it could have turned out badly. You know what I mean."

"Yes. I might have come back to life with an inexplicable desire to feast on human brains."

She felt a wave of relief when she saw Tung's grin. She did not want her new mentor to be nervous or unhappy.

"The thought did cross my mind. Seriously, though, I didn't know how much oxygen deprivation your brain had suffered, nor how much damage the blow to your head had caused. You might have been a vegetable, if not a zombie."

"Right. But it all worked out for the best. I'm firing on even more cylinders than before. I've always been a lucid dreamer. I think my recent brief foray into the afterworld flung open a portal that had always been slightly agape. Perhaps the visions will help us in our mission."

"I don't intend to go anywhere near an ocean, so the hurricane you've been seeing shouldn't impact us."

"No, but it may affect your friends."

"Yes, I will contact Amelia and Fergus about it soon."

"Everything and everyone is connected. We're all sinuous, meandering threads woven into a cosmic tapestry of incomprehensible complexity. It's fascinating. I'm thrilled to still be alive and to be a part of the adventure. I think Jessie...and you...made the right decision. It would seem I'm meant to be part of this saga."

"I think so too. I'm happy you're still with us." Tung glanced at her. "I know you're awake, Jessie."

She grinned. "When you talk to Amelia with your *scythen*, please tell her I miss her and I love her."

"Of course. Now it's time for sleep."

"Okay." She turned onto her side and closed her eyes.

She was soon asleep. Her state of consciousness quickly reached the level at which she could experience remote viewing. It didn't happen every night, but fairly often. It had happened several times in Kansas. She had seen and heard Isaiah and the people who were near him — Lootinent Martin and the Spider Lady — when they were approaching Liberty. Amelia told her to be very careful in these situations because it may be a two-way street. In other words, those people she saw during remote viewing may also be able to see her. She was supposed to hide if she felt they could sense her presence. That had happened with Isaiah, the Smiling Man. He had also possessed the talent and when he sensed her, she had scurried behind a dream tree.

Tonight she saw Amelia sitting on a yellow sofa. Jessie's heart filled with joy. Amelia was her most favorite person now that her daddy was gone. Before she could try to make Amelia see her in return, the view shifted. Now she was looking down at a notebook. Someone was writing in it, but because she stood behind the person, she couldn't tell what they looked like. There was a silver ring with a purple stone on the middle finger of the person's hand, a hand which was scribbling terrible things. She didn't read cursive well, but she could identify a few of the words: killing, poison, Angel of Death. She felt a surge of panic. What if the person writing those terrible things wanted to hurt Amelia? Her worst fears were realized when she saw the cursive version of her friend's name in the notebook — something about Amelia and her black bag. Before Jessie could try to decipher more of the words, the images shifted again. Now she was standing at the foot of someone's bed. Moonlight coming in through the window revealed an old lady lying there. There was a man next to her. He was awake, watching the woman as she tossed and turned. Jessie instinctively knew the silver-haired woman was clairvoyant, like Harold, and that she was having a vision of something that hadn't happened yet. Jessie didn't have that ability; hers was limited to seeing only what was happening in real life at that moment in time. Her mentors had explained the difference: remote viewing versus precognition. The old woman was dreaming about something that terrified her, while the man beside her watched. Starlight glinted off eyes that looked black in the gloom of the bedroom. His hair was like Harold's — gray and long — but this man's was thicker and there was some dark hair mixed in with the gray. Before she could get a sense of either the old woman or the old man, the images changed again.

She departed the state of consciousness that allowed her to see actual events unfolding in real time and transitioned into a normal dream. It was one she had often. She flew just above the treetops; the wind rushing to meet her felt exhilarating. The blue sky above was brimming with puffy sheep-clouds. Dream-Jessie dipped and soared in the air like a dolphin might do in the sea. The real Jessie smiled in her sleeping bag.

Chapter 28 — Amelia

Amelia had shown up for dinner that evening outside the Love Shack, but she wasn't able to relax and enjoy the socializing that went along with the meal. The kitchen staff cooked for everyone three days each week. The other days, people were expected to do their own cooking with food that was distributed by the supplies allocation people as well as anything they were able to catch, trap, or grow. Some people maintained personal gardens, but just as with the Colony's communal garden, most plants had been severely damaged from the recent hail. Nobody was going hungry yet, thanks to Ingrid's generous donation of food, but sensible people were spending more of their free time these days fishing and cultivating new seedlings.

She knew how to use a rod and reel; Tyler had given her a lesson several weeks ago. She had a knack for it too. At least one cast in ten hooked a fish. There were so few people left in the world that marine life was making a comeback. The ocean's bounty was one of the many reasons she had chosen to spend the rest of her days in the Colony. No matter what, she would be able to feed herself, and with better fare than cans of Spaghettios that had outlived their sell-by date.

Charlotte was a wonderful cook, but for some reason the thought of chatting with fifty other people tonight did not appeal to her. When she arrived at the Love Shack, she found Rosemary and made her excuses for not staying. She would go back home and see about doing a little shore fishing for her dinner.

So when she came back to her condo to find Lucas rummaging around in her kitchen cabinets, she wasn't surprised. Her *scythen* had been trying to tell her something was up.

"Can I help you?" Amelia said to Lucas's back. She felt some minor pleasure at his discomfort for being caught snooping in her home.

"Sorry, Amelia. Your name was at the top of my list. Howard suggested you were the cat killer. Maybe you wanted revenge."

"Please. If I wanted to kill someone, you would never know."

"That sounds like a challenge."

"It's not. I'm no murderer. I catch and release spiders, for goodness sake."

"So you say. Well, you're in luck. I didn't find anything incriminating here, so I'll just be on my way."

"You intend to search the homes of all the Colonists?"

"Won't need to. I'll find the perp long before I've gone through all the houses. By the way, please don't mention this to anyone. If you aren't the killer and you want the person apprehended, then you'll let me do my job without tipping people off about my searches."

"Very well," she said, then stuck out her hand, an olive branch of sorts.

He gave her fingers a gentle squeeze.

The Colony's head of security walked through her front door and onto the sidewalk of her building. Rather than turning right, toward dinner, he turned left. Amelia thought about who lived in that direction; she knew whose house he was going to next. She had seen Chin at the Love Shack and knew Lucas would have plenty of time to search the quirky little man's home.

He was probably wise in doing so. Chin was a loner and a bit of a misfit. Those qualities could be attributed to Asperger's or any number of personality disorders a percentage of Chicxulub's survivors shared, but they could also be red flags for something worse.

Lucas was unlikeable. Something about his maleness — so overt that it felt aggressive — put her off. But the handshake had given her three pieces of helpful information: he was not the murderer; he was an unknowingly strong transmitter to anyone with *scythen* who could receive his thoughts; and he felt a profound sense of responsibility in keeping everyone safe.

Amelia might not like the man nor his methods, but she could not fault his motivation.

She headed out to the beach with rod and reel in hand. It was going to be a spectacular sunset; a perfect balance of wispy and plump clouds riddled the sky, waiting for the fading light to paint them in a kaleidoscope of colors. When she saw a small figure walking toward her, she sighed, trying not to be annoyed by the interruption.

"Hey, Amelia."

"Hello, Kenny. I have another pole in my condo if you'd like to join me."

"Nah. I'll just watch you."

The teenager plopped down in the sand and gazed out at the water. It was glass-smooth this evening. When it looked like this, it was difficult to imagine how it would appear during a category-five hurricane.

She shrugged the thought away and tried to focus on the boy. Kenny wasn't easy to read, but tonight she could see he was bothered about something.

"I heard Charlotte made tuna casserole tonight..."

"Not really in the mood to be around people."

"Am I not people?" She smiled, then cast her lure. It plunked into the turquoise water thirty yards from shore.

"Daaamn, Gina."

"Gina?"

"Just a silly pop culture reference. Seriously, though, that was smooth as buttuh."

"Tyler taught me. Where is he, by the way? I didn't see him at the Love Shack."

Kenny frowned.

Seconds ticked by. She continued reeling in her lure with fluid motions.

"He left. Took Zoey, the Malevolent Little Mermaid, and sailed away."

"What? When?"

"Early this morning. I'm not supposed to say anything about it, but I figure Rosemary won't mind me telling you. She thinks you're the bee's knees."

"I think she's an impressive woman too. I guess I won't press you for more if you're sworn to secrecy. It's a shame though. I will miss him very much."

"Me too. When will Fergus be back?"

"I'm not sure. I hope not too much longer, though."

Kenny nodded, gazing out to sea.

"So you've been faking the Tourette's thing?"

A slow grin spread across the youthful face. He didn't respond.

"I think you may be an evil genius."

"That's what Tyler used to say." The grin faded.

Amelia sent another perfect cast into the ocean. The half-sun sinking on the horizon had turned the water to periwinkle and painted the cloud-washed sky in shades of peach and tangerine. Amelia breathed it all in. This place...this paradise was where she would spend her final days.

And she would do anything to keep it safe from anyone who would bring trouble here.

"How do you feel about Jupiter Inlet Colony, Kenny?"

"It ain't no ghetto."

"No, it certainly isn't, but how do you feel about it? Is it just a nice place or is it your home?"

Kenny pondered the question. "I suppose it's my home now."

"Even without Tyler?"

"Yes. I'll miss him, though. He was kind of like a big brother to me."

"I know. But there are many other good people in this world whom you will also grow to love."

"Yeah, but there are lots of nut jobs too. Blondie did the right thing, you know." He added, lowering his voice, even though nobody else was nearby.

"You mean with Zoey?"

"Yes. She was trouble, for sure. Now she's not, because of Tyler."

"Ah, I see. Rosemary sent him on a suicide mission, so to speak."

"Yeah. What a way to go." Eyebrows waggled above the black-rimmed glasses.

Amelia chuckled. Kenny's smile returned. He took a deep breath and let it out slowly.

"There's an empty unit next to mine," she said, "if you're interested. It smells like cat pee, but we can get it cleaned up in no time."

"I think I'd like that. I hope Fergus comes back soon."

"Me too, but even if he doesn't, you're where you should be for now. We both are."

Suddenly, she jerked the pole, then sped up the reeling. The next moment she flung a twenty-inch fish onto the sand.

"Grilled and blackened?" she said.

"Yes, ma'am. Thanks, Amelia." When he smiled this time, he turned to her. His face was wet with tears.

"You'll be fine, Kenny. I'll see to it." She squeezed his shoulder while he removed the lure from the gaping mouth. In doing so, she learned more about the boy than she had during all the months they had both been living on the island.

~~~

Amelia: Are you there?

Fergus: Yes, love. I'm bunking at the headquarters of the Terminators with the aforementioned giant and would-be tiny murderess.

Amelia: Are you safe?

Fergus: I am. The giant and the murderess are friends.

Amelia: So you've successfully infiltrated?

Fergus: Oh yes. We're thick as thieves.

Amelia: There's no possibility of having your cover blown?

Fergus: None whatsoever.

Amelia: Good. Have you determined the nature of Zoey's sister?

Fergus: I have. She is a psychopath.

Amelia: I believe that Zoey was as well.

Fergus: Was?

Amelia: Yes. Tyler has taken her out onto the ocean where she will, with luck, never be heard from again. I think he was our turncoat, if I'm understanding the situation correctly.

Fergus: Fascinating!

Amelia: Kenny has decided to move into the condo next to ours. We'll be taking him under our wing.

Fergus: I like that boy. He reminds me of a younger, dark-skinned version of myself back in the Old Country.

Amelia: He's smarter than you.

Fergus: That's one of the reasons I like him. Any news of the killer?

Amelia: No. I caught Lucas searching our condo. I think I've been eliminated from the suspect list.

Fergus: Excellent. If you had wanted to murder someone, they would never know.

Amelia: That's what I said to Lucas. He took it as a challenge, I think. By the way, I've changed my opinion of him. Or rather I've upgraded my loathing to mere distaste. He does have the Colony's interests at heart, and for that I will tolerate much. It is my home now.

Fergus: I understand. Its beauty suits you.

Amelia: When will you be leaving Tequesta?

Fergus: In a few days. I'm getting the complete tour in the morning. I want to get the full measure of their resources and weaknesses, and I need to know if and when they intend to invade the Colony. Rosemary will have a lengthy report when I return.

Amelia: You want to impress her.

Fergus: Have you seen those breasts? Who wouldn't want to impress those breasts?

Amelia: You're incorrigible. Be safe, my dear.

Fergus: I shall. Good night, darling.

~~~

Amelia lay in her bed, listening to the waves crashing outside her window. The wind had picked up after sunset. Hearing their roar made her think about the hurricane Ingrid saw in her vision dreams. She didn't doubt the woman's sincerity, nor her precognitive talents, so the matter of what was to be done about it was all that remained. Rosemary was smart to put together an evacuation plan, even though the Colonists refused to participate in drills. But despite how devastating the destruction, Amelia would return to this place afterward. It was her home in a way that Arizona had never been. It was her home in a way that even the Great Plains of the North American continent had never been all those thousands of years ago.

The thought of a monster storm sent a frisson of near-panic through her small body. She could imagine the catastrophic ruination of her paradise, and the image filled her with dread.

But perhaps it didn't have to be so.

She had been cast out of *Cthor-Vangt*, but she still had connections there. She might yet hold some sway with the *Cthor*, those ancient beings who possessed the technology to manipulate the very essence of humankind, as well as to orchestrate geological and meteorological events on a global scale. Recent examples included triggering the volcanic eruption of Pompeii, and further back, summoning an inundation of rainfall to bring about the Great Flood referenced in Christian-Judaea folklore.

The *Cthor* could mitigate a tempest as easily as they could summon one. The difficult part was to convince them to do so.

Chapter 29 — Ingrid

Ingrid watched Hector puttering about in the communal garden. She wore sunglasses and her favorite floppy sunhat so he wouldn't see that she was scrutinizing him. She admired the corded muscles of his arms, still well-defined; his thick salt and pepper hair, the envy of men half his age; and the expert way in which he tucked the seedlings into the prepared holes, then covered them with just the right amount of compost and soil. The man knew his way around plants, as well he should — landscaping had been his livelihood before the plague. Illegal immigrants coming from Mexico were practically destined for that career when arriving in the United States. It was a hot, dirty, low-paying job that most Americans didn't want.

She had scarcely noticed people like Hector before — the men who kept her yard mowed and trimmed; the women who kept her house immaculate; the workers who cooked her food in all those restaurants where she dined on Saturday nights. Rarely did she give a thought to their intellect. They were manual laborers there to provide services for people like her.

She sighed in disgust. In hindsight, she realized how narrow and self-absorbed her thinking had been. All people were equal, no matter the color of their skin, the job at which they toiled, or the language they spoke.

In Hector's case, he spoke more than a dozen. He was exceptional in all ways. She loved his companionship, and not just for the sex; their conversations were interesting and enlightening. You're never too old to learn something new. She couldn't remember the last time she had enjoyed being in someone's company so much, so the recent nightmare was particularly upsetting. The identity of the phantom chasing her had not been revealed. When she had reached up to move aside the hood, there was only a black hole surrounded by a glowing circular band, like the peak of a solar eclipse in the totality zone. What had disturbed her was Hector's absence amongst the fleeing throng. Dream logic told her that no one in the crowd was the Colony's murderer; Hector had not been among them. Rosemary, Amelia, Tyler, Fergus, and even Lucas had been running next to her. Her dreams had always been accurate in their messages — she owed her privileged lifestyle to them — but they were subject to interpretation. She didn't grasp the significance of the cobblestone path and why safety lay at the beach rather than her house, so perhaps there was something else she was missing as well.

Either way, the problem remained of what was to be done about Hector. She knew he had been picking up on her recent aloofness, but he would wait for her come to him when she was ready to talk. He never pushed her; it was another trait she appreciated about him.

"I know you are watching me." She could hear the smile in his voice. "Have you decided to trade in this seventy-year-old man for two thirty-five-year-olds?"

She laughed, despite her unease. "I can barely keep up with one seventy-year-old."

"Excellent. I would prefer to stick around a while longer. I think there is still a room or two in your palace that we have yet to christen."

The comment triggered a thought, bringing it forward into focus and out of that murky place reserved for less pressing issues. It was suddenly relevant.

"Why don't you move in with me, Hector? Or I could move in with you. Everyone knows we're sleeping together. Why must we keep our own houses? And why do you leave in the morning before the sun is up?"

"Are you afraid that I am a vampire? If that were so, my skin would be sizzling at the moment."

She didn't smile. He didn't look up, continuing down the furrows. Seconds ticked by.

Finally he responded. "I guess you are expecting an answer."

"Yes."

He straightened his bent back with a sigh. He wore polarized wraparound sunglasses so she couldn't see the dark eyes sparkling from within the web of crow's feet, acquired from a lifetime of laughter and working in the sun.

"I like having personal space and privacy. I did not want to say as much because I knew it would hurt your feelings."

He was right. She felt a petty stab to her ego. Why would he want privacy from her? Was he not also smitten?

"Let me finish," he said, holding up a hand when he saw she meant to speak. "I came from a very large family. Eight children. We lived in a two-bedroom house in Torreón. Can you imagine how cramped that was? I slept in a twin bed with two younger brothers. All night long I smelled their farts and listened to their snores. I shared one dresser drawer with them, not that I needed much room for my few possessions, but that wasn't the point. There was not an inch of space in our house that I could claim for myself. Not a corner, a crawlspace under the bed, or even a windowsill that was not already being used for something. I made a vow that if there were ever an opportunity to own a home in this great country, I would share it with no one. It sounds selfish, I know, but that is the way I felt and still feel. As much as I enjoy spending time with you in your house, I love — almost as much — walking in the front door of my own home. It is all mine. There is no one else in any of the rooms. There is no one else hogging my king-sized bed. My home is not grand, like yours, but it belongs to only me. All twenty-two hundred people-free square feet of it."

Ingrid allowed herself a few moments to consider his words. She decided she not only believed him, she understood and would not allow her feminine pride to find fault with his rationale.

"So there are no bodies buried in your basement?"

"We are at sea level. It is my understanding that basements would fill with salt water here, thus there are none within the Colony."

"Right. It was a joke and a bad one at that. I was trying to lighten the mood."

"The mood is heavy because you have something on your mind. A dream, I think, that you say you cannot remember."

She felt a twinge of guilt. She had lied to him after the dream and was lying to him by omission now. He wasn't a believer, though. He put no credence in her hurricane visions, so why mention the sickle-wielding specter?

"I barely remember it, Hector. Let's change the subject."

"It was not about a hurricane? Did it foretell another dire event? I do not believe so. I have a different theory: I think your Mexican dream lover appeared in a way that frightened you, which would explain why you look at me sideways when you think I cannot see you."

"You're very observant, old man."

"Indeed, beautiful lady. So if you do not want to share it with me so that I may defend myself, you at least owe me the courtesy of not judging me by it. Dreams are sometimes just dreams, you know. Our subconscious mind processing information. Nothing more."

She nodded. Perhaps Hector was right.

Chapter 30 — Rosemary

"You still haven't found anything?" Rosemary said to Lucas.

They were perched in the watchtower on the western side of the island. It was Lucas's turn for sentry duty. He felt he should set the example that no one was above doing the grunt work of watching the mainland. Falling asleep on the job was a serious offense; the penalty for committing it was necessarily unpleasant. The hapless guard on duty when Zoey swam across the Intracoastal had spent the next twenty-four hours in a sweat box on the beach.

A pair of high-quality Swarovski binoculars remained in the watchtower at all times, chained to the window ledge so they couldn't be carried off. From the mainland, anyone looking their direction would see a copse of royal palms and nothing more. Their 'deer blind' was hidden from view at that angle, and was austere for a reason: sentries weren't supposed to be comfortable while on duty.

Lucas peered through the lenses. "No, nothing so far. Amelia caught me in her condo, by the way. I expected her to be at the Love Shack for dinner."

"Amelia? Why the hell were you searching her house?"

"Who's the cop here? I have my reasons which I don't have to share with you. Don't micromanage me, Rose. I won't tolerate it."

She bit her lip. He was right.

She studied his handsome profile as he scanned the coastal terrain, back and forth, back and forth, hunting for signs of any activity that might suggest an impending invasion. The thought was always at the back of her mind, along with a million other problems to worry about. At least the Zoey dilemma had been handled, but the loss of Tyler and his expertise was a blow to the Colony. Everyone liked him and valued him for his extensive knowledge of all things relating to the ocean. There were others who would now do the deep-sea fishing and manage the aquaponics facility, and there was no shortage of boats to take the place of the *Celestial Seas*. But Tyler would be missed by everyone, and by Kenny most of all. The teenager was the only person on the island besides her who knew the real reason the couple had sailed away, and she believed he would keep the secret. Not for her sake, but out of respect for his friend. Kenny would not want people to know Tyler had been the Tequesta spy, and so her shameful past would remain private as well. The decision to send him away in the company of a sedated psychopath would benefit herself and everyone else too.

It had been the right call, but it made her feel nauseated when she thought about it.

"Whose house is next?"

"None of your business." He paused the back and forth motion. Something had caught his attention.

"You're right. I'm only the Colony leader, voted into that position of authority by a wide majority. You enjoy your job as head of security because of me."

"I enjoy it because I'm good at it and you would have been stupid let anyone else do it."

She appreciated his bluntness but could understand why others were put off by it. He didn't bother to sugar coat anything; never bothered to dress up whatever he said in tactful phrasing. He spoke his mind, always, even when doing so was not the best course of action. In that way, he reminded her of an autistic boy she had befriended in high school because nobody else would. The boy blurted out everything that popped into his head, no matter how hurtful or rude. Lucas was like that, but his talents compensated for the lack of tact.

The Colonists were safer with him than without him.

"Where did you send Fergus off to, by the way?"

"That's between Fergus and me. Why do you ask?"

"Because I just now saw a flash of spiky red hair moving around among the sea grapes and mangroves south of where the bridge used to be. I think I see a kayak stashed in the roots at the waterline."

Rosemary did a quick mental calculation and decided to explain the secret mission.

"Infiltration? Jesus, Rose. You looking to get the little guy killed?"

"We need information. We need to know what their operation is like, how many people they have, and whether they plan to invade."

"Right. And if Zoey was an indication of their leadership, I think you can assume he is in some deep shit."

"I don't think we have to assume that," she snapped.

"Yes, you do. I just saw some big guy catch him in the foliage. He's got a gun to his head."

"No."

"Yep. Here." He handed her the binoculars.

She watched as Fergus was forced back up the incline, away from the water and the hidden kayak which would have returned him to safety. His captor was enormous — perhaps two feet taller than Fergus. Rosemary's stomach turned into a ball of knots when she thought about explaining what she had just seen to Amelia.

Chapter 31 — Fergus

"What tipped you off?" Fergus was breathing heavily as he scrambled back up the steep incline. He had been ten yards from freedom at the water's edge when Lester caught him. Mangrove roots snagged his feet at every turn as he trudged back uphill; the last thing he needed was a sprained ankle when he was about to be interrogated and tortured by a psychopath. Worse than an injury was the look of betrayal on the face of his new friend.

"Aubrey said she got a vibe when you shook her hand. She gave orders to have you watched."

"For such a large fellow, you're remarkably covert."

"I'm disappointed, Fergus. I thought we were friends."

"We are friends, Lester. I just wanted to get away for a little while."

"You know that's not how it works. Once you're accepted into the Terminators, there's no leaving without permission."

"When you're a Jet, you're a Jet all the way?"

"I don't care for musicals. I never understood why breaking into song at random intervals throughout a film made any kind of sense. Where were you going just now? If your motives were innocent, why not tell me? That's what a friend would have done. Instead, you sneak away when you think no one is looking and make a beeline for a hidden kayak. Where would you have gone, Fergus? Back home to tell your people all the secrets you've discovered here?"

"I have no people. I was all in until the meat freezer, Lester. You must know that crosses a line."

"We've been over that. I think all the other benefits — the farm, the medicine, the safety in numbers, the *cheese* — should have compensated for the meat freezer. Friendship should have compensated for the meat freezer. How am I going to explain this to Annabelle? You were just going to abandon her, after everything she's been through?"

Fergus did feel remorseful about forsaking the giant and the little girl, but his first loyalties lay on the island to the west.

Amelia would be furious that he had gotten himself into trouble.

"I just needed to get away and think about things. I intended to return." He would stick with the lie until the end. He wondered if Aubrey was the waterboarding type or more of a bamboo-under-the-fingernails lass. He had been tortured before back in the Old Country; he knew he could withstand whatever methods they used, but he didn't relish the notion.

"I'm a loner, Lester. I don't have a home to go back to, nor people to whom I report. There's no tribe, no rival gang that's looking to move in on your territory. It's just me, struggling with whether I wanted to be part of a society that eats people."

"And yet when you approached us, you said you were tired of being alone. Wanted to become part of a group."

"I had hoped to hook up with non-cannibals."

"I told you that's a temporary solution. Once the livestock is built up, we'll do away with it. I'm dismayed that an intelligent man like yourself can't get past a societally imposed taboo and see the practicality of it. Meat is meat. We've talked about this before. I tried to prepare you."

"You did. I'm sorry I didn't pay closer attention during our philosophical discussion, although at the time I thought your talking points were hypothetical."

Lester prodded him from behind, not ungently. They walked on the blacktop highway now which led to the Costco warehouse.

"I have to take you to Aubrey."

"I know."

"She'll have you whipped, at the very least. Or she may do it herself."

"I assumed that. She's a psychopath, you know."

"Yes, but she is a sensible psychopath. Both she and her sister are self-aware. You saw their books? They restrain that part of their psyche that prompts them to do monstrous things. Instead, they channel those...impulses...into organization and productivity. When we started, there were ten of us, half-starved and half-crazy. Now there are forty-seven highly skilled, fully fed people who have found a modicum of happiness in this post-apocalyptic world. I think that's admirable."

"I suppose you're right. But at some point they will do the unspeakable because that is their nature. They have no conscience, no empathy. What if Annabelle were to cross them?"

"I've thought about that. I hope I never have to choose between the sisters and the child. Perhaps if the day comes when their liabilities outweigh their usefulness, I will dispose of them. But in the meantime, they serve a purpose. Remember our conversation?"

"About the good man who will do harm in the future?"

"We are still in the part of the story where the man is doing good deeds for the benefit of many."

"The needs of the many outweigh the needs of the few."

"Or the one. You're a *Star Trek* fan too. Damn it, Fergus, it will break my heart to see you tortured."

Fergus's beard twitched.

***

"You read my mind when we shook hands?" Fergus said to the woman who was wearing an expression of intense pleasure. The anticipation of torturing him was practically orgasmic, it seemed.

"It's not mind reading. My sister and I have that twin thing. We're often aware of each other's thoughts when we're not together. It's similar to that, but with other people when we touch them. It doesn't happen with everyone, and it's not precise. It's more like a vibe. You know?"

"Yes, I know about vibes. I'm having one now. It's telling me you intend to cause me a world of pain."

A throaty chuckle. Under different circumstances, he would have found it captivating.

"Tell me the truth and I won't hurt you. Much."

"I have been telling you the truth. I know you want to believe I'm a devilishly handsome double agent, but I'm sorry to say I'm not nearly so interesting. I'm just an ill-fated wanderer who managed to get himself inducted into a group of people who eat other people."

"Meat is meat. Why such a hang-up about it? We're not killing them to get their meat; we're just utilizing what's been made available."

He sighed. "Yes, I've heard all this before. I guess I'm just a cannibal bigot."

"Very funny." She stood, then walked around the desk, stopping in front of him. He forced himself to look up at the exquisite face and not ahead at the equally exquisite eye-level breasts; he did not want to further antagonize the psychopath standing a hands-width away. He summoned every ounce of intellectual strength he possessed to erect a mental barrier between his thoughts and the woman placing her hands upon his chest. He felt a tingling sensation when she touched his sweat-stained shirt; it intensified when she released the top button and brushed her fingertips against his skin. He closed his eyes, sensing the tentative, probing *scythen* of a neophyte. She had raw talent, but it was untrained, undeveloped...an infant wriggling in its crib yowling that it was hungry without knowing how to ask for a bottle.

She frowned, removing her hands from his chest. "Well, it's a damn shame. I think you would have fit in here."

"I still can. Perhaps we can forget about this little faux pas? In the future, I promise I won't question from whence come the meaty chunks in the Sunday stew."

"It's too late for that. You broke the rules, you pay the price. If I let you get away with an attempted escape without suffering any consequence, what sort of example would that set for everyone else? People will think they can just come and go as they please."

"What's so terrible about that?"

An unlovely snort. "That's not how we operate here. This works," she said with a gesture indicating everything outside the air-conditioned office, "because of tight discipline. That's why we're more successful than all those other losers out there."

"I see. So what's to be my punishment? Paper cuts and lemon juice? Bikini wax? Skinny jeans?"

"It's tailored to the individual. That's what makes our punishment system such an effective deterrent."

Fergus felt a stab of alarm.

"I've been talking to Lester to get a better handle on you. He says you're quite the Chatty Cathy. Says it would be hell for you to be isolated for any length of time. When you walk out of this room, you're going into another very small one. It's called The Box."

"The Box? That's unfortunate. I've always rather liked boxes up to now. You make this one sound as if you should be twirling a Snidely Whiplash mustache when you say the word."

"You won't like it, but it will take a while for you to realize how much you don't like it. After several days, you'll wish I had just whipped you and gotten it over with. Pity about that. I was looking forward to watching you bleed. It's been a while since I've given a good whipping." There was nothing attractive about the shark smile on the flawless face.

"Take him to The Box, Lester. I'm bored."

Lester prodded him through the doorway and out into the warehouse.

Annabelle stood a few feet from the identical guards. "What happened? Is she going to kill him?"

"No. He's going into isolation."

"Fergus, why were you running away from us?"

"I'm sorry, love. In hindsight, I wish I hadn't. After a few days they'll let me out and we can pick up where we left off with the *Little House* books. In the meantime, I'm sure Lester will be happy to read to you."

"I don't need someone to read to me. I can read myself, you know. I just like the way your voice sounds during the parts where Charles Ingalls is talking. It reminds me of my grandpa."

This was one of the drawbacks of being above ground and involved with people. Sometimes you let them down.

"You have me to thank for this, you know," Lester said as they walked down one of the cavernous aisles. "Aubrey wanted to flay you with the metal-tipped whip she keeps in her desk drawer. The last person she used it on developed an infection from his wounds and died. Law-breakers don't get Cephalexin."

"I guess I should express my gratitude, then.

"You better do it now because after several days you won't be in the mood."

"The Box is that bad?"

"It's...disagreeable. I'm sorry, Fergus. Maybe if you're still sane when you're released, we can be friends again. Through here." He opened an innocuous-looking door.

Just enough light from the warehouse filtered in to reveal a tiny space that had been larger at some point in its former history as a small breakroom or janitorial closet. Metal sheeting on all sides now formed a cube. In one corner sat a bucket; the roll of toilet paper on the floor next to it indicated its purpose. In another corner was a case of bottled water and three boxes of Ritz crackers. There was nothing else — no cot, no pillow, no light source. The stench was prodigious. He wondered if the bucket had been emptied since the last occupant.

"Lester, this is going to suck balls."

"Mind the naughty words, please."

"Sorry, child."

Annabelle darted forward and kissed his cheek above the wiry red beard.

"I'll miss you, Fergus. Please don't go crazy while you're in there."

"I shall do my best." He stepped inside.

His last glimpse of the world before darkness consumed him was of a giant man and a curly-haired adolescent wearing matching mournful expressions.

The door closed and then locked with the solid thump of a deadbolt. He sat in an absence of light more complete than anything he had ever experienced.

***

An unknown amount of time passed. It might have been hours or days. Probably only hours because he hadn't had to use the bucket yet. He was thinking about the pat-down Lester had given him before they reported to Aubrey. He smiled in the dark when he thought of the utility knife in the pocket of his cargo shorts. Lester's deft fingers had moved past it, which told him their friendship was still very much two-sided. It wasn't possible that he had overlooked it, and Fergus pondered the implications of the intentional oversight; he had plenty of time to do so at the moment.

A niggling sensation scratched at his brain. It was what he had been dreading. He would have to pull off the performance of a lifetime to keep Amelia's *scythen* from discovering that something was amiss.

~~~

Amelia: Are you there?

Fergus: Yes, love. How are things in the Colony?

Amelia: Never mind that. What's wrong?

Fergus: Nothing is wrong. I'm lying on my bunk reading Gaiman's American Gods *for the tenth time. All is well here. I expect to be home in a few days. I still need to discover a timeline for when the Terminators will invade the Colony. That's my prime directive, you know.*

Amelia: I'm picking up on something else. Are you in distress?

Fergus: Not at all. Perhaps some other person's distress is bleeding into our communication.

Amelia: Hmmm. Perhaps.

Fergus: Has the murderer been apprehended?

Amelia: Not yet. I think Lucas may be closing in, though.

Fergus: And what of the impending tempest? Is Ingrid still having the visions?

Amelia: Yes. We just discussed them. They're getting more frequent and more precise. She says the island will suffer a direct hit, which of course we cannot survive. Rosemary is wise to coordinate an evacuation plan. However, I have an even better idea. One that will circumvent the destruction of our home and all the hard work we've accomplished these past months.

Fergus: Do tell.

Amelia: I'm going to contact Tung. He is above ground with Jessie and a British fellow named Harold who was harvested at the same time as Jessie.

Fergus: Interesting. And what will you say to Tung?

Amelia: I'm going to have him ask the Cthor *to deflect the hurricane.*

Fergus: Why would they? You're persona non grata in Cthor-Vangt *these days.*

Amelia: That doesn't mean I'm not still doing their work. We have several exceptional people here who may well be candidates for recruitment. We won't have time to vet them before the storm arrives.

Fergus: Clever! Are there truly several or are you fudging a bit?

Amelia: I've done more laying on of hands the last few days than a faith-healing preacher. People must think I've lost my mind. I haven't seen evidence of strong scythen *or* langthal, *yet, but I know Zoey had some self-healing ability at the very least. I watched her broken finger straighten itself before my eyes. Perhaps her sister Aubrey has it too.*

Fergus: Aubrey does have a modicum of scythen, *but I'm not sure how robust it is, and I've seen no* langthal *from her. At any rate, Zoey is bobbing about somewhere in the Atlantic and they're both monsters, which makes them rejects for* Cthor-Vangt.

Amelia: Yes, but the sisters prove there is a concentration of extraordinary people here...even more so than in Liberty, Kansas. And that will be my strategy. I just have to convince Tung to convince the Cthor *to mitigate what would be a catastrophic storm. It won't be easy. He's such a by-the-book person.*

Fergus: He is that. Maybe you could get Jessie to help. Have you made contact with her?

Amelia: Not yet. Her scythen *still isn't up to speed. Perhaps I will try again.*

Fergus: Excellent idea. When do you plan to do this?

Amelia: Soon. I want to examine a few more people. The more candidates we have, the better.

Fergus: Agreed. Good luck, my dear.

Amelia: Thank you. Good night, my love.

~~~

The connection was gone. He had caught himself just before he sent the thought, *Oh, it's night, is it?* For the first time in his life, he had lied to Amelia. He knew when the Terminators planned to invade — Lester had mentioned it the second evening in Tent Town while sitting around a communal fire pit. But he couldn't tell Amelia just yet. Otherwise, she would expect him to promptly return to the Colony, and he was not in a position to do so.

He blew out an explosive breath of air in self-disgust, then instantly regretted having to refill his lungs with the putrid oxygen. Lester underestimated him. He would not go insane in The Box, although he would be uncomfortable during his time here. He would put the hours to good use, and he would not think about the cheese just a few aisles away. The Box served as a sensory deprivation tank. He wasn't floating in warm water, but he pretended to be to achieve the same effect. The result was a significant improvement of his *scythen*, similar to a blind person's enhanced auditory and tactile abilities.

He would send it out and see what was to be seen. In this way, he would stay sane. Only his body was imprisoned.

His mind was free to go wherever it fancied.

Chapter 32 — Anonymous

Dear Diary,

I'm afraid my time here in Paradise is coming to an end. I grow bored of pretending to be kind and helpful, but even more pressing is the Need; it is coming frequently now. As my True Mission becomes clearer, the figurative walls of the Colony close in on me. Those imagined barriers keep others out and everyone, including myself, in. They represent civilization, order, cooperation, safety...life. They are the antithesis of everything I am now. I put up with being oppressed and limited by circumstances and geography during my old life; I won't tolerate it now.

I'm not leaving quite yet, though. I've set some tasks for myself before I go, and I will need to prepare for life on the road as well. I remember my time 'out there' before arriving on the island and before I had fully realized what I was. I went hungry more times than I can count. Fortunately, I know where I can acquire food for my travels. Pilfering a bit shouldn't be too difficult, if I'm stealthy. And the Angel of Death is indeed stealthy.

In the meantime, the Need is calling. Its siren song is as sweet as that of the lone night bird's melody wafting in through my window even now.

It is not to be denied. Not tonight.

Chapter 33 — Jessie

"This is the way to travel," Harold said from the front passenger seat.

"I wish we had found horses instead of a working car." Jessie had to admit to herself that the cool air conditioning did feel wonderful.

They had been traveling in eastern Kansas during late July in temperatures that hovered near a hundred degrees. When they had found an abandoned Jeep Wrangler with a 'stick shift,' containing a full tank of still-good gas, and with no mummified bodies inside, Harold had laughed in delight. He was old and all the walking was beginning to wear him out. He never complained, though. He was so happy to be alive, he never complained about anything, even after checking dozens of cars with no luck.

She knew she had made the right decision in bringing him back from being dead. Tung still worried about it, but not like he had at first. He seemed to like Harold as much as she did. Unlike Amelia, it was hard to read her new mentor. Tung was very smart and also a little distant most of the time. He had the best *scythen* of anyone and every night they worked together on training hers. Harold's was also quite good; actually even better now that he was clairvoyant. Tung didn't seem jealous that Harold's *scythen* rivaled his own. She thought he might feel a little relieved not to be the only one who was so good at it.

"Have you ever ridden a horse, Jessie?" Harold turned to look at her in the backseat. He wore an expression of intense curiosity, like she was a fascinating puzzle and he very much wanted to understand how all her pieces fit together. He looked at everyone like that. Harold was the smartest person she had ever met, and he wanted to understand everything. He had probably always been that way, but now that he was part of *Cthor-Vangt* and knew all the secrets of how the Ancient Ones had been managing the rise and fall of humankind for almost forever, he was in hog heaven. That was a phrase her daddy used to describe someone who was really happy.

If she ever got to see Amelia again, she would be in hog heaven.

"Once at a carnival in Flagstaff I rode one of those ponies that goes in a circle. It was fun, but I felt bad for the pony. I don't think he liked his job, being around a lot of loud kids and walking in a circle all day."

"No, I imagine that is not the life a pony would prefer to lead."

"I'd like to have a horse someday. A real one, not just a pony. I like those Appaloosa horses with the black and white spots. I would call her Apples."

"Apples would be lucky to have a girl like you for her best friend."

"I would live in the barn with her. I would sleep on a sleeping bag right next to her stall. I would brush her and keep the barn clean for her. I would muck out her stall every day. That's what it's called, you know. Cleaning out the poop and leftover hay."

"Yes, that's exactly right."

"But now that I'm in *Cthor-Vangt* most of the time, I don't know if I'll ever get to have Apples."

"We don't have horses down there, Jessie. We're not set up for animals. Just people." Tung kept his eyes on the road ahead when he spoke.

They were making excellent time now that they were in a car that contained non-oxidized gasoline. They would avoid the larger cities, like Springfield and Nashville, on the way to their destination in Tennessee. The people Tung wanted to investigate lived in the Smoky Mountains near a town called Pigeon Forge. Jessie had never been to Tennessee. She really wished they could drive right past Pigeon Forge and on to Florida.

"Have you talked to Amelia?" she asked.

"Not yet. I'm waiting until we get a little closer. Makes the quality of the communication better. Nuance isn't overlooked. You know what that word means?"

"Yes, I know nuance." She paused...concentrating now... struggling to recapture a memory hovering on the edge of conscious thought. She pictured her mind as an insect net, and the elusive memory a fluttering monarch butterfly.

She snared it the next moment. "I just remembered that I saw her in a dream last night. She was sitting on a yellow sofa."

"Was it a remote-viewing dream?" Harold's eyes were bright with interest.

"Yes. That part was nice. I was going to try to communicate with her, but then all of a sudden I was somewhere else. I saw a person writing terrible things about poison and killing. I think that person is near Amelia."

Tung sought her out in the rearview mirror with a frown.

"Are you sure, Jessie? That sounds serious."

"Yes, I'm sure. The person wrote something about being the Angel of Death. It was in cursive, so I couldn't read it all, but it was bad, I can tell you that."

"How do you know the person is near Amelia?"

"Because their window was open as they were writing in the book and I could hear the ocean noises, just like when I saw Amelia sitting on the yellow sofa. Her window was open too."

"Very well. I will contact her on our next stop."

"Can't we do it now?"

"I want to get through this stretch of highway first. It doesn't look like a safe place to stop. We're near Poplar Bluff, which appears to be a sizeable town. Those are always the worst places to stop or even slow down."

"Can I help talk to her when we stop?"

She could see he was thinking about it, then he nodded. She felt a surge of happiness. She was going to get to speak to her beloved Amelia after all these months. She thought she might burst with joy.

Harold smiled at her from the front seat.

"Getting to talk to Amelia is almost as good as mucking out horse stalls?"

"Yes!"

"You love her very much, don't you?"

"She's my favorite person in the world now that my daddy is gone."

Jessie watched Harold focus intently on Tung who seemed to sense the older man's laser gaze on the side of his face.

"We're not driving to Florida, Harold. Especially not after your prophetic dream. My mission is to keep the two of you safe."

"It is also to teach and mentor and perhaps help others along the way."

"Yes, but safety comes first. Allowing Jessie to grow up a bit comes second. Mentoring comes third. Observation comes fourth. Then if there's something we can do to help the survivors, we will do so if it can be done safely."

"You have that." Harold pointed at the futuristic weapon on the car's console.

"That won't stop a hurricane."

"The thing about hurricanes is you get plenty of advance notice."

"You're making this more difficult."

"I just want Jessie to be happy. She's endured more than any little girl should have to."

"I know, but Florida is not one of the safer places for her."

She listened to the back and forth between the grownups. She was trying not to get her hopes up about seeing Amelia. The worst thing is when you thought you would get to do something wonderful and then it was taken away from you.

"Who's to say the Smoky Mountains will be safer? I've never been there, but as with any forested mountain area, there will be dangerous animals — cougars, bears, bobcats, wolves."

"Ah, but that," Tung gestured to the weapon now, "will work on all those creatures."

"It won't stop an avalanche."

"I don't think they have avalanches in the Smoky Mountains, but even if they do, I don't plan on wintering there. We'll be heading back to the Midwest by autumn."

Harold sighed dramatically. "I tried, Jessie."

She blinked very fast so the tears wouldn't spill out, but there was no stopping them. She wiped at the wetness with the back of her hand, catching Tung looking at her in the mirror. His mouth was a thin, unsmiling line. She was afraid she had done something to upset him.

"We'll talk to Amelia when we stop for the night. I'll get details of her situation there. I'm not saying you should have hope, Jessie, because I doubt I will change my mind about this. It's not always easy doing the right thing, you know. I don't want to disappoint you, but I have to consider your well-being before anything else, including your happiness. Do you understand?"

She nodded. At the very least, she would get to talk to Amelia. If everything went well, she might get to visit her too. She figured the odds of that happening were better than getting to muck out Apples' stable.

***

"Close your eyes and let the physical world fade away," Tung said.

He sat next to her on an outdoor table made out of logs. They had stopped for the night at Bullwinkle's Rustic Lodge near Poplar Bluff, Missouri. Harold told her that Bullwinkle was a famous cartoon moose, so she had hoped they might see a real one, but they only spotted a few deer and caught the stinky scent of a nearby skunk. Tung had done a thorough search of the buildings before he would let his charges out of the car; he had encountered no people. The area was wooded and pretty, and there was a pond with lots of ducks swimming in it.

The sun had set and the small fire they'd built in the blackened pit near the picnic table had burnt down to embers. They had eaten dinner, and it was time to contact Amelia.

She closed her eyes.

"Now imagine you're floating in a big bathtub of warm water. The temperature is perfect, and the water is buoyant. You're able to float without even trying."

They had done this a number of times before. Each time, Tung would create a different version of the scene he had just described. Sometimes it was drifting in space; sometimes it was lying on one of the soft puffy-sheep clouds she so loved. The bath water was nice too. Hers had bubbles. She pictured the tub as one of those old-fashioned ones with feet that looked like dragon claws.

"Now send out your *scythen*, like we've done before, but this time picture Amelia's face when you do it. I'll help you. We'll do this together."

She imagined Amelia sitting on the yellow sofa, as she had seen her in the remote-viewing dream. She sensed Tung's *scythen* next to her, like an invisible cable running in tandem with her own, both connecting to telephone poles down a stretch of dark highway. *Scythen* was kind of like that — thoughts traveling along cables that no one could see, and instead of connecting to wooden poles, they connected to people.

When she found Amelia, she felt a jolt of white-hot energy, like when you accidentally touched the metal part of an electrical plug as you pushed it into an outlet. Unlike electricity, this jolt didn't hurt.

~~~

Amelia: Well, hello, child.
Jessie: Amelia! I'm so happy to hear you!

Amelia: I'm happy to hear you, too. Tung? She's coming along quickly, I see. Well done.

Tung: (smiling) Thanks, Amelia. Scythen *training is one of the many services I offer.*

Amelia: You are the Cthor's *most treasured asset, you know.*

Tung: Only as long as I keep my two charges safe and viable.

Amelia: How is the British fellow?

Tung: He's fine...now.

Amelia: I sense a story.

Tung: Not one I'm inclined to tell at the moment.

Jessie: Harold died and I brought him back to life!

Amelia: Goodness. That's impressive, Jessie. I'm not sure anyone has ever done that before. He was completely gone, Tung?

Tung: Yes, but he's fine now. More than fine, actually. He's clairvoyant.

Amelia: Ahhhh. Like Maddie after her head injury.

Tung: Yes, but there's something you should know.

Amelia: Let me guess. He's been dreaming of a tempest destroying the little island that I've decided to call home.

Tung: You know about that?

Amelia: Yes. There's a woman here who is experiencing the same vision. She and others are possible recruits for Cthor-Vangt, *by the way. There is a concentration of them here.*

Tung: Have you been performing the tests?

Amelia: As time allows. I'm not nearly finished, and now I have to deal with the prospect of our island being destroyed along with those would-be Cthor-Vangt *recruits. Oh, and there's a killer on the loose here as well.*

Tung: It seems you have your hands full. I was considering bringing Jessie down for a quick visit, but it doesn't sound safe.

Amelia: The storm is days away, according to Ingrid's dreams. As for the murderer, I assume you brought a weapon with you? Jessie and Harold will be fine as long as they stay with you. I believe we're closing in on a suspect. Between the head of security conducting house-to-house searches and me touching everyone I can get my hands on, it's only a matter of time. We have new clues in the case, too, since another person was killed last night. It's very sad. He was a lovely man. Ingrid, the clairvoyant, is distraught. It was her lover and companion, Hector, who was the latest victim.

Jessie: I saw the killer writing in a diary. There was something about your little black bag and poison.

Amelia: Interesting. Well, a murderer is something we can control and contain. A hurricane is not. Tung, I was hoping you could help with that.

Tung: How so?

Amelia: As I mentioned, we have several candidates and I won't have enough time to evaluate them before the storm.

Tung: Where is Fergus? Can't he help?

Amelia: Fergus is on a mission at the moment. I can tell you more about that later. More pressing is the impending hurricane.

Tung: I hope you're not suggesting what I think you are.

Amelia: Why not? The Cthor can deflect it, send it off to the north Atlantic. It doesn't have to make landfall. That would solve the problem, Tung. It would give me time to assess these people as well as keeping my home intact. I only have twenty or thirty years left, you know. I'm no longer a near-immortal like you. I want to spend my remaining days on this tropical paradise, not on a sandbar that's been scrubbed clean of everything useful and beautiful. You know you could convince them if you wanted to.

Tung: Oh, Amelia. You always manage to put me in the most awkward positions.

Amelia: Just think about. Come down here and see for yourself before you make a decision. The people are quite exceptional. It would be worth your time.

Tung: I'll consider it only if we can find more gasoline for our vehicle. It's becoming quite difficult to find any that is still usable these days.

Amelia: Yes. We're utilizing bicycles in the Colony and saving the precious gasoline for the fishing boats. Soon there won't be any left. I hope you can find some. I think you'll want to see this place before you go back to Cthor-Vangt. The sunrises over the ocean are breathtaking.

Tung: I get the sense there's something you're not telling me.

Amelia: (hesitating) You'll need Fergus's help to get here from the mainland. He's there now on the mission I mentioned, so the timing is good. He'll bring you over.

Tung: I haven't agreed to come yet, but I will contact you again, if so. Good night, Amelia.

Jessie: Good night, Amelia! I miss you very much!

Amelia: I miss you too, child. Be sure to let Tung know how much you'd like to come visit.

~~~

"That little woman is going to get me in trouble one of these days," Tung said.

"They could do it though. Right?" Jessie's heart was pounding in her chest after the excitement of talking to Amelia.

It was full dark now. A crescent moon had risen above the Ponderosa pines and the crickets were making music. Jessie imagined all those bugs rubbing their scratchy legs together to make the noise she found so comforting. She would miss that sound when she had to go back under ground. Maybe she would ask to have a recording made that she could listen to in her room at *Cthor-Vangt*.

"Yes, they could do it if they wanted to. The *Cthor* have been able to manipulate the weather and other forces of nature since long before my time. Harold, I assume you were tagging along just now?"

Jessie had sensed Harold's *scythen* next to Tung's. He hadn't been specifically invited, and he didn't contribute to the conversation, but she didn't mind that he had eavesdropped. "Indeed, I was. This sounds like an opportunity to accomplish several objectives. We can head to Florida now, then make contact with the Tennessee group on the return trip."

"At what point did I completely lose control here?"

There was exasperation in Tung's tone, but also amusement, which was a good thing. Jessie liked when her mentor was amused; he usually said 'yes' to whatever she wanted to do. She also knew that Amelia had been one of his favorite people in *Cthor-Vangt*. It made him very sad that she no longer was allowed to live there.

"It's your decision, of course. But I wouldn't want to be the one to disappoint a certain little girl."

"If we can't find enough usable gasoline, I'll be forced to disappoint her."

"Right. It's a numbers game, though. Although rare, it is still to be found, and we'll have to check a lot of cars before we find more. But we will. I know it."

"I can help with that," Jessie said. "I know about sucking gas with a hose. Pablo really hated doing it, but I don't mind. There was an old man named Alfred who told us how to do the match test to tell if the gas still worked. He was the one who gave me Gandalf the Grey. I miss my kitten."

It was true that she missed her kitten, but she also knew mentioning it would make Tung more inclined to let her have her way. Sometimes it was okay to manipulate people if you were doing it for a good reason. Seeing Amelia was the best reason of all.

Tung frowned. She acted like she didn't notice, staring off into the woods on the other side of the duck pond. The crickets seemed louder when nobody was talking. Jessie counted a hundred heartbeats before her mentor replied.

"Fine. We'll head out at daybreak. Now off to bed."

"I'll sleep on the floor, Tung. I don't mind. You and Harold can have the two beds." She tried not to smile when she spoke. The other rule of manipulating people was not to be smug when you got your way.

She felt happier than she had been in a long time. Tomorrow they would be driving to Florida and Amelia. She was so excited she doubted she would be able to fall asleep, but soon after her head touched the pillow on the floor, she began to dream normal-people dreams.

Chapter 34 — Ingrid

"Ingrid, I can't even begin to say how sorry I am."

Rosemary sat on a patio chair next to Ingrid's small vegetable garden. Lucas was beside her. Ingrid watched him focus on everything almost at once: the neatly trimmed lawn (Hector had been using one of those old manual push mowers), the martin houses perched on top of thirty-foot poles, the colorful lantana so loved by the hummingbirds, the newly planted seedlings, and finally on her own face which was carved in granite at the moment.

She would not cry in front of this man.

"Please start at the beginning." The former police detective's voice was as kind as she had ever heard it. She didn't care. Nothing would make her like him.

"He left here before dawn, as was his habit. I had been trying to get him to move in with me, but he insisted on keeping his own home, for reasons that are none of your business. I expected him to return by lunchtime, so when he didn't, I went to his house and found him. He was lying in the entryway. I think he had just arrived home when the killer..."

"You don't have to talk about that part. We're just constructing a timeline which will be helpful when I begin questioning witnesses and potential suspects."

"It just makes sense that the killer was there waiting for him to walk in the front door, as if he knew Hector's routine. We're old. We like to keep a schedule."

"Who would be out that early to even know his routine? Most people are still in bed asleep."

"Most young people are still in bed. Old people like us are up before the sun. We only sleep a few hours at a time. Bladder issues are one of the many delightful benefits you youngsters may look forward to, if you're lucky enough to become as old as we are. As old as I am, I mean."

"Ingrid, you're only seventy, not ninety," Rosemary said. "And you're the spryest seventy-year-old I've ever known."

"Save your compliments for someone who needs them," she said, then immediately regretted her rudeness. "I'm sorry, dear. Some of my less desirable old habits tend to resurface. Hector was helping me with that, you know. I wasn't always the likable woman you see before you." Her smile trembled; she pressed her lips together to make it stop. "I can't imagine why anyone would want to kill him, of all people. Howard I can understand. He was a boor and an impediment to progress. I realize that sounds appalling, and I don't care. That is another benefit of being old. You get to say whatever you want with impunity. Hector didn't have an enemy in the world. Why him?"

"It's about the act itself, not the victim," Lucas said. "I think he provided an easy opportunity. My guess is the killer had spotted him returning to his house on several occasions, tucked that information away for the future, and then utilized it when the need to kill could no longer be restrained. That's how it is with serial killers, you know. It's a compulsion. They can't stop even if they want to, which they don't. I've never interviewed one who had regrets or who would have done anything differently, other than not getting captured. That's one of the reasons I enjoyed living in Louisiana. We had the death penalty there."

"These days I guess our only option is to slap their wrist and kick them out of the Colony. Sending someone away as punishment for murder is pathetic. The monster will simply migrate somewhere else and kill again. Hector deserves better. Unknown strangers deserve better."

"We decided this a long time ago: no capital punishment here. It's barbaric," Rosemary said.

"Slicing the throat of one of the kindest men that ever lived and watching his blood pool on the floor of his own home is barbaric."

"You're right. It's beyond horrible. But this isn't about homicidal maniacs. It's about us as a society choosing a more civilized method for dealing with bad people than the way it used to be."

Ingrid felt all the fight drain out of her. She was not up to a battle of will or words with the Colony's leader at the moment. She needed time to process what had happened and time to grieve. Then when Lucas caught the killer, she would be ready. She agreed with Rosemary in theory, but now that Hector was dead, the notion of his murderer walking away Scot-free wasn't a notion she could stomach. And she wouldn't. Rosemary was right about something else: Ingrid was in excellent shape, not only in body, but mind and spirit as well. There would be a more appropriate reckoning than banishment when the time came.

"Is there anything else you need from me? I'm very tired. I would like to go lie down."

"No, that's all for now. If I have any more questions, I'll let you know," Lucas said. "Again, I'm very sorry. I will catch the person responsible. You have my word."

His tone was grim and determined. She nodded her approval.

The rest of the afternoon, she puttered about her cavernous home. A black hole seemed to be expanding in her chest, sucking away all the good emotions she had been experiencing since becoming romantically involved with Hector. Had she been in love with him? Probably not. She enjoyed his company and also the taboo aspect of their love affair — it had felt naughty and exciting.

It didn't matter now anyway whether she had been in love with him. He was gone, and she would get on with her life, just as she had after every other heartbreaking episode in her life these past seventy years.

Ingrid was a survivor. She would be fine — sooner than most after enduring such a loss — and the sooner the better. She had two missions now: convince people that her hurricane vision was to be believed and acted upon, and avenge Hector's death. She found some minor, twisted pleasure at the thought of the second task. Focusing on revenge would ease her grief. She smiled, imagining the surprise on the killer's face at the sight of her loaded revolver. As she lay in bed, she reached a hand out and slid open the drawer of the bedside table. Her fingers touched the reassuring metal. She tried not to think about the empty space next to her.

It was early evening and the sun had yet to set, but she found herself getting drowsy. Within a few minutes her eyes closed against the golden sunlight streaming in through the sheer curtains.

Soon she was dreaming of surging waves and cloaked assassins.

Chapter 35 — Rosemary and Amelia

"Hi, Amelia. I'm sorry to barge in like this, but there's something I have to tell you."

Rosemary stood in the open doorway of Amelia's condo. Kenny had moved in next door and stood in the hallway, watching the two women with interest.

"Can I join the party?" he said.

The Colony's leader studied the young face, noting the intelligent eyes behind the Clark Kent glasses. She thought about everything this kid must have gone through and the recent loss of his best friend. Tyler probably wasn't dead. Perhaps he was even enjoying his sailing adventure with Zoey, but the truth was they would never know. Kenny would never know what had become of his friend.

"Sure, Kenny."

Amelia frowned. Rosemary saw concern on the face of the tiny woman as she ushered them into her living room.

Rosemary took a deep breath. "Lucas and I were in the watchtower and we saw a large man...very large...capturing Fergus as he was attempting to leave the mainland. His kayak was hidden in some dense brush near the water. We think he must have finished his assignment and was trying to come home. We're speculating, of course, but that's what it looked like to us. I'm sorry."

Amelia shook her head. "I knew something was up," she muttered to herself.

"What do you mean?"

"Nothing. What's the plan then?"

"You mean a rescue? I haven't come up with anything yet. It's been a crazy day, what with Hector's murder. I was on my way to talk to you earlier about Fergus when I heard Ingrid's screams."

"How long ago was that?"

"Several hours."

"Hmmph. There's not much time, then."

"What do you mean?"

"I mean I'm going over there to get him," she said as she stood.

"Don't be impulsive. The last thing we want is to lose you too."

"Yes, I'm sure that's true. I'm the only person here with medical knowledge."

"That's harsh."

"But true."

"We don't want to lose you — or anyone else, for that matter. Please, sit down."

The small woman reluctantly sat back down on the yellow sofa.

"Give me twenty-four hours to come up with a strategy. That's all I ask."

"Fergus could be dead in twenty-four hours."

"Fergus could be dead now. Either way, would he want you to come charging to his rescue and get yourself captured or killed too?"

"Of course not."

"Then give me the time."

"Very well."

"I mean it. Don't do anything on your own. Going against a direct order could lead to banishment."

Amelia snorted in disdain, then said, "I won't. Now please leave and get to work on a plan. I need to think."

A minute later Rosemary stood by the ocean, basking in the salty breeze that cooled her skin, watching the sun inches away from plunging into the turquoise water.

She loved this place. She would do whatever necessary to keep it and her people safe, even if it meant pissing off Amelia, to whom she had become attached. She was fond of Fergus as well. She would tackle the logistics of planning a rescue mission in between helping Lucas identify their murderer, working on the details of their hurricane evacuation plan, and keeping people from going hungry. It was a lot for one person's plate, but fortunately for the Colonists, there was no better person for the job. Rosemary was a consummate juggler. It had been a crucial talent in her former life.

***

"I know that face," Kenny said with a grin after Rosemary left. "That face is telling a different story than the one you gave Rosemary."

"I agreed that I would do nothing on my own. I'm not going to do anything on my own. You're going to help me."

"Damn straight, shortcake. What's the plan?"

Chapter 36 — Fergus

Fergus heard a mouse-like tap on the locked door of The Box. He had been dozing, or rather a combination of dozing and something like astral projection. When he opened his eyes, there was no discernible light. His claustrophobic cube-shaped world was utterly dark; he might have been wearing a dozen sleeping masks. Or perhaps just one coated with Vantablack, the most opaque pigment ever invented. It was so black, it gobbled up laser light and flattened reality.

He shook his head to clear his thoughts. His mind was wandering again.

Following the tap, he heard the clink of the deadbolt lock. He squeezed his eyelids together, knowing how painful even subdued light would be to his dilated pupils.

Through the thin flesh of his eyelids, he saw the inky blackness lighten to something not so all-consuming. He kept one eye tightly shut and allowed the other eyelid to open a centimeter...then two centimeters, until the pale light was tolerable.

"How are you doing in there, little man?" Lester's deep voice was a whisper.

"I've been choking the chicken more than usual. That's what too much free time will do for you."

The bass chuckle made him smile.

"How long have I been in here?"

"How long does it feel like?"

"About two weeks, so it's probably only been three or four days."

"Very good. It's been ninety-three hours."

"How much longer, Lester?" He was pleased that his own whisper sounded steady and strong, not the shaky, weak voice of a beaten man...or a lunatic.

"Aubrey says at least another day or two. She's conflicted about you. She was disappointed that you tried to leave. The only reason you weren't executed is because she's taken a liking to you."

"With friends like her..." he said. "Well, I suppose I should be flattered."

"You should be. Aubrey doesn't like many people."

"Psychopaths rarely do."

"I'm taking a chance by checking on you like this. It's not technically against the rules, but it's understood that for maximum suffering, people in The Box have no outside contact. How are those Ritz crackers holding up?"

"Holding up or plugging up? I'm happy to report that I haven't had to use the bucket for number two since I checked in. I plan to give this place a scathing review on Travelocity, by the way. The view sucks, the maids have yet to change the bed linens, and room service never answers the phone."

"You'll be fine. Just imagine you're somewhere pleasant...a mountain meadow filled with wildflowers...a white sand beach at sunset. Wherever is your happy place."

"It's hilarious hearing the Incredible Hulk talk about happy places."

"I've been in The Box before. I know what works."

"Really? I'm surprised. I thought you were Aubrey's right-hand giant."

"I am, but Zoey doesn't like me. I expect her back any time now. I admit I've enjoyed her absence."

"How could someone not like you? You're delightful."

"Agreed. I think she's jealous of the regard in which her sister holds me."

"Ah, I see. I'm not eager to meet the twin, then. Is she a psychopath as well?"

Of course he had met Zoey and knew the answer; Amelia had verified it. He wished he could tell his friend that he didn't have to worry about the young woman returning to vex him in the future.

"Yes. She has even less humanity than her sister. The...contents...of the meat freezer — that was Zoey's idea."

"So for all your 'meat is meat' rhetoric, you don't embrace the notion?"

"Between you and me, I'm still on the fence, regardless of how I wax philosophical on the subject."

"Interesting." Fergus smiled in the dark.

"Just hang in there, my tiny friend. And stay frosty." An oversized hand reached through the doorway and tapped the lowest pocket near the knee of Fergus's cargo shorts. The next moment the door closed, the deadbolt clinked into place, and he was again consumed by blackness.

"Stay frosty," Fergus mumbled to himself, puzzling over the meaning of the words as well as the gesture acknowledging the overlooked knife. Was Lester expecting trouble? What was happening out there in Costco world? He hadn't had time to ask about Annabelle. He knew she would be safe as long as she was under Lester's care, but he would still fret.

The apocalypse was no place for children, no matter how bright and self-reliant.

Chapter 37 — Jessie

"Go ahead and do the test, Jessie," Tung said. "I'm optimistic. This time it doesn't smell like turpentine, which is a good sign."

The three travelers stood beside a Ford Explorer, gazing at a puddle of gasoline. They were on a stretch of highway just north of Marietta, Georgia. When Tung had taken the exit for Interstate 75 south toward Atlanta instead of north toward Pigeon Forge, Jessie breathed a big sigh of relief. It was really happening. They were going to visit Amelia and they would arrive the next day if the match test was successful. It was the seventh such test so far. The needle on the Jeep's gauge was below the quarter mark, so they must find gas soon. She wished with all her might that the puddle would ignite quickly and burn cleanly, rather than produce oily black smoke and leave behind a sooty residue.

She gave Harold a hopeful look. He smiled back, still holding the siphon hose. She pulled the Bullwinkle's Rustic Lodge matchbook from the pocket of her jean shorts. They had grabbed a handful because they would come in handy, and also because she loved looking at the cartoon moose on the cover.

"Here goes!" She tossed the lit match.

Even Tung shouted happily at the sight of the clear flames. The tank was almost full; the bodies inside were ignored. There was no need to disturb the dead.

Jessie always got sad when she saw bodies, but this time she was so excited about going to Florida, she didn't stay sad for long.

An hour later they were back on I75 after skirting Macon on secondary roads. She hummed the song that Pablo, Maddie, and Amelia had made up on the drive out of Arizona two years ago. She was so happy, she began singing the lyrics Pablo had written. He said they were cheesy but she didn't agree. She thought they were quite nice.

> *If I said I was certain she's waiting*
> *You'd know I was lying for sure*
> *But I feel all my sorrows abating*
> *I can sense that our love will endure*
>
> *So I packed up this rusty old Chevy*
> *I gave my two weeks to the Man*
> *My heart no longer feels heavy*
> *The best of life finally began*

Arizona in the rearview mirror
Every passing mile takes me nearer
I swear I can already hear her
That sweet angel's whispers of love

"That was exquisite. You have a lovely voice, which does not surprise me. Is there anything you can't do?" Harold said.

"I can't dunk a basketball. Maybe when I'm older I'll be able to."

The older man laughed. "I doubt professional basketball is in your future anyway. Oh, what's that?" He frowned. "Do you sense that, Tung?"

"Yes. Let me pull over."

After the Jeep was parked on the blacktop, Tung scanned the terrain for any signs of danger. Then he leaned back against the driver's seat and closed his eyes. Harold followed his lead, then Jessie did the same. She had been feeling a scratching sensation in her brain, but her *scythen* wasn't advanced enough yet to know what that meant.

~~~

Amelia: Tung?

Tung: Yes, I'm here. What's wrong?

Amelia: It would be quicker to list what isn't wrong.

Tung: Start with the most pressing problem.

Amelia: Fergus has been captured by a group in Tequesta. That's the town on the mainland close to the island of Jupiter, my home.

Tung: Are these Tequesta survivors bad people?

Amelia: Unknown. That's what Fergus was trying to find out. Two of their members came here. One was a lovely young man, the other a remorseless tyrant. So perhaps they are a mixture of good and bad. The man who was seen capturing Fergus was gigantic.

Tung: Have you contacted Fergus?

Amelia: No. I didn't want to tip him off that I'm planning a rescue mission. I wouldn't want him to do anything impulsive to stop me. Also...I was afraid to. If I can't make contact with him, I'll know he's gone. I couldn't bear it.

Tung: Are you asking for my help? You understand that my hands are full keeping my precious cargo safe.

Amelia: Yes, damn it. I understand that. Do you think I would ask you to do something that would put Jessie in danger?

Tung: No, I'm sorry. I know you wouldn't. But I do know the depth of your feelings for our friend.

Amelia: What I need from you at this moment is two-fold. I need that weapon you've placed on the console of the vehicle you're driving, and I need to have Jessie nearby in case someone gets hurt.

Tung: Amelia! You know the rules. I can't ask her to do that. It would be against protocol.

Amelia: Yet she brought your English charge back from the dead. That must also be against protocol.

Tung: I didn't give her permission to do so.

Jessie: I don't need permission. I'll do it again, if I have to. I'll do whatever I can to help you, Amelia.

Amelia: (smiling) Hello, child. Your scythen has improved even in the last day.

Jessie: We're on our way to you now. We found some good gas and there is enough to drive all the way to Florida. We have a road atlas. We know right where you are.

Amelia: Child, you are more special to me than you can ever know.

Tung: Wait a minute, you two. I haven't agreed to any of this. I only said I would take Jessie to Florida for a quick visit. Not to put her in danger.

Amelia: Tung, you have a heart of gold. I know you will do the right thing.

Harold: Hello, Amelia. I'm the English charge you mentioned. It will be my pleasure to help in any way I can. How do the skies look to the east?

Amelia: Hello, Harold. There are dark clouds forming. It looks like we may have some rain tonight."

Harold: Oh dear. My expertise in anthropology and ancient languages is extensive, but not so in the area of meteorology. I do think the rain may be a harbinger, though.

Amelia: Perhaps, but the more urgent issue now is Fergus. We must act.

Tung: You are testing the limits of my patience, Amelia.

Amelia: I know, my friend. I wouldn't ask if I had any other choice. I'll be at the Jupiter Hills Golf Club in north Tequesta tomorrow at dawn. It's off Federal Highway, just west of the Blowing Rocks Preserve. You'll see it on the atlas. I assume there's a clubhouse somewhere on the property.

Jessie: We'll be there, Amelia! I promise!
Amelia: Thank you, child.

~~~

Amelia ended the communication. Jessie got the impression she had done that so Tung wouldn't have the chance to say no.

"Jessie, we need to have another talk about rules."

"I'm listening," she said from the back seat while wearing a huge grin.

Tung sighed. Harold turned his head and gave her a wink.

"I know you're listening, but I wonder if you're understanding why the rules were put in place to begin with and why they're so necessary. Breaking them may have terrible consequences. Do you understand that?"

Jessie nodded. "I do."

"Do you realize we'll have to travel at night to get to Amelia's meeting place by morning?"

There was exasperation in his tone but also affection. Jessie knew Tung loved Amelia almost as much as she did. They had been friends for thousands of years.

"I know. And I know you don't like traveling at night because it's dangerous. I'm sorry."

Tung was not to be mollified so easily. "Once we arrive, we shall listen to her plan, and I will make the decision whether I am in a position to help or not. You and Harold will have no part in it. But you will get to see Amelia as promised."

Jessie hesitated. "I understand."

Tung studied her in the rearview mirror, then gave a little shake of his head.

She was walking a fine line. She would help Amelia in any way she could and Tung wasn't going to stop her, but he could make it difficult. She wasn't big enough to drive a car, so she needed his help getting there. After that, she would see how things went.

For all Tung's talk, Jessie knew she held the cards. She knew her value. The *Cthor* believed there wasn't anybody on the planet like her. Amelia had gotten herself kicked out of *Cthor-Vangt* because she broke the rules, but Jessie had *langthal* and other talents nobody else had. Jessie knew there was nothing she could do that would keep the *Cthor* from taking her back.

She would help whomever and however she could when the time came.

Chapter 38 — Amelia

"We're getting wetter than a whore on dollar night," Kenny said.

Amelia and the teenager had waited until full dark, then they donned black clothing and stole a kayak from the Colony's fleet. It was midnight now and they were paddling north on the Intracoastal Waterway, which, at their current location, was also part of the Indian River. They would have been less conspicuous traveling on the Atlantic side of the snake-shaped Jupiter Island, but the first outer bands of the hurricane had arrived and Amelia had no desire to venture into the ocean. A mere fifty yards of land separated the Intracoastal from the sea in some places. Formerly, the area had boasted some of the wealthiest residents and priciest real estate in the country, but Chicxulub was an equal opportunity killer. The odds were that nobody lived in those palatial homes. They saw no lights nor any other indication of life.

The weather was more of an inconvenience than a danger at this point, and the clouds and drizzle provided excellent cover. As long as they didn't encounter people, they should be fine. Nevertheless, Amelia had strapped a sheathed long-knife to her back. She was no warrior, but she knew how to use the thing. She wouldn't hesitate to kill anyone who tried to harm those she cared about, which included the boy behind her. She hadn't had a chance to test for unseen talents, but at the very least, Kenny was an Einstein-level genius.

"I just noticed you're not wearing your glasses. Is that because of the rain?" she said in a low voice, turning her head slightly to glance behind her at the boy.

A snicker wafted from the back of the kayak.

"They're just a prop. I can see fine."

"So it's like the fake Tourette's? Why all the shenanigans?"

"The Tourette's outbursts are fun, and you have to admit it's a great way to make your point without taking heat. Only a total asshat would start a fight with a disabled kid."

"True. What about the glasses?"

"I read a long time ago that people who had bad eyesight were more intelligent on average than people with good eyesight. Think of all those Asian eggheads. I shit you not, there wasn't anyone in my gifted classes who didn't wear glasses. I figured the specs would help me fit in with the smart kids. Then after a while, I realized I enjoyed wearing them. I think they make me look older and wiser."

"If you say so. Are you sure you don't have a boy crush on Clark Kent?"

"Listen, Sacajawea, Kenny don't swing that way. I'm into chicks and only chicks...all colors, all sizes. And all ages," he added in a lecherous tone.

Amelia snorted. "We're almost there. We'll pull onto the shore by that large banyan tree and hide the vessel in the mangroves." She pointed to a cluster of trees with one leafy leviathan protruding out the top.

"Damn, Gina. The lady knows her trees."

"I have made a point to learn as much about the Mother's gifts during my lifetime as possible."

"The Mother? As in Mother Nature?"

"Of course."

"I'm guessing you're not the religious sort then? I think I like you even better now."

"What's not to like?" She grinned in the gloom as they paddled up to the shore. The water was a sinister inky-black this time of night. "Time to put your rubbers on," she whispered.

"Well, aren't you a frisky little mare."

"I mean your waders."

"Oh right. Putting them on now."

"We don't know what's in the water. Perhaps snakes."

"Why does it always have to be snakes?"

"That was from a movie, yes? You're quite entertaining. I see why Fergus likes you so much."

"What's not to like?" he said, mimicking Amelia's voice.

She was impressed; he had gotten her subtle, ambiguous accent down perfectly and even managed to hit the correct octave. His impression of the actor in the snake movie was probably also superlative, but she had never seen it. She wasn't the film aficionado that Fergus was. She wondered what other talents might be hidden behind the boy's comic façade.

The kayak slid onto the narrow beach, crunching a bit on the bottom as it struck sand, rocks, and tree roots. The vessel was lightweight, and the two pulled it into the foliage with little trouble. They walked a short distance up the bank to the blacktop known as Highway 1, which ran north along the coast to the Georgia state line and south to the Florida Keys. This section was also called the Federal Highway and the A1A. Jupiter Hills Golf Club lay on the western side of the roadway.

The two small figures darted across the wet asphalt and onto a grassy stretch that was the prelude to the Jupiter Hills community. Amelia had studied one of the many maps she kept in her condo and had committed everything to memory. They would cut through a residential neighborhood as a shortcut to the clubhouse. She expected that would take no more than fifteen minutes, so they would arrive early, ahead of the sunrise by at least an hour. They might be able to take a quick cat nap before Tung arrived. She hoped so. After hours of paddling, she was exhausted. She turned to say something to Kenny but he was no longer trudging along beside her.

"Kenny," she hissed into the night. The relentless drizzle muffled all sound. Did she hear his footsteps? Where had the boy gone, and how had he disappeared so silently and completely? She scanned the area, shielding her eyes from the rain, but could see little beyond twenty yards in any direction.

"Kenny!" she called, louder now. She hated to think of who or what might be alerted to her presence. She stood in place, weighing the options of what to do next, when a voice floated toward her from the direction of the river.

She would blame the mental and physical fatigue for overlooking the two people hiding in the tangled mass of mangrove roots and sea oats near the spot where they had pulled the kayak ashore. She didn't know they were being tailed until she heard the voice.

"Stop there. Hands up. Don't make any sudden moves."

She lifted her hands toward the night sky. "I have some food and a bottle of water in my pack." She had begun shrugging out of her backpack so she could get to the long-knife, when the deep voice spoke again.

"Stop, woman. I am generally averse to hurting females, but my partner here isn't so inclined."

"May I turn to face you?"

"Slowly."

Two figures stood in the misty darkness. The female held a firearm. The man was colossal and carried no weapon that she could see; his size was intimidating enough.

I'm bunking at the headquarters of the Terminators with the aforementioned giant and would-be tiny murderess. Luckily, the giant and murderess are friends.

The woman wasn't a child, but could this man be the giant Fergus had mentioned?

"Where did the boy go?" the woman asked.

"I was just wondering that myself."

"What were you doing on the river, and where are you going?"

"You two are Tequesta Terminators, aren't you?"

Amelia had decided to take a leap of faith. She hoped the ploy might buy her some time and perhaps even get her inside the Costco in which Fergus was surely being held against his will. Doing it that way rather than with Tung's help might save some bloodshed.

Fergus better still be alive to benefit from her intervention.

"So you've heard about us?" There was pride in the woman's voice.

"Spaz, no talking, please."

Amelia heard a note of irritation in the man's response. She took another leap of faith, one that could span an ocean.

"I bet you're Lester."

The behemoth did a good job of covering his surprise, but she could tell from even ten feet away that she had sparked his curiosity.

"How do you know my name, Lilliputian?"

"Because we have a mutual friend."

"Let me guess. Red hair, blue eyes, stands about yay tall?" A large flattened palm gestured at waist-level.

"That's my Fergus."

"Interesting. He said he had been traveling alone for some time before he came to us. He's been with me almost every minute since then. When could he have told you about me?"

"That's the part that truly is interesting." She was about to violate one of the most sacrosanct rules of *Cthor-Vangt* — she would explain *scythen* to a normal human. She had no doubt the titillating information would get her entrée into the Terminator headquarters.

She was preparing to launch into a compelling explanation, when both the woman and the man made sudden swatting motions at their backsides.

"What the fuck?" the woman said, just before her legs turned to rubber. She crumpled to the ground.

The male stayed on his feet twenty seconds longer than the female. Amelia watched a variety of unidentifiable emotions flit across the chiseled face before he collapsed too, a redwood felled by a woodsman's axe.

Kenny materialized out of the drizzle.

"And that's how it's done," he said with a big grin.

"What did you do?"

"I poison darted their asses."

"What was in the darts? Please tell me it was only a sedative."

Kenny frowned at the alarm he heard in her voice. "Yes, part of the mixture I use is fentanyl."

"A fast-acting opioid with immobilizing effects in larger dozes."

"Right."

"What's the other part of the solution?"

"Wolfsbane."

"Aconite. Oh dear. What were you thinking, Kenny?"

"I was thinking to disable people who wanted to harm us."

She sighed. "I know you were trying to help."

"Damn straight. When I realized those two were behind us, I made myself invisible, then nailed them with the darts. I think the woman was going to shoot you. She was pointing that GI Joe gun right at you."

"What do you mean you made yourself invisible?"

"Not literally. It's just a talent I developed for fading away into the background to keep myself safe."

"I see. Well, the problem is I believe the man is Fergus's friend."

"Why do you think that? Do you know him?"

"No, but Fergus told me about him."

"I'm confused."

"Never mind about that now. Things are going to become even more confusing in the next few hours. Help me drag this man to the clubhouse."

"You still haven't told me why we're going there. Do you have a hidden weapons cache? A small army? How the hell are we going to save your boyfriend?"

"I'll get to all that later. Grab the left arm and I'll take the right."

"What about the woman?"

"I don't care about the woman. Fergus didn't mention her."

"So the issue isn't that I probably killed two people with my darts, it's that I probably killed a friend of Fergus?"

"Yes. It will be all I can do to save the life of the man, if that's even possible. How much aconite is in those darts?"

"A lot."

"It is a slow-acting poison, thankfully. We just might save him."

"I don't see how, unless the Jupiter Hills Golf Course clubhouse is supplied with antiarrhythmic drugs."

"You know your poison cures."

"Just like you know your trees. I'm a smart kid, Amelia," Kenny said with a grunt as they began dragging the man through the wet grass.

"You're much more than a smart kid. Soon we will discover all your talents, some of which you may not even realize you possess."

***

Amelia ignored the look of intense disapproval on the face of her dear friend. Instead, she focused on Jessie. She would not coerce the child to do anything immoral, unethical, or against the *Cthor* protocol. Jessie would have to make the decision to save the life of Fergus's friend — or not — all by herself.

Harold said, "That may be the largest human being I've ever seen in person. Evolutionarily speaking, he's quite an anomaly. Imagine how he would have stood out in a crowd ten thousand years ago when the average male was barely over a meter and a half. This fellow must be two meters, thirteen. That's about seven feet to you Americans. Fascinating!"

A small group of people encircled the man, who lay unconscious on the plush carpet of the Jupiter Hills clubhouse. Tung stood with his arms crossed, looking displeased. Kenny also had his arms crossed, but he wore an expression of utter confusion. Harold, Tung's British charge, was as delightful as Amelia suspected he would be.

Jessie hadn't left her side since their arrival fifteen minutes earlier. Amelia hadn't realized how much she had missed the child. In her former line of work as a mentor, observer, and occasional recruiter for the *Cthor*, she tried not to get too emotionally attached to people. That rarely worked out.

"How do you know he's the one Fergus told you about?" Tung said.

"His size, obviously. Also when I asked if his name was Lester, he displayed surprise."

"But he didn't affirm that was his name?"

"He didn't have to. I could tell by his reaction that it was. We can use his help getting inside the building where Fergus is being held."

"You aren't even certain Fergus is still alive."

"True, but you know we can confirm that before we go."

She watched the almond-shaped eyes dart toward Kenny, then focus on the ceiling in exasperation. She was pushing the limits of his patience and taking advantage of his fondness for her.

She decided to take the third leap of faith of the day.

"This one," she gestured to Kenny, "is one of those that I told you about yesterday. I think it will be fine to talk in front of him."

"Have you conducted the tests? If not, it is reckless for you to be discussing such things."

"I told you, I haven't had time, but I would bet my life, even shortened as it is, that he is a candidate."

"What the hell is going on here," Kenny said , using his own voice for once. "It's one thing to be talking shit that I don't understand, but it's another to be talking shit about me that I don't understand. Amelia, what gives?"

"Tung, there's nothing more the *Cthor* can do to me. I have nothing to lose."

"Have you forgotten about that recent request you made regarding a weather event? I'm still considering proposing it to them."

"Tung, please."

"You've become a loose cannon. You know how much you mean to me, but I can't condone this complete disregard for our rules."

"It's Fergus." She heard the plaintive tone, and she didn't care. She would beg on her knees if it would help.

She watched an array of emotions flit across her friend's normally inscrutable face. She could almost read his thoughts as he considered all the data alongside potential outcomes of any number of decisions. Finally, his focus shifted away from her to the floor where the large man lay dying. Tung's eyes opened wide in alarm when he saw that Jessie was kneeling beside him, her small hands placed on his chest.

"Jessie, what are you doing?"

"Shhh. I need to concentrate. The poison is spreading fast."

"I didn't give you permission to do this."

"I know. But this is really important."

"You mean it's important to Amelia."

"It's important to Fergus too. And he's still a citizen of *Cthor-Vangt*, so helping him in a roundabout way shouldn't be against the rules. Now please be quiet so I can do this."

Amelia bit off a sudden manic outburst of laughter, but her friend's *scythen* picked up on the emotion.

"Yes, it's hilarious, isn't it? The child has adorably usurped my authority. I don't know why I'm even needed any longer."

"I'm your witness," Harold said with an affectionate pat to Tung's back. "There was no stopping her. I assume that's how she was with me as well."

"Yes. Even more so."

"Where did Kenny go?" Amelia noticed the boy had disappeared again, practically under their noses and into thin air.

"I don't know," Harold said. "He was standing here next to me just a minute ago."

Tung arched an eyebrow. "What is this?"

"It's one of his talents," Amelia improvised. "He did it earlier too...just vanished. Of course it's not true invisibility, but he has a gift for making himself disappear into the background. He's done it for years as a way of staying under the radar. I have only just discovered the talent. Do you remember how Dani and

Sam were able to move about like ghosts? We'll add it to his list of qualifications in addition to an intellect that I daresay exceeds yours and mine."

"Before he can be a candidate, he has to be located. Harold, you're not going anywhere. Amelia, you may go search, and if you find him, bring him back here. We'll conduct a fast-track analysis. If he passes, then we will contact Fergus to make sure he's still alive before we launch this rescue mission."

The exasperation was gone, replaced now with Tung's normal low-key, competent manner.

She was out the door the next moment.

"Kenny," she called, stepping into the early morning drizzle. She wondered how long these rain bands would continue and then intensify before the hurricane arrived. Why did everything always have to happen at once? She thought about how nice that nap would have been before facing a day that would demand all her physical and mental strength.

"Girl, you got some 'splaining to do."

"There you are. You did your disappearing trick again. Someday you'll have to show me how you do that."

"I could show you, but then I'd have to kill you. Now what the hell is going on in there? Who are those people and what is Thorvant?"

"*Cthor-Vangt*. It's a place. Kenny, you're going to have to trust me. Do you think you can do that?"

"I'm not an inherently trusting person," he said, sounding twenty years older, "but I do trust you for some reason. I get a good vibe from you."

"That does not surprise me. Okay, here's what I need you to do…"

***

"What's happening?" The giant said from the floor.

"Hi, Lester. I'm Jessie. That's Amelia, Kenny, Tung, and Harold." Jessie removed her hands from the big man's chest. She wore a tired smile.

"Where's Spaz?" the man asked.

Amelia replied, "She did not survive the poison dart. Your bulk was partly what saved you."

The huge man struggled to sit up. "Where am I?"

"You're in north Jupiter and in no imminent danger. We need your help to gain access to the Terminators' headquarters."

"Why would I help you? You poisoned my partner and almost killed me."

Amelia squatted so she could look the man directly in the eyes.

"Fergus spoke highly of you, so I know you must be an honorable person. I know that he tried to escape and you caught him trying to leave Tequesta. I know that your leader is a psychopath, and I suspect she is holding him prisoner. We need your help to free him."

"Again, why should I help you? For that matter, why shouldn't I just kill you?" With surprising speed, he encircled Amelia's throat with fingers that felt like iron bands.

She smiled. "Hear us out before you throttle me."

***

Amelia: Fergus, are you there?

SILENCE.

Amelia: Fergus, are you there? Please answer.

Fergus: Hello, my darling. I'm here.

Amelia: Are you in distress? Are you injured?

Fergus: No, no. I'm fine. I'm just doing some light reading.

Amelia: Cut the crap. I know you tried to escape Tequesta in the kayak and Lester captured you and took you back to their headquarters.

Fergus: There's no point in denying it then.

Amelia: What is your situation?

Fergus: I'm being held in a tiny room. There is food and water, so I'm not in distress, but I'm terribly bored and more than a little horny.

Amelia: Thank goodness. We're coming to get you. Your friend Lester is with us.

Fergus: He is? Is Annabelle with him?

Amelia: No. A woman named Spaz was with him. She was a casualty of war. Is Annabelle the tiny would-be murderess?

Fergus: Yes. Lester is supposed to be taking care of her. Amelia, I don't need to be rescued. I'm fine. I'm being punished, not tortured. Aubrey the psychopath has taken a liking to me. I just need to take my medicine like a good boy.

Amelia: That's what Lester said you would say. He knows a lot more about what's going on inside that Costco building than you do. We'll get Annabelle too, then.

Fergus: I hope you're bringing the cavalry. They're well-armed.

Amelia: We don't need the cavalry. We have Tung's weapon.

Fergus: Impressive! I can't believe you talked him into this.

Amelia: I've had help from Jessie in managing Tung. I'm sure I'll pay for that later in some unpleasant way. Lester will be coming too. He's with us now.

Fergus: By 'with' do you mean he knows about us?

Amelia: Yes, as does Kenny.

Fergus: My darling, determined Amelia. I imagine Tung is not a happy camper at the moment.

Amelia: That is the understatement of the millennia.

Fergus: What is your ETA?

Amelia: I can't say for sure. Just be ready for us.

Fergus: I shall. Be careful, my dear. Stay alive. No matter what occurs, I will find you.

Amelia: That's from a movie, isn't it?

Fergus: Of course. The Last of the Mohicans. *Madeleine Stowe...now there's a beautiful woman. And I have to admit, Daniel Day-Lewis is a fine-looking man.*

Amelia: Goodbye, Fergus. I'll see you soon.

Chapter 39 — Ingrid

"This is it. You realize that, right?" Ingrid said to Rosemary. She stood in a puddle of rainwater in Rosemary's kitchen, her clothes soaked through. She had barged in through the front door, which wasn't locked — how careless of the Colony's leader, considering there was a murderer on the loose — to talk about last night's dream.

"You mean the rain? Yes, it very well could be the first bands of a hurricane."

The woman before her was exhausted. Deep vertical wrinkles were etched between the well-shaped eyebrows.

Stress will age you. That was the price Rosemary was paying now for shouldering all the problems of their fledgling society. Ingrid felt no sympathy for her; this is what the woman had wanted, and she was getting it by the bucketful.

"Of course I mean the rain. I've lived here for decades. This type of precipitation is what precedes a hurricane."

"I've lived in Florida for a long time as well. I know about tropical weather."

"What are we going to do?"

"About the evacuation? Nothing at the moment. It's too early anyway. And besides, maybe it won't be as bad as you think."

Ingrid's eyes narrowed. "I had another dream. I guarantee it will be as bad as I think."

"Would you like a towel?"

Ingrid took a deep breath. It would serve no purpose to alienate this woman whose help she needed to save the lives of the Colonists.

"Yes, please. I don't suppose you have any coffee?"

"I do. Room temperature, though. I made it yesterday in the Love Shack."

"That will do. A bit of sugar as well, please."

"Of course. It's your sugar, after all."

"Indeed." She sat in one of Rosemary's kitchen chairs. "I know people don't want to leave. Even before the plague when we had access to Doppler radar and could see these monsters out in the Atlantic, people didn't want to leave. I was one of them. My house was constructed with reinforced concrete. It can handle the winds, but not even a fortress can withstand the storm surge."

Rosemary sat down across the table from her. "Is that what you saw? Flooding?"

"A frothing, relentless tide consuming everything after the winds have demolished most of the trees and structures. Do you remember the pictures of Puerto Rico after Hurricane Maria?"

Rosemary nodded. The etched lines deepened.

"This will be worse. There will be nothing left but floating debris and floating bodies. I've seen it."

"I know you believe this prophetic dream of yours will come to pass. I'm not so sure, though."

"Damn it, don't start that with me. I've told you before the dreams are accurate."

Rosemary leaned forward, sudden and fierce. "Every single time? Have you never had one that didn't come true? Be truthful. I'll know if you're not."

Dark brown eyes bored into her. She resisted the urge to look away from their intensity.

"There have been some that didn't...fewer than five, I would say. In more than forty years, fewer than five."

"Well, there you have it." The Colony leader slumped back in her chair as the ferocity from seconds ago drained away. "The logistics of evacuating over fifty people in terrible weather while adversaries are ready to swoop in during our absence, or worse, attack us as we're fleeing...it's a freaking nightmare. I've done the math. Our odds are better staying in place and weathering the storm. By my calculations, we'll lose fewer lives in that scenario than in any other."

A jolt of panic ran through her seventy-year-old body. "You're not following through with the evacuation then?"
"No. It wasn't a popular notion before, and it's even more unpopular now. People want to hole up in their houses, cover their gardens, secure their belongings, and hunker down in place."

"Then they will die."

"We don't know that."

"I know that."

"What we do know is that leaving our homes, abandoning all that we've built this past year, is something nobody wants to do. We have no idea what we'll even find out there." She gestured to the west. "You didn't experience the full brunt of the collapse of civilization. You didn't fight for scraps of food to keep from starving. You didn't drink ditch runoff and suffer from dysentery because there was no clean water to be found. You didn't knife a man in the testicles because he was about to rape you."

"No, I didn't. I had a relatively easy time getting through the end of the world. And do you know why? Because I knew disaster was imminent. I had seen it in my dreams. I used a significant portion of my wealth to prepare for it. Do you know what people said about me behind my back when they saw all those boxes of food being delivered to my house? What they whispered about me at cocktail parties after the well was dug? The nickname they settled on when word got out that I'd put a secret room in my house for storing my supplies? Crazy Ingrid the Doomsday Prepper. Crazy Ingrid. That's what they called me. And do you think I cared one whit? No. Because I had faith in my dreams then, and I have faith in them now. This storm will kill everyone who doesn't evacuate. I know it with every fiber of my being. And I can't get people to leave without your help."

Rosemary sighed and closed her eyes. "So we'll be taking the killer with us on this mass exodus?"

"Is that what you're worried about?"

Rosemary barked a laugh. "That's one of the many things I'm worried about."

Ingrid studied the younger woman as her mind raced. "If I catch the killer, will you consider evacuating then?"

"How do you plan to do that?"

"There have been times in my life when I programmed my subconscious to focus on a particular event or person so as to determine the future."

"And does this work?"

"Not always, but sometimes it has. When I try to dial in like that, it's not as reliable as when I allow the future to show me what it wants to. It's almost as if whatever has given me this power does not want me to abuse it. Does that make sense?"

Rosemary gave her a slow blink.

Ingrid stifled the sudden rush of anger. "I will attempt to do so tonight when I go to sleep. I hope to have the name of our murderer for you in the morning. If I do, promise me you'll go forward with the evacuation plans. That's all I ask."

"And how will I know that the name you give me is correct?"

"You'll send Lucas to verify it. He'll go to this person's home and find the tools of his...or her... trade."

"Just like that. You make it sound so easy. You know Lucas has been covertly searching houses this entire time."

"Of course. Nothing happens in this place that I don't know about. He's clever, that young man of yours. I will admit that, even though I don't like him."

"Gee, thanks. I'll tell him you said so. It'll mean a lot to him."

Rosemary had never spoken so rudely to her before. Ingrid let it slide, seeing it as a symptom of the woman's exhausted state.

"Tell him if you want. I don't care either way. But tomorrow, if I give you a name, you may rest assured that it is the name of our murderer."

"How do I know that you won't just pick a name of someone you don't like?"

"I am many things, young lady, but I am no liar. And I would never bear false witness." She used the imperious tone she had cultivated during a lifetime of giving orders.

"You're right. I know you would never do that. Fine. Give me a name in the morning, and I'll have Lucas check it out. What do we have to lose?"

"And if I'm right, you agree to evacuate?"

"I'm not agreeing to that outright, but I will say that I'll push harder for an evacuation knowing that we don't have a killer in our midst who could make the process even more dangerous."

"I suppose that's all I can ask for then. I'll say one more thing before I leave. I have never evacuated in advance of a hurricane. Not once since I've been living on this island. And whether or not the rest of you are coming with me, I will be leaving soon, even if I have to paddle my own boat. That should tell you how certain I am of my dreams. You know me, Rosemary. You know I'm no coward." She leaned forward, taking Rosemary's hands in her own. "The hurricane will destroy everything that remains. I know this with certainty, and I'm more afraid than I have ever been in my life...even more than when everyone around me was dying from the plague. This storm is leviathan. It will be the end of us all."

Chapter 40 — Anonymous

Dear Diary,

I am down to days, perhaps even hours, before escaping this oppressive paradise. I had planned a rather showy going-away celebration for the Colonists — several large pots of poisoned gumbo — but the weather is not accommodating. Nobody wants to come to my party in the rain. It has also created some logistical problems in terms of procuring supplies for my expedition. Everyone is staying inside, so there are people occupying the two places to which I require covert access: Ingrid's secret room and the Love Shack. How I loathe that ridiculous name...almost as much as I detest my time spent there in the persona I invented to 'blend in.'

It chafes, it annoys, it nauseates...but not for much longer.

I will wait for the kitchen staff to exit the Love Shack, and then I will ransack it. Afterward, I will take the footpath to Ingrid's house and gain entry by whatever means necessary. There has never been a door that could keep me out for long. I daresay the old woman doesn't always remember to check every lock in that garish monstrosity. I know she leaves the upstairs bedroom window open. I've often stood in the shadows below and watched the gauzy curtains rippling in the night breeze.

It appears that I won't get to kill everyone before I go, but I shall at least enjoy snuffing out that old bird. She represents two things I despise: wealth and privilege. As a child born into poverty and ignorance, I had to fight for everything. I had to use the utmost stealth while acquiring the knowledge my intellect demanded; if I was discovered reading library books under my threadbare bedcovers at night, I would be beaten. Education wasn't revered — it was feared. It was deemed 'uppity' and 'snooty,' and anyone who desired it was scorned.

Can you imagine such? No, Diary, I think not. Only those who have lived in the inbred backwater of Appalachia have an inkling as to what a gifted little girl would have suffered.

And, oh, how I suffered. I have the switchin' scars and the absent teeth to prove it.

It's a shame that I have only so recently come into my own, a battered Lepidoptera shedding its restrictive larval form and emerging as the glorious creature it was meant to be. I will make the most of what remains of my time on earth as the Angel of Death. Even now I perceive magnificent obsidian wings sprouting moth-like from my shoulders. I sometimes feel lightened by their silent fluttering movements, as if my feet barely touch the ground while going about the chore of pretending to be someone I'm not.

Those days are soon coming to an end. When I leave this place in my sublime new incarnation, I will set off on my solitary journey and never again assume a persona other than my own.

But first, there are a few minor tasks to complete...

Chapter 41 — Fergus

"Stay frosty...stay frosty...those words and the gesture toward the knife in my pocket...they mean something."

Fergus had lost count of the hours and days he had been inside The Box, or as he had come to think of it, Lucifer's Anus — surely there was nothing more disgusting than the anal cavity of the most powerful fallen angel. He had acquiesced to the demands of his body and filled the bucket. He was used to the smell, and as bad as it was to him, it would be much worse for whomever was charged with the task of releasing him. This thought prompted another: when would he be released? His punishment seemed to be going on for too long. Had something happened? He knew that his skyscraping friend was not out there, surreptitiously protecting him, because Lester was with Amelia. What if everyone else had abandoned the building and he had been forgotten? Amelia was planning a rescue mission, but what if something happened to her on the way? That little woman was a force of nature, but she was still human and therefore fallible. He tried to remember how long it had been since they had last communicated. Three hours? Twenty-four hours? It was impossible to tell.

The Ritz cracker cartons were empty and their wax paper liners licked clean. His stomach had been rumbling nonstop for a while now. His thoughts had become foggy and detached. Sometimes it was difficult to discern if he was sitting in a metal cube in the Tequesta Costco building or in some stinky, cosmic backwater black hole. Probably in the vicinity of Uranus.

He shook his head, struggling to clear his thoughts. These bizarre mental wanderings had been happening frequently. He hadn't lost his mind, but he felt it fraying around the edges.

"Stay frosty...hmmmm. And the knife bit...hmmmm."

He shook his head again with such force, it felt like something dislodged inside his skull.

"You're losing it, mate. The food is gone, the bucket is full, and there's a marked absence of naked women in here. It's time to go."

He realized he had been subconsciously contemplating a prison break, but the notion hadn't fully coalesced in his brain. He wouldn't wait for a rescue that may not come. Besides, there would be much less danger for Amelia and Tung if he were to amble up to them on the road, all safe and sound before they arrived at the Terminator headquarters to bust him out.

He reached for the device in the pocket of his shorts was no simple switchblade, but rather a Victorinox Swiss Army multi-tool, boasting several blades, scissors, a wire cutter, two screwdrivers, a bender, a scraper, and a prying implement, all folded into a four-inch metal ruler. You could build a bomb or deliver a baby with the thing, and he would put it to good use now on the door of The Box. He hadn't been lying to Aubrey when he told her he could pick any lock this side of a maximum security prison. And since she didn't strike him as someone who would forget a significant detail, he suspected she might be having The Box watched, waiting for the exact move he intended to make now: escape.

He ran his hands over the surface of the door, then the knob and locking mechanism, then the aluminum casing of the doorway. He closed his eyes — even though there was no discernible difference between when they were open or not — and pictured the structure in its entirety, fleshing out all the details in his mind. Then he visualized the specific movements the multi-tool would make to free him, like a red-haired turd squeezed from the bung hole of Lucifer himself.

Twenty minutes later, he was free, and breathing in a lungful of undefiled air. He surveyed the perimeter and saw no one. Perhaps the building had been abandoned, as he had feared.

The rubber soles of his cross-trainers emitted faint squeaks as he headed toward the back of the building. There would be fewer guards at the back door leading out to Tent Town than at the front door near Aubrey's office. At least he wouldn't have to worry about Spaz, the Linda Hamilton wannabe; although if he were forced to engage in hand-to-hand combat with a guard, he wouldn't have minded having a go at her.

"Focus, Fergus," he muttered to himself. He stopped at the end of the aisle, peering around the corner to the door with the EXIT sign and the crash bar. As expected, no sexy woman wearing a black tank top and toting a semi-automatic rifle stood sentinel. Instead, one of the two twins who normally guarded Aubrey's office was stationed there, wearing a bored expression and running the fingers of his left hand along the cartridges in the crisscrossing bandoliers covering his chest. The M16 hung at his side. The index finger of the right hand was placed above the trigger. The safety was off.

Fergus pulled his head back around the corner and contemplated his next move.

"I didn't know you were getting out today," a child's voice whispered through the stacks of paper towels which separated Fergus's aisle from the one next to it.

"Annabelle, my dear. You scared the shi...you scared the bejesus out of me."

"What's bejesus?"

"I have no idea, but it just squirted into my underpants."

He smiled at the giggle.

"I think I know what bejesus is now."

"That's because you're a smart cookie. Tell me about the situation here."

"What do you mean?"

"Lester is gone, yes?"

"Yes. He left a day ago to track some people that had been spotted going up the river."

"I see. And was he alone?"

"No, Spaz went with him. They should be back soon, though. I know he'll be happy that you're out of The Box. Was it terrible in there? I'll understand if you're not up to reading to me until you've recovered. You'll want to get a bath too," she added.

"You can smell me from over there?"

"Yes. Have you ever been to the monkey house at a zoo?"

"Say no more, child. So other than Lester being gone, everything is normal?"

"Yes. I've been hanging out with Aubrey a lot. I think she really likes me."

Fergus frowned. "Indeed? What have you two ladies been up to?"

"She's been telling me stuff. About how everything runs here and why she has to make difficult decisions sometimes."

"Like what?"

"Sometimes she has to make decisions that not everyone likes. Like the meat thing. At first people weren't happy about that."

"Understandably so."

"But then after a while they got used to the idea. If they didn't, they had to be dealt with. You can't have order without discipline, and you can't have discipline if people are allowed to complain."

Annabelle's parroted words had come directly from Aubrey's lips. With a creeping sense of disquiet, he wondered how much time the child had been spending with the psychopath while he was in The Box.

"I know you're impressed by her, Annabelle. But as smart and pretty as she is, she doesn't know everything. She's not right about everything, either. What would your mommy have thought about eating people?"

He heard a shuffling of small feet on the other side of the paper towels. "She wouldn't have minded. Before she died, she told me to eat her after she was gone if I got really hungry. So I did. She kept me alive until I got good with my gun and could shoot squirrels."

Fergus felt the bile rising in his throat.

"Oh, Annabelle. I'm so sorry. That is not something a child can do without being forever changed by it."

"It's okay, Fergus. She was right, and so is Aubrey."

"Stay put. I'll come around to your side."

"No you won't," a woman's voice said from behind.

He had been talking into the paper towels, intent on his conversation with Annabelle, and had let his guard down in the process. He pivoted slowly, dreading what he would see.

"Good job, Annabelle. You did exactly what I told you."

He looked down the barrel of a Heckler and Koch 9mm handgun. Annabelle scampered up the aisle to stand next to the psychopath.

"Well, bollocks," Fergus said. "I did not see that coming."

"Didn't think you would." Aubrey smiled, patting the blond head affectionately.

"I'm Aubrey's understudy now. She's teaching me everything I need to know. Someday I may be in charge if she and her sister ever want to take a vacation."

"I see. So what's to be done with me?"

He watched the little girl look up into the face of the lovely woman, waiting for a difficult decision, no doubt.

Suddenly he felt a scratching sensation inside his brain. He barely managed to keep from smiling.

"We'll take you out back for a public execution. We're going to make an example of you. Let people see what happens to people who try to escape. Annabelle, go tell everyone except those on guard duty to be at the shooting range in ten minutes."

A quick bob of the blond curls and the child was gone.

"Don't try anything. I'm very good with this." Aubrey brandished the handgun.

"Yes, I imagine so. It seems that many people are these days."

"Keep those hands up and walk toward the back door."

"Very well. I don't suppose there's any point in groveling for mercy. You don't strike me as the merciful sort."

"You got that right. If you're born completely lacking in empathy and compassion, you can't develop them."

"Neither you nor your sister were born with those traits?"

"Correct. Keep moving. Turn left here. We knew what we were when we were nine-years-old. The same age as Annabelle."

"How can such a young child know that she is a monster?"

"Because it was the only thing that made sense."

Fergus nodded. He supposed that was true. He remembered the psychology books in the woman's office. She had studied about herself in those books; had probably come to terms with her psychopathy years ago. Perhaps even embraced it.

Some monsters are happy being monsters.

"Open it," she said to the man guarding the back door.

Fergus stepped out into a drizzling, overcast day. He couldn't tell if it were early morning or late afternoon since the sun was obscured by thick gray clouds. They hung low and oppressive in the sky, the waterlogged roof of a child's abandoned blanket fort.

"Hands up!" Aubrey said from behind.

He had been lowering his arms a fraction with each step. He had hoped she wouldn't notice, but of course she had. Psychopaths possess a superior intellect as well as excellent observational skills.

"What's to stop me from running? My odds of survival would be better than to submit to a firing squad."

"Because if you run, I'll put a bullet in your knee and then I will slowly torture you to death. If you behave, you'll be shot in the head. Quick and painless."

"How could you shoot such a handsome man?"

"I won't be doing the shooting. Annabelle will."

Suddenly he thought he might need to vomit.

"This way. Past the tents."

He was being ushered toward the open grassy area beyond the sleeping quarters. It was where the Terminators conducted training exercises and target practice. A chain-link fence, adorned with curly-cued razor wire along its top, encircled the perimeter. Curious onlookers appeared in the openings of tents as he and Aubrey walked by. He studied their faces and saw a mixture of sympathy and excitement. He thought about his philosophical conversation with Lester; it seemed as if it had taken place a lifetime ago.

Are there mostly moral or immoral folks in your organization?

He knew he could expect no help from any of the Terminators; Aubrey's hold on them was too secure. Fortunately there were others in the vicinity who had never met the beautiful monster. The question was, would they reach him in time to stop his execution?

"Keep walking. See the target in the middle? Stand there and keep your hands up like you have them now. Don't lower them little by little like you were doing in the building. I'm not an idiot."

"You are many things. An idiot is not one of them."

Aubrey stopped fifty yards from the bullet-scarred plywood on which human-shaped silhouettes had been painted. These weren't for game-hunting practice. Fergus continued on, trudging through the weed-choked field as slowly as possible. His clothes were soaked. Mud sucked at his sneakers with every step. He wondered how long it had been raining. Was it a precursor to the tempest Amelia was so worried about?

The notion seemed absurd at the moment. You could easily avoid a hurricane; not so easy to dodge a bullet sent from a sharpshooting, tiny would-be murderess. Annabelle had been killing squirrels with her rifle for months. It must require considerable skill to hit a moving target that small. She would have no problem hitting his stationary, red-haired head from half a football field away, even in the rain.

He reached the plywood at last. The human figure drawn on this one was small. He imagined his body filled in the empty space perfectly. He turned, preparing to face his miniature one-man firing squad. During his slow walk to the targets, a congregation had gathered near Aubrey. He recognized the rat-faced pharmacist and a few other people to whom he had been introduced prior to going into The Box.

His stomach felt like a bowling ball floating in battery acid. He knew he was in trouble. Amelia's last communique had revealed her location. Tung's weapon would not arrive in time.

"Lucifer's Anus is looking rather appealing right about now," he muttered, then caught his breath when he saw Annabelle's blond curls emerge from the crowd.

He had an epiphany.

"Lester knew," he said out loud. "Lester knew Annabelle would turn. He was leaving and knew I might be in danger in her presence. That's what he had meant with his 'stay frosty' warning. Damn it, Fergus. You fell down on the job. You got distracted by that adorable little killer, and now you're about to pay the ultimate price for your carelessness."

He watched the little girl say something to Aubrey, then saw Aubrey nod. He watched her load the weapon that looked much too big for such small arms.

He knew better, though.

He watched the barrel rise. In a few more seconds, a bullet would be coming to claim him.

He pinged Amelia again, noted her minor progress, and sighed.

"I love you, my darling." He sent the message with his *scythen*, having no idea if she received it or not.

"I've had a good, long life. Perhaps I'll meet up with Thoozy again. That would be lovely. We'll have a nice chat about women — the ones we've loved, the ones we've lost, and the ones who wanted to kill us."

He took a deep breath, resisting the temptation to close his eyes. He needed to see the bullet. It would be what carried him to Thoozy.

His eyes widened at the unexpected tableau unfolding before him. Annabelle's rifle had been pointing at him. The blond curls hovered near the scope. He didn't see the small finger move toward the trigger, but sensed the action's imminence...was bracing for it.

So he was surprised when she pivoted suddenly and shot the real-life Little Mermaid. Was surprised again when she twirled in the opposite direction and fired at the two bandolier-wearing men who were charging her. By the time she had taken out the guards posted on the roof of the Costco building, he was no longer surprised.

Annabelle's small back faced him now, rifle pointing at the stunned crowd. Her childish voice cut through the downpour and the distance.

"Anybody else? I have five more rounds. Come on, mother fuckers!"

Fergus didn't know whether to laugh or cry. He did neither, but instead began running toward the small form.

"Lester would not approve of that word," he said when he reached her.

"I know. But he's not here, so it's okay. Anybody else?" she yelled. "Bring it, cocksuckers!"

"Annabelle!"

"What? Is that a bad word? I'm don't know what it means, but I heard my mommy say it when she hit her thumb with a hammer one time."

"Yes, it's a very bad word. Promise you'll never say it again."

A shrug of the small shoulders. "We'll see. Sometimes using bad words is effective. Aubrey told me that."

"Yes, well, she's no longer relevant." Fergus glanced down at the dead woman with the perfect dime-shaped hole in the center of her forehead. Unseeing eyes stared at the sullen sky.

"Was this your plan all along?" he said.

"Not exactly. I kind of winged it. All I knew was that I had to let Aubrey think I was with her so that I could help you and Lester if I needed to. I hope he'll be back soon. I miss him."

"And he has missed you," a deep voice said from behind.

Fergus turned to see that the cavalry had arrived. The next moment he was in Amelia's arms.

He was vaguely aware of guns being fired, but his brain was still fuzzy from his time in The Box and being a hair's breath away from dying. Amelia didn't seem to be concerned about the commotion, so he chose not to be as well.

"Oh, that was too close."

"Tell me about it. I was preparing my pithy banter with Thoozy on the Other Side."

His heart swelled when he heard her familiar laugh.

"No offense, love, but you smell like a sewer." He heard the smile in her voice.

"A modern, well-maintained sewer in an advanced society or a medieval sewer in the red-light district of London? All sewers are not created equal."

"Get a room, you two," someone said.

He opened his eyes at the sound of the teenager's voice. Kenny was grinning from ear to ear.

A quick scan of his surroundings revealed carnage that wasn't as excessive as it might have been. In addition to the Terminators whom Annabelle had shot, five more now lay unmoving on the wet ground. Standing ten yards away were a giant man and a tiny murderess, both holding firearms with the ease of professional killers.

Fergus was grateful to count them as friends.

"Hello, Tung," he said.

"Hello, Fergus." Tung held the weapon from *Cthor-Vangt* boldly in front of him, which was significant. Tung, in this small yet significant way, was defying his masters by doing so. He had always been fond of Tung, but this minor act of rebellion elevated him several degrees.

"Did you have to use that thing?"

"No, thankfully."

"You're not very happy with us, are you?"

"Not in the slightest."

Fergus kissed Amelia on the cheek and released her, studying the people in the subdued crowd. If not for Lester, this coup d'état would not end well. His enormous friend was well-respected within the organization. Now that Aubrey and her sister were gone, leadership would transfer to him, if that's what he wanted. He watched Lester now with keen interest.

"Aubrey was a genius." Bass notes resonated through the drizzle, felt by the subdued gathering on a subharmonic level as much as heard on an auditory one.

"She and her sister saved most of us from starvation, injuries, illness, and even worse. But every one of us knows — has always known — that she and her sister were also something not so admirable. I won't be disrespectful of the dead, but I will say this: every good thing they have achieved here will not end today. We will go forward with plans to improve the quality of life for everyone, and in so doing, will dispense with the darker side of being a Terminator. As of today, we will no longer raid. We have always known it is wrong to steal from others, especially so when it means starvation for our victims. Another practice we will eliminate pertains to certain contents of the freezer — you know the ones I mean. Even more than the raiding, we have always known in our hearts that what we were doing was an abomination. I can see by the looks on your faces that I have struck a nerve."

Lester's focus seemed to be on everyone at once. For an introvert, he was a compelling speaker. Fergus smiled, mentally adding another talent to the big man's lengthy repertoire.

"Friends, from now on, we will lay our heads on our pillows at night with a clear conscience when we think of what is *not* in that freezer. The third modification to the former protocols is about freedom, and we will start with that one immediately. If there is anyone who wishes to leave, you may do so with impunity now or at any time. Our walls and razor wire will remain to keep us safe, but not to keep us prisoner. Finally, all newcomers will be welcome, no matter whether they can offer anything in return. With these changes and others, we will retain our humanity."

"What about Zoey? Will she be allowed to come back?" the rat-faced pharmacist said from the back of the throng.

Lester tilted his colossal head in thought. "There should be a limit to our beneficence when it requires we open our door to an established threat or danger. So the answer is no. If you have a problem with that, you are free to leave. Any other questions?"

The only response was a rumble of thunder from the oppressive clouds. Fergus tried to gauge the mood of the remaining water-logged Terminators, studying one face after another. His beard twitched.

"I think that's about all I have to say. My office door will be open to anyone, with no guards standing in front. Let's bury the dead now, friends."

Some sporadic applause began at the back and soon spread throughout the gathering. The Terminators — a mixture of both moral and immoral people — were cheering.

Chapter 42 — Jessie

Jessie had not been happy about having to stay hidden with Harold in the trees. She could have defied her mentor and charged out onto the field with the others, but something told her she needed to obey his command this time. She couldn't explain why. Maybe it was because everything had turned out all right without her help. Nobody that she loved or that Amelia loved had been injured or killed. Had Jessie somehow known that would be the outcome? It was impossible to say. As far as she knew, her psychic talents only included remote viewing and her *scythen,* which was getting better every day. She didn't have prophetic dreams like Harold was having about the hurricane, so she couldn't say for sure that her instinct to mind Tung's order was because she knew something bad would happen if she didn't.

"What are you thinking about?" Harold wore his fisherman's hat, but it and the rest of him were soaked, as was Jessie herself.

Tung had told them to stay hidden in the trees until he came back to retrieve them. He hated leaving them alone and vulnerable, but he would only be gone a few minutes. Even now she could see that the situation behind the Costco building was under control. She couldn't hear what was being said, but the body language of Amelia and Tung seemed normal and relaxed. She hadn't spent enough time with the giant man or the teenage boy to know what was normal for them, but she knew she liked them both. Lester was nice, and Kenny was funny. She hoped she would be able to stay long enough to become friends with Lester. It seemed Kenny had passed the quick tests put to him back at the golf club, so she would get to know him on the way back to *Cthor-Vangt.* Also, she was intrigued by the little girl with the curly blond hair and the gun. She looked to be about Jessie's own age, but she shot that rifle like the men in the old western movies her daddy watched. Those cowboys never missed when they aimed their guns at the bad guys.

"Nothing," she said.

"I'm not so sure about that. It appears everything is going to be okay. Look, Tung is already coming back to get us."

"Are you still having the hurricane dream?"

Harold frowned. "Yes."

"Is it going to destroy Amelia's home?"

Harold's frown turned into his sad face. She did not like that face one bit. "I'm afraid so. At least, that's what I'm seeing."

Tung was getting closer and closer. She had been working out a plan in her head but hadn't gotten many of the details figured out yet. Until now. Maybe Harold would help.

"You know he isn't going to talk the *Cthor* into stopping the hurricane."

He hesitated a few seconds before answering. "I don't know that for sure, but I admit, it doesn't seem likely. In the history records I've been studying during my time in *Cthor-Vangt*, I have seen no evidence of them manipulating weather events except on an earth-cleansing scale. I can't imagine they would deflect a storm simply to please Amelia."

"But it wouldn't be just to please her. She says there may be other *Cthor-Vangt* candidates on her island."

"Yes, but I think we both know she might be stretching the truth...for leverage. You know what that word means?"

"Yes, of course."

Tung was getting closer by the second. Her mind raced. She grabbed Harold's knobby hand in her own small one and gazed up at him with beseeching sea-green eyes. She knew the effect it had on people when she did that. She had learned the technique a long time ago.

"If you and I are on that island, the *Cthor* will stop the hurricane from destroying it."

"I don't think they would for me, but they certainly would for you. I think I know where this is going."

"Tung won't allow it. You know he won't. So we have to run. Now."

"What happens if I say no?"

"Then I'll go without you. I'm very fast. You would never catch me."

Harold laughed. "Goodness, child, I'm beginning to understand poor Tung's exasperation. You are a force of nature, aren't you?"

"Just like Amelia," she said with a grin.

"Very well. We'd best be on our way, then."

***

"This is going to be much more difficult than we anticipated." Harold had to raise his voice to be heard above the heavy downpour and strong wind. The weather was getting worse by the minute.

He and Jessie stood on a slippery, grassy bank next to the river that Jessie knew was called the Intracoastal Waterway. The current seemed to be moving very fast. She had the first stirrings of doubt about her plan, since it would require they get over that fast-moving water and onto Amelia's island on the other side. When they arrived there, she would use her *scythen* (with Harold's help) to send a message to Tung, telling him to have the *Cthor* stop the hurricane or she and Harold would perish. Tung would be furious with her in that quiet way of his. She hated to upset him, but it couldn't be helped.

She had sensed the level of desperation Amelia felt. That land on the other side of the river was her home now. Jessie had caught glimpses of it during their recent communications. It was a paradise, and it was where her beloved Amelia wanted to live out the rest of her life, which would only be a few more decades. Compared to the near immortality of the residents of *Cthor-Vangt*, decades were less than a drop in a bucket...more like a drop in that big ocean on the other side of Amelia's island.

"We have to do this. It's the most important thing to Amelia."

"Not more so than your life."

Jessie ignored the remark. She knew she was taking advantage of him — his fondness for her and his kindhearted nature — but she had to do this. For Amelia.

"There's a surfboard!"

"Not a surfboard. That's a paddle board." Harold followed the direction of her pointed finger. "Which would be only slightly less dangerous to get both of us across than a surfboard. We should find something a bit more substantial. And we need to hurry. I think the rain is intensifying."

Her keen eyes scanned the bank in both directions. She spotted a structure nestled among some trees with strange roots that looked like squirming snakes from this distance. It seemed to be some kind of boat. She thought she could see a paddle next to it.

"There. Do you see it?"

"No, dear. My vision is not what it once was, and it certainly isn't as acute as yours."

"Follow me!" She took off running.

"It's a kayak," Harold said several minutes later, slightly out of breath. "And luckily for you, I know how to operate one of these things. I often took my summer holidays in Mallorca. That's what we Brits do on holiday...we escape our rainy, cold England and flee to warm, sunny destinations. We're also lucky this is a two-person kayak."

"I only see one paddle."

"No worries. Go on. Get in the backseat."

Jessie scrambled in. Harold pushed the vessel into the shallow water near the shore, then eased into the seat in front of her. She was impressed. For such an old man (sixty-seven seemed ancient to her), he was in good shape and still strong. She knew he had been doing 'calisthenics' at *Cthor-Vangt* during his time there, and it seemed the exercise had paid off. He had told her that after being holed up in his flat in Twickenham for a year, he was ready to get his girlish figure back. Then he laughed. Jessie hadn't understood what he meant by that, but when Harold laughed, she always laughed too. A flood of gratitude filled her as she watched him maneuver the vessel like an expert. He really must have done a lot of kayaking in his old life because they navigated that treacherous-looking river in under fifteen minutes.

She would never had made the crossing without him.

The bottom of the kayak crunched on the rocky beach of Amelia's home. The bodies dangling from the crosses were even more sad and disgusting close up. They were mostly bone, but bits of flesh still clung in places and looked slimy from all the rain.

"Not much of a welcome," Harold said, pulling the kayak all the way up onto the sand.

She studied the perimeter of the beach, noting the wooden shack built into a giant palm tree and the wires that ran along the shoreline.

"Watch out for the wire," she said, just as Harold was about to step on it.

"Clever. These look like percussion tripwires. See that stick over there? It's a shotgun shell. When someone invades their island, they'll be notified by the sound of it exploding. By the way, does your plan include a way to avoid being shot on sight?" he added, as they watched a man running toward them pointing a gun at Harold's head.

"What's our cover story?"

Jessie barely managed to get the words out before the man with the gun arrived.

***

"Your story seems farfetched," the pretty black lady said to Harold.

They were in the lady's kitchen, drying off with some towels she had given them. Her name was Rosemary, and she was the leader on Amelia's island. The man with the gun was her boyfriend. He sat on the sofa and scowled at them.

"Indeed it does, but it is nonetheless true."

Jessie thought Harold's accent had become even more British-sounding. She wondered if he was doing that to charm the pretty lady.

"Why would you risk crossing the Intracoastal in these conditions?"

"As I mentioned, we were headed toward the Costco building and what we thought might be sanctuary. People we had encountered on the road told of a small, organized colony there, which we hoped to join. Just as we approached the building, we heard gunfire coming from the back. So we ran and ended up on the waterway. We had the idea, as I'm sure many of your citizens here did, that we would be safer on an island than on the mainland. When we found the kayak, it felt significant, almost like a sign pointing toward your island. Right, Jessie?"

She nodded, taking the lady's hand in hers and gazing up into the intelligent brown eyes. She arranged her own face to appear innocent and compelling, just as she had done with Harold earlier and a thousand other times before with other people.

"Please, Miss Rosemary, may we stay? We don't eat much, and we can work to pay for it. I'm little, but I'm strong. Harold is old, but he's strong too and very smart. If you send us away, I don't know if we'll make it."

She hid a smile when she saw the reaction to her speech and then, finally, a slow nod.

"Yes, you may stay for now. What kind of a person would I be if I turned my back on a little girl and an old man?"

"I'm only sixty-seven." Harold grinned. "I don't have a foot in the grave quite yet."

Rosemary laughed. Jessie could tell she liked them both. Harold was naturally charming and even more so when he worked at it. She could tell Rosemary's boyfriend did not approve of the decision, though. She knew before he opened his mouth that he was about to object.

"Rose, seriously? We barely have enough food for everyone as it is. Plus, according to Ingrid, we're about to be blown away by a hurricane. This isn't the time to accept new people."

"They're staying, Lucas, at least for now while I decide what to do about an evacuation."

The good-looking, unfriendly man shook his head in disgust.

Jessie walked over and sat down on the sofa next to him. The man watched her, like her kitten Gandalf the Grey would watch the birds in the trees. She did not take his hand, but instead sat a few inches away and sent out waves of happy thoughts. He was close enough to receive them. She watched their effect on him as the scowl softened into something that looked mildly disapproving instead of outright hostile.

She had been honing this technique for a while without understanding what it was. She knew it was an extension of her *langthal* — the ability to heal herself and others — but rather than affecting a person's body, it affected their mood. She didn't even need to touch the person with her hands when she did it. She had discovered this talent a few months ago and was cultivating it without Tung's knowledge. She knew it might come in handy someday on him or others in *Cthor-Vangt*, so she had decided not to tell anyone, not even Harold. When you did something like that, it was called 'not tipping your hand,' which was a poker term her daddy had told her about. She understood the concept even though she had never played poker in her life.

"Fine," Lucas said after a minute. "I suppose two more mouths to feed won't make that much of a difference."

Jessie smiled.

Three loud knocks came from the front door, then a grandmother-looking lady barged in without waiting for Rosemary to answer.

"Well, it didn't work," she said, then noticed Jessie. "Who the hell is that?"

Despite the rudeness, there was something about the older lady that she liked right away. She couldn't explain what it was, though, especially since the woman was scowling at her just like Rosemary's boyfriend had been doing. Perhaps if she could get her to sit down on the sofa...

At that moment the older lady saw Harold, who was still standing in the kitchen. Jessie watched the sour expression transform into one of surprise.

"It's you!"

Harold wore a similar expression: surprise mixed with a hint of awe.

"It is me. And it is also you."

They stood looking at each other from across the room, unwilling or unable to break the spell that seemed to have been cast between them.

"Ingrid, you know this man?" Rosemary said.

That did the trick. They walked toward each other, as if an invisible lasso was being tightened around them.

They stood a foot away from each other now; both might have been seeing the prettiest sunrise or the most beautiful flower they had ever seen. It made Jessie feel wonderful just to see their happiness on such obvious display.

"No, I don't know him. Not in real life, I mean."

Ingrid was smiling now. She must have been lovely when she was younger. She still was, even with the wrinkles. Her silver hair looked magical. The Queen of the Fairies would have hair like that.

"I have been dreaming about you for so long," Ingrid murmured. "I didn't know if you were real or not."

Harold was grinning the biggest grin she had ever seen. She realized suddenly that he was handsome in an old-man way.

"I always knew you were out there somewhere; I just didn't think I would ever find you in this big world."

"What the hell is going on?" Rosemary's voice was annoyed and tired. Very tired. She must have a lot of responsibility on Amelia's island.

"I've seen this man in my dreams for decades. Ever since I've been having them. The special ones, I mean," Ingrid replied.

"And she has been in mine as well, but much more so now that I see the hurricane too."

"You're having the hurricane dream?"

"Yes. That's also why we're here. We were hoping we might warn everyone. I wasn't lying about the gunfire, though." He glanced quickly at Rosemary. "However, I didn't think you would believe me if I led with that angle." He flashed another charming grin. "So I suppose you could say our reason for being here is twofold."

"It's inevitable, then? The destruction?" Ingrid said.

Harold frowned, glancing at Jessie. She held her breath. Harold would be in serious trouble if he told anyone about the *Cthor* and *Cthor-Vangt*. They might not let him come back.

"I'm not sure."

"Someone please explain what this is all about," Rosemary said in a tired voice, sitting down on the sofa next to Jessie, who patted her leg and sent her some happy thoughts.

Ingrid ignored her. "What is your name?"

"Harold Clarke. I was an anthropologist in the UK. And you're Ingrid? Do I detect a faint German accent? I always dreamed of you in Berlin or perhaps Munich. And also here in Florida."

"Munich. And I dreamed of you in London and various places around the world, which now I know to be archaeological dig sites, yes?"

Harold smiled. "Yes, that's right. Yours are much more specific than mine. I admit, until very recently, you were the only dream phenomenon I was having. After getting hit on the head and coming quite close to dying," he winked at Jessie, "I began to see you with more clarity. And then the hurricane dreams began."

Rosemary studied the two old people. Jessie could see uncertainty on her face. It would be a difficult decision moving everyone to a safer location. If they went to all that trouble and the storm wasn't even that bad, it would have been a waste of time. People could get hurt or even killed on the way to higher ground. But if she didn't move them and it did come, everyone might be washed into the sea.

Amelia believed in Ingrid's dream and Jessie believed in Harold's dream. Without intervention from the *Cthor*, the hurricane would arrive. There was no question.

Rosemary said, "Ingrid, don't say anything else. I don't want this man's version tainted by yours. Mister Clarke..."

"That's Doctor Clarke, but you may call me Harold."

"Harold, tell us about your dream."

For the next five minutes, Harold described his visions, during which Ingrid nodded every few seconds in agreement.

"They're the same as mine, Rosemary. You can't deny that."

"This is fucking insane," Lucas said from a corner of the room. He had gotten up from the sofa and had been pacing the floor for a while now. The effect of her happy thoughts was wearing off.

"Lucas, language."

"Rose, you can't make a huge decision to move people from the safety of their homes based on some stupid nightmares. That's madness, and you know it."

"Ingrid, when you first came in, you said it didn't work," Rosemary said, ignoring her boyfriend.

The older woman nodded. "Yes. I tried to direct my dreams last night, hoping to unveil the identity of the killer, as I said I would. But nothing came to me. I went to bed hungry and dreamt of gumbo much of the night. Anyway, we'll just have to take the murderer with us, I guess."

Rosemary smirked. "Nice try, Ingrid. I haven't decided yet."

"As I told you before, I'll be leaving with or without you and everyone else. I know how it will end here. And while I'm distressed at the thought of abandoning my home, I don't want to die. Not yet."

With that, she entwined her arm with Harold's and gave Jessie a stern look. "Come with us, child. You'll be staying at my house until it's time to leave."

Jessie looked at Harold, who wore a dreamy smile, then at Rosemary, who was frowning, then at Lucas, who was scowling again.

"Okay," she said. She planned to contact Tung as soon as they were settled at her house. The *Cthor* would receive Tung's request to divert the storm, Amelia and Fergus would return to the island, and she could have a nice little vacation before going back to *Cthor-Vangt*.

It was an excellent plan.

Chapter 43 — Anonymous

Dear Diary,

There has been a delay in my exodus, but I think it will prove serendipitous. The rain has foiled my plan to poison the entire Colony, so I was prepared to settle for the killing of just the old female tyrant. But now I have been presented with a new opportunity for orchestrating the deaths of everyone on the island.

The rumor mill tells me the so-called leaders of this cloying little utopia believe the weather is a precursor to a catastrophic hurricane. It also tells me this belief is based on the prophetic dreams of the despised old female.

Surprisingly, it seems that our fearless leader has decided the prophesized event poses an actual threat, and is considering a mass evacuation of the Colony.

Do you know what is required for such an endeavor, Diary? That's correct.

Boats.

One needs a boat to get from Point A to Point B. All the watercraft were transferred months ago from the marina, which faces the mainland, to the beach near the Love Shack. What would happen if a certain someone cut the nylon ropes of the Colony's ragtag flotilla? What if that same someone also jettisoned four of the Colony's five kayaks into the Atlantic? How convenient it will be to wander out to the beach, saw in hand, and hijack the Colonists only means of escape! It needs to be done quickly though, because I heard the old tyrant plans to leave soon.

Once I've done so and loaded up the fifth kayak with supplies, I'll row row row my boat gently down the stream.

I'm excited about this new idea. I won't get to witness the demise of the Colonists in person, as I would have with poisoned gumbo, but I will imagine their terror, stranded on their tiny island while the storm surge washes them out to sea. I'm picturing them now, like so many corks bobbing in a sloshing bucket...their arms flailing, their mouths gaping, gasping for air as the relentless waves drag them under...once, twice, twenty times, until their tired wittle bodies can no long keep their pinheads above the water.

You might ask why I'm inclined to believe in paranormal nonsense such as prophetic dreams, and my answer is this: I've dreamt of the hurricane as well.

It. Is. Inevitable.

Chapter 44 —Amelia

"I'm sorry, Tung. This is all my fault," Amelia said.

"Yes, it is one hundred percent your fault. Jessie is trying to make you happy by coercing the *Cthor* to preserve your home. She believes they will divert the hurricane if she is in harm's way."

He was angrier than she had ever seen him. They had been sending out their collective *scythen* to locate Jessie and Harold since the moment Tung had discovered them missing in the copse of trees behind the Costco building. They followed the ignored pings to the Intracoastal Waterway, white-capped and churning from the strengthening wind.

"If I lose her, I will be personally devastated. And it may well result in my expulsion from *Cthor-Vangt*."

"I will be too, Tung. I don't know if I could bear it. The *Cthor* will never expel you, though. You're their favorite."

"Let's try to avoid that possibility. How do we get across?"

"The kayak I left here is gone," Fergus yelled from below. He stood amongst a tangle of tree roots. The river surged and roiled like a living creature inches from his sneakers.

"What now? We have to get to her before it's too late."

"Why not just communicate with the *Cthor* now? It would save a lot of trouble," Amelia replied.

"Because then they will know how supremely I have fucked up."

She had never heard him use swear words in any of the languages they both spoke. She took two small steps back from the hostility she saw and felt. In the process of trying to get what she wanted for herself, she had likely squandered his friendship. It was regretful, of course, but she couldn't change it. Fergus was alive and well and even now scrambling back up the grassy incline to stand beside her.

Kenny observed the scene from a few feet away. He had said little since mastering the battery of expedited tests back at the golf club. He probably thought they were suffering from a shared delusional disorder. He didn't possess *langthal*, but his ability to 'disappear' was extraordinary. It was not actual invisibility, of course, but a clever magician's misdirection. Even more relevant, his intellect was off the charts. She had enjoyed seeing Tung's stoic expression shift to one of astonishment at the boy's test results.

The nerdy black kid standing a few feet away was perhaps the smartest human being left on the planet. The *Cthor* would be thrilled to harvest his DNA for their next batch of genetically engineered humans.

Amelia hated herself for where her mind went at that moment, but introspection could wait until everyone, and her island, was safe.

"Tell them about Kenny too. Do it now. It's not just about getting Jessie back and saving your own hide. The simplest solution is for that storm to be diverted or diminished."

"My hide is in jeopardy because of your selfishness."

"I know, my friend. And I'm sorry, but that doesn't help us now. Please, Tung. Contact them."

Three drenched, bedraggled people stood in the rain on the river bank watching a fourth drenched, bedraggled person as he closed his eyes and sent out a communication. Amelia's heart was in her throat. Everything depended on this; everything came down to this endeavor, and she would pay a high price for its success. She knew she had used up all her friend's good will with this favor, and the knowledge filled her with sadness.

She waited.

Minutes passed. She was picking up some of the transmission with her own *scythen*, but Tung operated on a level superior to everyone in *Cthor-Vangt* except for the Ancient Ones themselves.

A sense of unease crept in.

She studied his exotic, perfectly symmetrical face; watched his eyelids flutter; watched his mouth turn down in a frown; watched his head nod once, a subconscious response to a direct order from the *Cthor*; watched his eyes open again, unfocused at first, then tinged with sorrow when they rested on her.

"I'm sorry. They won't do it."

Amelia felt the words like a physical blow. Her knees almost collapsed beneath the sudden weight she felt.

"Why not?" she said when she could finally speak. "What about Jessie?"

"They will not be negotiated with nor manipulated in this way. Their decision is final. There will be no diverting of the storm, and it is beyond your station to have presumed you could make such a request. You have overreached."

"What will happen now? To Jessie? I can't believe they would risk such a priceless commodity."

"They regret it, but they have downloaded her genome, of course. While they prefer to have both the host and its DNA, they don't need Jessie herself, just her blueprint." There was a bitter note to his words.

"We have screwed the pooch, haven't we, darling?" Fergus said. Leave it to her beloved to make himself complicit in her manipulative schemes.

"No, we haven't. I have, and I'm terribly sorry. For everything. Now we need to figure out how to get Jessie and Harold off that island. And anyone else who will listen."

"That is your problem now. My job is to get Kenny to *Cthor-Vangt*."

"Whoa there, Jet Li," the teenager said, mimicking Tung's deadpan inflection. "I haven't agreed to that. I'm not even sure you people are sane."

"Kenny, you know in your heart we're sane," Tung said. "I've sensed it. You know in your heart that what we've told you is true. You saw Jessie heal Lester from your own poison dart. You know what you put in that cartridge, and you know the man should be dead."

"True 'dat. Still, it doesn't mean I believe this *Twilight Zone* episode." Kenny switched to his own voice now.

"Yes, you do," Tung insisted. Amelia saw him glance down toward his pocket, retrieve the weapon from *Cthor-Vangt*, and adjust the setting. Her heart sank. She gazed out at the turbulent water, her mind racing now on a plan for rescuing Jessie and Harold. Fergus followed her gaze, no doubt pondering the same thing.

When she turned back to watch Tung sedate the teenager, Kenny had vanished.

She barked an involuntary laugh. "I so wish he would show me how he does that."

"Perfect, just perfect," Tung said. "I can't leave without him."

Amelia felt bad for her friend. He seemed so resigned now, as if his fate were beyond his control. She supposed it was. That was the price one paid for virtual immortality.

"Give him some time. He'll come back. He just needs to think about such a big decision. In the meantime, you could help us with Jessie and Harold. They're still your charges."

"Technically, they are not. My responsibility is Kenny now."

"How can you be so callous, Tung? That's not like you," Amelia said.

Fergus spoke up, "He's having a bad day, Amelia. Perhaps we should cut him some slack."

"You're right. Good grief, I've become someone I don't much like at the moment. Very well, Tung. Do what you need to do."

"I intend to."

At that moment, all three received a communication from Harold and Jessie.

~~~

Harold: I guess you've discovered where we are by now.

Jessie: Don't be mad at Harold. I made him come with me.

Amelia: Jessie, I appreciate what you've done for me, but it is for nothing. The Cthor *have refused to divert the storm.*

Jessie: Uh oh.

Tung: That's right. Uh oh. Child, you are in serious trouble. And you've put Harold in danger along with yourself.

Jessie: I'm sorry! I was just trying to help.

Amelia: We know, dear. We need to get you both off that island now. By what method did you cross?

Harold: A kayak. The policeman took it to the beach on the Atlantic side, though. That's where they keep all the sea-faring vessels.

Tung: Can you get to it?

Harold: I believe so. There will be three of us, although I think Jessie can squeeze in between the two adults.

Amelia: Ingrid? Yes, that makes sense. You're both having the same dream.

Harold: Jessie and I are with Ingrid now, at her house. She has been planning to evacuate whether the Colonists decide to or not.

Amelia: After all she's done for them, they can't refuse her the use of one of their kayaks.

Harold: That's what she said! She's a firecracker, that one. And we have a connection that goes beyond sharing the prophetic dreams. I will explain all that later. I have to say, I'm having the time of my life. A white-knuckle crossing of a tempestuous river, talking my way out of being shot, meeting the aforementioned firecracker, and now orchestrating our escape from a catastrophic hurricane. Tung, I'm so happy to have accompanied you and Jessie.

Tung: Glad to be of service. Now, please get to the vessel immediately. We'll be here waiting for you.

Harold: Will do, sir. And please, don't be angry with Jessie. I could have tried to stop her.

Jessie: No, you couldn't. I'm much faster than you.

Amelia: Jessie, promise you'll do exactly what Harold tells you to do.

Jessie: I promise, Amelia. I'm sorry your home is going to be destroyed.

Amelia: There are other islands, child. Be safe and hurry!

~~~

The transmission ended.

One former and two current residents of *Cthor-Vangt* stood in silence on the saturated bank of the Intracoastal Waterway. With every passing minute, the unrelenting wind and torrential downpour seemed to intensify. Despite the warm temperature, Amelia shivered.

Chapter 45 — Rosemary

"Come on, Lucas. You must have some idea who the murderer is," Rosemary said, shrugging into a plastic yellow poncho. Annoyingly, Lucas still lounged on the sofa after Ingrid had left with the two newcomers.

"Maybe I do, but it would be irresponsible to accuse anyone without proof. That's how it works."

"That's how it worked before. Everything is different now."

"It wasn't different a few days ago when you told me you wanted empirical evidence."

"That was before this downpour started and I became more convinced about the hurricane. Especially now after that stranger showed up and corroborated Ingrid's visions."

"Yeah, that's a weird coincidence," Lucas said, grudging acceptance in his tone.

"Oh, you believe it now?"

"I didn't say that. Let's just say I think there might be something to it. There is some strange shit happening lately."

"I just wish Fergus had come back to let us know what we're facing in Tequesta. The British fellow confirmed the group is still there, and the gunfire he heard is troubling. So the question now is, if we do evacuate, where do we go? It can't be just a straight shot across the Intracoastal because we could run right into the Terminators. So do we go north or south? What will we find when we arrive? God, I hate not knowing things."

"Where are you going?"

"To the Love Shack to inventory our supplies and check on the power grid, then I'm going to the beach to inspect the boats. What will you be doing?" She opened the front door, letting the rain pour onto her tiled entryway. The reality of its acceleration disheartened her. She would have to make a decision soon.

Lucas gave her the roguish smile she usually found sexy.

"Don't worry your pretty little head about what I'll be doing. Got your pepper spray? Got your knife?"

"Yes." She fingered the lumps in the pocket of her capris, then stepped out into the rain.

"Keep them handy!" he said as she closed the door behind her.

When she arrived at the solar panel field a few minutes later, the pepper spray and knife were still in her pocket. Chin was there checking on the equipment, clucking and humming as he moved from one panel to the next.

"How is the system?"

She decided he was ignoring her after a full minute passed without a response.

Finally he said, "Looking okay, for now. Not so good if salt water gets there." He gestured to the outbuilding that held the 12-volt batteries and inverters.

"No kidding. Are the panels secure?" she said, then almost laughed at the blatant look of annoyance on the man's face. His hands were on his hips now as he glowered at her.

"I no tell you how to do your job. You no tell me how to do my job. I go home for now. I not a goddamn duck."

She was chuckling to herself when she opened the door to the Love Shack. She was surprised to see Charlotte there, rummaging through one of the freezers. The woman was dripping wet and had left a trail of sand and water from the doorway to the kitchen.

"Hey, Charlotte. Listen, don't worry about cooking for now. People can get by on their own food until the weather improves."

"I don't feel right about that," Charlotte replied without turning around.

"It's okay. You're such a trooper for coming out in this and trying to feed people. I think you've spoiled us."

A snicker came from the thin woman. It was an unusual sound, nothing like Charlotte's normal laugh. She continued to ferret through the foil-wrapped contents.

"I mean it," Rosemary said, frowning now. "We should save the juice in the batteries for more critical things."

"Is that a direct order, oh Fearless Leader?" Charlotte said, pivoting to face her now. She wore a macabre, Jack-O-Lantern grin.

Rosemary had two thoughts at that moment — one crazy and the other unsettling. First, she imagined placing a tea-light candle in the woman's mouth so it would shine through the gaps left by absent teeth. Second, she realized the Kentucky accent was gone.

She was looking at the killer. She remembered the pepper spray and knife in her pocket and fumbled for them now under the rain-slicked yellow plastic.

The grin widened, as Charlotte's hand moved toward a canvas bag slung over a bony shoulder.

"Your timing is unfortunate," she said, then darted across the floor faster than Rosemary would have thought possible.

The blade was so sharp, she barely felt it slice through the hand she had instinctively raised. The second blade was serrated. She felt its progress from left side to right as it slashed her throat. There was surprisingly little pain; more concerning was the abrupt absence of oxygen.

Her trachea had been severed by the grinning monster before her.

Her knees collapsed. As she lay on the gritty, wet floor, she thought about the man she had befriended in her old life, saw him dangling from his dining room chandelier. No matter how much good she had done since that day, it would never be enough to make up for his suicide. As her body began to shut down, she experienced a moment of clarity: this was what she deserved. It felt right...proper...fitting. She didn't resent her premature death. It was the price she always knew she would pay for her transgressions.

"*For the Angel of Death spread her wings on the blast, and breathed in the face of the foe as she passed; and eyes of the sleepers waxed deadly and chill, and the hearts but once heaved, and forever grew still.* That's Byron. Apropos, yes? I had to change the pronouns from male to female, of course."

They were the last words Rosemary would hear.

Chapter 46 — Ingrid

"I think it best that we leave now, before the weather gets worse," Harold said soon after they arrived at Ingrid's house. He and Jessie had asked for a moment alone to discuss their situation, and she had respected the request. She had no idea what the two were talking about, and while it shouldn't be her business, she felt piqued at being excluded.

She had been dreaming of this man for years. He was her soulmate; as cliché as that term was, it applied to him. How else would you describe a person you had never met but had been in love with for decades? She always suspected he dreamt of her as well, but to discover the truth of it was the most gratifying moment of her life.

"Yes, I agree. I won't wait until Rosemary decides we're right about the hurricane. By then it may well be too late. We'll gather some supplies and head down to the beach where the kayaks and boats are kept. You're skilled with water craft?"

"I'm an Englishman, so the answer is yes, of course."

"I'm still trying to wrap my brain around all this." She felt shy suddenly. They stood inches apart now. Jessie's owl eyes watched from across the expanse of the living room. Ingrid barely noticed her presence, enthralled by the flesh-and-blood version of her dream man standing in front of her.

"So am I. And I eagerly await the opportunity to fully explore our…connection. But that must wait until we are off the island."

She loved that his gaze lingered on her lips an extra moment before traveling back up to her eyes. She had always been secretly proud of those lips; they were still full at her age, and damn few old-lady lines framed them.

"You're right, of course. Let's be about our business, then."

For the next half hour, she directed Harold and Jessie's activities as she prepared to leave her home. A pragmatist would not bring jewelry boxes filled with diamond rings and strands of cultured pearls; nor unwieldy photo albums; nor sentimental keepsakes. A pragmatist would bring easy-to-carry food, bottles of water, and a loaded revolver.

Harold pulled the wagon down the cobblestone footpath behind her and Jessie, who darted covert glances her way every few seconds. The child was lovely, but those large green eyes were unsettling. There was something not quite right about the little girl, but the riddle of Jessie would also have to wait.

The sustained winds were not screaming yet, but they seemed intent on that goal. She wished she had done a better job of convincing Rosemary to evacuate. There were a few people in the Colony whom she genuinely liked; she hoped they would follow her lead.

A figure appeared twenty yards ahead. In the heavy rain, it was difficult to make out who it was. She squinted through the downpour.

"Oh, it's you," she said as the woman approached.

Charlotte wore a black rain slicker. The pale, homely face seemed to float inside the hood. Ingrid felt something tug at her memory, but she dismissed it. No time for ruminating or chit chat.

"Where you goin'?" Charlotte said when they were within speaking range.

"We're headed to the kayaks. We're getting out of here, and if you're smart, you'll do the same."

The thin woman snickered. It sounded strange to Ingrid's ears, but it didn't matter now. She was on a mission.

"Good luck with that," Charlotte said. "Who are your friends?" She saw intense interest in the woman's face, and also something else. Amusement, perhaps? What the hell was there to be amused about at a time like this?

"None of your business." For some reason, Ingrid felt the need to reach for the revolver in her knapsack.

"I'm Charlotte," the Colony's cook said to Jessie, thrusting a skeletal hand toward the child.

Jessie's eyes opened wide when she looked at the hand; a silver band with a purple gem encircled the middle finger. "Harold, my dream. You remember the one?" Jessie said, looking at Harold in alarm. Something passed between the two...some private message to which Ingrid was not privy.

Charlotte chortled again — an odd muffled sound she had never heard come from the woman — then skittered off, up the path and away from the beach.

"What just happened?" Ingrid said.

"Jessie has been having some nightmares."

"Harold," the child said, tugging at his sleeve and giving him a frightened look. "I saw the ring. And the terrible cursive words written on the paper."

Harold squatted down next to her, wrapping the small hands in his. "Jessie, Amelia is safe. She's waiting for us now, and if you want to see her, we must leave at once. Do you understand?"

Ingrid felt like a clueless outsider. Not only did she have no idea what the two were talking about, she felt a stab of jealousy at the camaraderie they shared.

And how the hell did these people know Amelia?

She was about to ask when Harold waved her off. The gesture almost felt like a physical blow.

"Jessie, we can't help everyone. My job now is to save you. That's all that matters. And you know why."

Seconds ticked past.

"You're right. Let's go," the child said finally, turning her back on them both and darting down the cobblestones toward the ocean.

Ingrid gave Harold a cool nod and went after her. She didn't bother looking back to see if he followed. She knew he did, but was it because of Jessie or her?

***

Harold: An unfortunate development here.

Tung: What is it?

Harold: All the watercraft have drifted out to sea. It appears the anchor lines were severed.

Tung: This is the worst possible news.

Harold: You're telling me. I'm the one stuck on this doomed island.

Tung: Stay put, then. We'll come to you.

Harold: Best hurry. The storm is getting stronger by the minute.

Tung: Yes, Harold, I'm aware of that. I'm still standing on the bank of the waterway, soaked to the skin and as miserable as a human can be.

Harold: And that is because of me and Jessie. I realize that, and I'm very sorry, Tung.

Tung: Don't forget Amelia's complicity. Stay safe until we can get there. I'll communicate as soon as we've found a suitable vessel.

***

"Harold!" Ingrid yelled to her dream man, who stood near the shoreline in the pouring rain with his eyes closed. The boats and kayaks bobbed about in the surging, frothing waves — much too far out to consider swimming, even if she were forty years younger. She had seen storms in the Atlantic, but this one would be unlike any before, and now there was no escaping it. Perhaps she had known this would happen all along. It felt appropriate, somehow. She would either survive it, or she would not.

There were worse ways to go.

"Sorry, my dear. I was contemplating our strategy."

"Our only strategy now is get away from the water's edge, out of this downpour, and into some dry clothes. My house is the safest place on the island."

Harold nodded. "Perhaps we'll be rescued," he said with that charming grin.

"Who would rescue us and why? Never mind that now. I'm drenched. I just want to go home." When she spoke the words, another impression from the shrouded-killer nightmare flashed through her mind: safety was to be found on the beach, not in the direction of her home. Well, that might have been the case before all the boats were liberated from their anchors. Now everything had changed. There was no choice.

Jessie and Harold followed her back up the cobblestones. As they approached the Love Shack, she decided to warn anyone there about the absent fleet. Then, they would go by Rosemary's house to inform her there would be no escape for the Colonists. After that, she would wash her hands of the matter and focus on keeping herself, Harold, and the child as safe as possible.

"Oh dear lord," she whispered moments later.

Rosemary's body lay in a sea of blood. Her arms stretched out Christ-like on the tiled floor; her head turned toward the doorway; her lifeless eyes stared at something no living person could see.

"It was that lady who did it. The one with the ring," the child said.

The puzzle pieces clicked into place. The shrouded killer from her dream was Charlotte in a hooded black slicker.

"I think you're right." Ingrid couldn't stop staring at Rosemary's body. She had developed respect — even some fondness — for the strong-willed woman. Rosemary had spearheaded most of the advancements and improvements in their community. She didn't deserve this ending.

"I think you should retrieve that revolver now," Harold said.

She pulled it from her knapsack in a daze, handing it to him.

"My hands are shaking too badly to aim it. We need to tell Lucas. He won't take this well."

Jessie tugged on Harold's sleeve again. "Should I...?" she whispered.

Harold gave a curt shake of his head.

Again, Ingrid felt like an interloper. There was much more than just a profound kinship between these two. And if she lived through the hurricane, as unlikely as that was, she intended to get to the bottom of it.

Chapter 47 — Jessie

It was a good thing she didn't try to help Rosemary; she was too far gone, unlike Harold had been. Jessie couldn't imagine what would happen if she brought back someone whose brain had begun to die. Would the person act like the zombies in those horror movies her daddy wouldn't let her watch? Or would she just be slow and not very smart since part of her brain no longer worked?

She shook her head to clear her thoughts and followed Ingrid up the path. It was raining hard, and even though it was warm, she shivered. Harold was behind her pulling the wagon. They were going to tell Rosemary's boyfriend about their discovery. Jessie thought she would get close to the policeman and send him waves of happy thoughts to help with his grief. She knew he would go after Charlotte the killer and was glad about that. Then the lady with the missing teeth and the bony hands couldn't hurt Amelia or anyone else ever again.

Ingrid stepped off the cobblestones and onto a residential street. After passing a few abandoned dwellings, she veered toward a pale pink structure. It looked like a doll house. If she ever got old enough to live above ground by herself, she would like a home just like this one.

There might be room for a horse in that backyard.

Ingrid knocked on the front door. After a few seconds, Lucas opened it. He wore a gray raincoat, rubber galoshes, and a belt with a holstered gun. Jessie felt a tap on her shoulder when she started for the front door.

"Perhaps we should let Ingrid handle this by herself. It's the worst news someone can receive. Lucas might not want other people to see him upset. Do you understand?"

She nodded. They watched Ingrid speak to the good-looking man; watched her pull him close in a hug; watched her say something else to him and kiss his cheek, then turn and walk back down the sidewalk toward them.

"It's done. Let's go home."

Harold's girlfriend (as she had come to think of Ingrid) looked like she had aged a decade after delivering the bad news. For some reason, that made Jessie like her even more.

"Leave your wet things by the front door. I'll tend to them later," Ingrid said as they entered the welcome dryness of Ingrid's palace. It was the biggest and prettiest house Jessie had ever seen. She wouldn't be surprised if a princess lived upstairs in one of those rooms that had a balcony. She had seen those balconies from outside and imagined Rapunzel unfurling her long blond hair over the railing.

Maybe she would get to sleep in one of those rooms...

"Stay where you are and I'll bring some towels and dry clothes. They won't fit well — Hector was a foot shorter than you — but they'll do. Jessie, I have some clothes that my grand-nieces left the last time they visited. Stay put, both of you. I don't want you tracking water all through the house again."

Jessie smiled when she saw Harold gazing at Ingrid's backside as she darted up the curved staircase. She was very graceful and moved fast for an older lady. Harold was probably thinking the same thing.

"Are they coming for us?" she whispered.

"They're going to try. They have to find a boat that's large enough to carry all of us and that they can operate. I know they're talented people, but I'm not sure captaining watercraft in a storm is among any of their skill sets."

"Are we in big trouble?"

"Oh, yes. Me more than you. I'm the grown-up. I should have known better."

Harold's smile was back. He didn't seem to mind being in trouble as long as he could be with Ingrid.

"What if they don't let you back in?"

"To *Cthor-Vangt*? I think that's a distinct possibility. I suppose it wouldn't be as awful as it might have been before."

"Because of Ingrid?"

His grin widened. She had never seen him so happy, which was saying a lot because Harold was a happy guy already.

A knock at Ingrid's door startled them both. Harold reached for the revolver he had laid on a marble-top table in the foyer. He opened the cylinder part that held the bullets, saw that there was one in every hole, then opened the door.

A drenched Kenny was standing on the porch, grinning like a maniac.

"You gonna let me in, homey? I'm as wet as a beaver's pocket."

"How did you get here?" Jessie was pleased to see the teenager whom she had liked since their first meeting at the golf course. He was very intelligent and perhaps as special as she was herself, but in different ways.

"I jacked a sailboat."

"You sailed here? In this weather? Incredible."

Kenny snorted, then mimicked Harold's British accent when he replied, "I did indeed, old chap. I know a thing or two about yachting from my days at Oxford."

Jessie giggled. The boy sounded just like Harold.

"Clearly Oxford is not where you learned about sailing — we have specialized schools for that — but I am impressed, nevertheless."

"My friend Tyler taught me. He knew everything about boats and fishing. I miss him. He's out on the Atlantic somewhere with a smoking hot, crazy bi...uh, crazy woman. Maybe he'll come back someday if that chick doesn't kill him."

"Are you here to rescue us?"

"Oh, hell no. I barely made it here alive. I ain't going back out on that water."

"Then why risk it just to get yourself trapped here?" Harold asked.

"I'm finishing what the two of you started. If all this insanity is true, those big kahunas who live underground won't want me to die. I'm the smartest person on the planet. That Asian guy was blown away by my test results. He has an excellent poker face, but I'm an excellent poker player. That's how I put myself through law school. Okay, that last part was a lie, but the other parts are true."

"You're hoping the *Cthor* will divert the hurricane to save you instead of Jessie?"

"That's what I'm banking on since they don't have my DNA yet. You're welcome, by the way."

"Oh dear. I can only imagine how distraught Tung will be. Does he know you're here?"

"Nope, but you're about to tell him with that Vulcan mind meld thing you guys do. Better hurry up, Prince Charles. The wind is blowing like a hooker on her period."

Jessie didn't know what that meant, but Kenny was right. The storm was getting worse by the minute. She was shivering again and wondered what was taking Ingrid so long bringing the dry clothes.

Chapter 48 — Ingrid

"I wish I had more time to enjoy this moment, but with your new friends downstairs, I'm forced to exhibit restraint."

Charlotte had lost all trace of her southern accent. The voice whispering into Ingrid's ear was cultivated and elegant.

"So you're the killer. I should have seen it."

"How could you have seen it? My performance as a backwoods hick was perfection. I had plenty of examples to study growing up."

"Did you knock those missing teeth out just to complete the façade?" Ingrid said, then drew in a sharp breath as Charlotte's knife pressed more forcefully against her carotid artery.

"That wasn't very nice."

"You killed Hector."

"I did. The opportunity presented itself, which I interpreted as a divine message. The services of the Angel of Death were called upon."

"You're insane."

"Perhaps. I have fun, though."

"So you plan to murder me?"

"I'm afraid so. Wait a minute. That part was a lie. I'm not afraid of killing you at all. I'm quite relishing the notion."

The longer she stalled, the better the chance that Harold would come up those stairs with her revolver.

She hoped his hands didn't shake like hers.

"What have I ever done to you? For that matter, what did Rosemary ever do to you?"

"Oh, you found her, did you? By the way, I know what you're doing. You're stalling for time. I'll indulge you by supplying the short version of my motivations. You're a snooty rich bitch and Rosemary was an uppity nigger." During the last sentence, Charlotte had regressed back to her Kentucky accent. Ingrid didn't know if that was intentional or not.

"Those are terrible reasons for taking a life. I don't blame you for poisoning Howard, though. The man was insufferable."

A ghoulish snicker wheezed out of the gape-toothed mouth.

"Indeed. He was special, though. He was my first human kill. In a way, I owe him my gratitude. He helped make me what I am today."

"A murderess? That's nothing to be grateful for."

"On the contrary. I'm thankful for his help in my metamorphosis."

"Hmmph. If you say so."

She felt the outer layer of skin give way to the knife's edge. Harold wasn't going to arrive in time.

"I think we've drawn this out long enough."

Ingrid closed her eyes, so didn't see from which direction the bullet came that knocked Charlotte backward onto the four-poster bed. By the time she opened her eyes, there was blood all over her pristine white duvet. A perfect hole had appeared in the killer's forehead.

"Crazy broad," Lucas said from the balcony doorway.

"You're getting water all over my bedroom floor," Ingrid said. Then her knees buckled.

***

"After you told me about Rose, I went to Charlotte's house and found the cat tooth. I had intended to go there anyway, after you mentioned your gumbo dream. That should make you feel better, Ingrid." Lucas looked diminished, somehow. He still exuded the authority of a former New Orleans homicide detective, but his fire was gone. Ingrid wondered if it would ever return.

He continued, "I also found a Zip-lock bag with some hair in it. I'm sure it was Howard's. Serial killers like to keep trophies. Then I went to the Love Shack." The handsome face was a mask of anguish. He swallowed hard. "I found a kayak hidden nearby filled with food and water. I assume that was how she planned to escape after she cut loose the other boats. Then I tracked her here, to your bedroom balcony."

They were downstairs in Ingrid's living room now with Harold, Jessie, and Kenny, whom Ingrid was delighted to see. He hadn't been coming around as much since Tyler had mysteriously sailed away with Zoey.

Too many unexplained events had been happening lately. It vexed her, but at that moment, as the hurricane bore down on them, she experienced two minor epiphanies: she should not always strive to control everything in her world, and she did not need to know everyone's secrets. Some things were best left as mysteries.

"So we have one kayak to transport more than fifty people off the island," Ingrid said.

Lucas rolled his eyes. "Nobody is going anywhere. It's too dangerous. I think the best thing is to hunker down and wait out the storm."

"You've never believed there was anything to my dreams."

"I just told you about the gumbo thing, Ingrid. I'm not saying I don't believe any of it, but I don't believe all of it. Sorry."

She bit her tongue. The man had just saved her life.

"Will you excuse me a moment?" Harold said suddenly.

She nodded and watched him walk down the marbled hallway to the powder room.

She sighed. How tragic that she and her dream man would only share a few hours together before being washed into the sea.

"We should gather everyone here," she said. Now that Rosemary was gone, she supposed it was acceptable for Lucas to take charge. That made more sense than an old rich bitch calling the shots. "My house was built to withstand the very worst storms. It won't save us from relentless storm surge, but it will hold up against flying debris."

"I'll get the word out if the weather gets worse," Lucas said, standing. "I need to go take care of a few things. She's still there...at the Love Shack. Can you handle getting the body out of your bedroom?"

"Yes, of course. Do you need help with...?"

Lucas shook his head, then was gone the next moment.

"That dude ain't so bad," Kenny said. He perched on a bar stool in a corner of the room. His position on the tall seat and the amused, keenly interested expression on his face, made Ingrid think of a friendly gargoyle.

"I agree." She noticed Jessie sitting on the sofa, her owl eyes traveling back and forth as she listened to the conversation. The child couldn't be more than ten years old. Ingrid wondered about the horrors she must have endured during the last two years.

"Jessie, I know for a fact that Kenny loves chocolate, and something tells me a certain little girl does too. Do you like to read? My grand-nieces left some books about horses."

At the mention of the books, the child's face transformed into something that took Ingrid's breath away.

Chapter 49 — Amelia

~~~

Harold: You're going to hate me more than you already do.

Tung: Just tell me, Harold. What now?"

Harold: Kenny is here on the island. He found a sailboat and managed to get himself across the river in this raging storm. I know you realize how smart he is, but he is much more.

Tung: This day just gets better and better. We haven't located a suitable vessel yet for a rescue. I have no idea where Kenny found one.

Harold: As I said, the boy is exceptional. Perhaps to the same degree as Jessie. And the Cthor *do not have his DNA.*

Tung: Ahhh, more extortion. Amelia has subverted you as well, I see.

Amelia: Not directly.

Harold: You tested him, Tung. His intellect is just the tip of the iceberg. I can guarantee his...value. They won't want to lose him.

Tung: You people will be the death of me. Or at least, the expulsion of me. I like the notion of living for millennia even if you don't.

Amelia: Tung, please...

~~~

The connection was severed. Tung scowled at her now as they stood under a covered porch attached to a palatial house on the bank of the Intracoastal Waterway. Fergus stood next to her, not offering any verbal assistance. His proximity was all she wanted.

Amelia didn't need anyone to fight her battles for her.

"Give me some privacy, please," Tung said.

She ushered Fergus over to some patio furniture next to a wall of windows, not the best place to be in a hurricane. Tung better hurry.

"What do you think will happen?" Fergus said, gazing out at the pouring rain and turbulent river.

"I don't know. I regret just about everything except the decision to liberate my beloved from a metal box, even though he apparently didn't need my help.

The stench in there must have been something." She sniffed.

"Sorry about that. I've had no opportunity to bathe yet." His blue eyes sparkled.

Sometimes the tide of emotion she felt for this man threatened to pull her under, extinguishing the spark that was hers alone. Ferocity in all things — but particularly in matters of the heart — could topple mountains as handily as it could scale them. That unbridled dedication to getting what she wanted, despite the danger in which she placed herself and others, was what had gotten her ejected from *Cthor-Vangt*. It was also what made her who she was. She was too old to change now, but perhaps some modifications were in order.

Or perhaps not.

"If they won't do it, Jessie may perish. Are you prepared for that?"

"No. I would lament it for the rest of my life. Oh, Fergus. I'm so worried."

"I know you are, love."

Minutes passed, each one slipping into a parallel dimension and stretching to a hundred times the length of those in her world.

Tung's communication with the *Cthor* was taking forever.

Finally, he walked back toward her and Fergus, exuding exhaustion from every inch of his face and body. There were new frown lines between his brows, and the almond-shaped eyes no longer looked upon her with affection.

"They are profoundly disappointed in us all, but as long as I deliver Kenny to them, I still have a place in *Cthor-Vangt*. Amelia, you are never to ask for my help again. Fergus, you are on probation. The *Cthor* will mitigate the hurricane so that Kenny, Jessie, and Harold will be safe. I am to gather them up and convey them to the *Cthor* right away."

Amelia rushed to him and kissed him on the mouth.

"I'm still angry with you."

"I know. And I promise I will never ask for your help with anything ever again."

"Good. That way I won't have to say no." He didn't smile. "They want you to leave immediately," he said to Fergus. "On your way back to *Cthor-Vangt*, you are to stop at the settlement in Tennessee and evaluate its members. That was supposed to be my job until I allowed all this nonsense to derail me."

He turned his back on them and walked away.

Fergus frowned as he gathered Amelia's face in his hands and gazed into her eyes.

"It seems our tête-à-tête has come to an end. For now. Go back to your island, my love, and bask in heaven on earth until I can return to you."

Amelia blinked away her tears. She had been expecting this moment for weeks now. She was grateful that he had stayed as long as he had, and she would relive every moment they had shared until he returned. If he returned.

In the meantime, she had plans for the Colony...her home. Like the unrelenting surge of sea water in a tempest, the joy of contemplating all she would accomplish there began filling the sad recesses of her heart. Amelia would find happiness no matter where she lived or with whom she spent what remained of her life. There was no other way to live.

But it didn't hurt if she could spend those years in paradise.

Chapter 50 — Ingrid

"I don't understand any of this. How can you ask me to just accept that Kenny and Jessie are leaving with this stranger?"

Ingrid was furious. She had become attached to the little girl in a very short time, and she had always adored the brilliant teenager and his caustic wit.

She scowled at the Asian man standing in her open doorway, framed by a cloudless, cerulean backdrop. If she were honest with herself, that flawless blue sky also made her angry, as convoluted as that was. How could her prophetic dream prove so inaccurate? Lucas would never let her live it down. She supposed she should be grateful that she was still around to be ridiculed. She was also elated to have a few years — maybe even a decade or two, if her seventy-year-old body held out — with her dream man.

"Darling, you will just have to trust me on this," Harold said. "There are mysteries in life that we are not meant to understand." He gave her that irresistible grin.

"You're sure you don't want to come with us, Harold?"

"He said he's staying here," Ingrid snapped.

She watched the almond-shaped eyes crinkle at the corners. Was this impertinent newcomer amused?

"I'm quite sure, Tung. Thank you. Perhaps we shall meet again someday."

"Perhaps. It has been a pleasure. You will be missed. Kenny, Jessie, it's time."

Kenny pecked her cheek as he darted out the front door. Jessie approached wearing the pink backpack Ingrid had given her. It was stuffed with horse books. The child wouldn't let them out of her sight.

"Thank you, Ingrid. I hope you and Harold are very happy together."

For years to come, Ingrid would picture that face — those huge sea-green eyes and the stunning smile — and wonder about the woman the little girl had grown into.

When the door closed, the sudden quiet might have felt lonely and oppressive if not for the man standing beside her.

"I have so many questions," she began, then forgot what they were the next moment when he kissed her for the first time.

Ingrid was no prude. Despite never having married, she had enjoyed a healthy sex life with a variety of attractive and charming men for years before her romance with Hector. Those men, and the kisses she shared with them, were a sputtering match flame compared to the raging bonfire kiss of her dream man.

There would be many more kisses to follow, and more happiness in those remaining years than she had experienced throughout her entire lifetime.

Chapter 51 — Tyler

"That must be La Palma. Do you see it?" Zoey shielded her eyes from the intense glare of the sun reflecting off the ocean.

The water this far from land was the cobalt blue of a Mexican margarita glass. The thought evoked a squirt of saliva in his mouth; a frozen marg would hit the spot after weeks of being at sea. Not that Tyler had minded the journey to the Canary Islands. He loved to sail, and after weathering a nasty squall off the Florida coast, the weather had been perfect.

The best part was how quickly Zoey had adjusted to her predicament. Like a nuisance bear in an Alaskan suburb, she had been tranquilized and was now being relocated to a place where she couldn't do harm to others.

Zoey was more dangerous than any grizzly, though. Tyler would never forget that.

"It's spectacular. I didn't know there would be mountains."

She flashed the smile that never failed to make his knees weak. Lately he had been making a point of not letting her see the effect she had on him. He had been cultivating a kind of indifference when he spoke to her, which, he hoped, gave him some leverage. If his relationship with a psychopath was going to work long term, they must be equals.

"You know the best part about those mountains? The volcanic soil. That's coffee country, my dear."

"Oh, now you're talking. I wonder if there are people here. It would be easier in the beginning to raid, you know. It will take months for us to grow crops."

"There will be plenty of food growing there already. Plantains and bananas. Lots of bananas. In this country, the seeds Ingrid gave me will thrive. We still have rations in the cargo hold and a never-ending supply of fish. We won't have to raid."

"Hmmm. Perhaps." She shot him a sly look.

He pretended not to see it.

Chapter 52 — Jessie

"Thank you for letting me say goodbye to Amelia," Jessie said to Tung.

He had been wearing his stressed-out face for several hours now, on their journey back to *Cthor-Vangt*. He barely looked at her from the driver's seat. His hands held onto the steering wheel in what her daddy would have called a 'death grip.' His almond-shaped eyes had not crinkled at the corners for a long time. She decided her new goal was to make Tung smile before they reached the elevator in the alien-looking cottonwood trees.

Thank goodness for Kenny. He had been making her laugh ever since the tearful farewell with Amelia.

"I don't miss her nearly as much now that I got to see her and talk to her," she continued.

Tung said nothing.

"I'm gonna miss that Cherokee chickadee," Kenny said in his own voice from the back seat. Jessie thought he probably didn't want to aggravate their mentor further by doing his Tung impersonation. She hoped he would do it later, though, when they were alone. It was perfect.

"Not Cherokee," Tung said, keeping his eyes on the road ahead. "Hualapai."

"Wall Uh Pie? Mmmm. That sounds delicious. Are there cookies in *Cthor-Vangt*? A brother's gotta eat, and this little dude loves him some cookies. My favorite is chocolate chip. You'll need to know that if you want to get on my good side."

Jessie giggled. "The food is good. It tastes different than normal food, but you'll like it. I'm glad you're coming with us, Kenny. I'll miss Harold, but I'm happy to have a new friend who's close to my age. We'll have lots of fun together, and the furniture is really comfortable. I'll show you how it works when we get there."

Kenny looked at her with sudden interest from the back seat. "Yeah, I'll believe all that when I see it with my own peepers. If it's true, though, and we're the only kids in the joint, and if we're as kick-ass awesome as everyone says, can you imagine how we'll shake things up when we're older?"

Jessie giggled again, despite seeing Tung's unhappy face suddenly become even more unhappy.

Epilogue — Fergus

"You look comfortable sitting at Aubrey's desk, except for the fact that it's three sizes too small for you. Leadership suits you."

Fergus sat in a chair facing Lester across the desk that had formerly held tidy stacks of inventory paperwork, but was now covered in black-and-white marbled composition books.

Lester was writing again. Perhaps when Fergus returned to visit Amelia in a year or two, the giant might let him read some of his work. He doubted it, though. Lester said his words were for him alone. It was an intriguing notion to write only for oneself. Perhaps he would try his hand at it too.

"Leadership is nothing more than utilizing the most effective methods for getting others to do your bidding," Lester said. "A monkey could do it, if that monkey understood human nature."

Both men glanced at the shelf in the corner which still contained psychopathy books, but many others now, too. Lester's burgeoning library threatened to fill the entire office.

"Annabelle is just like them, you know." Delivering that message was one of two tasks he intended to accomplish before leaving for Tennessee. He felt an obligation to advise his friend, who was understandably blind to the child's predisposition.

"I realize that, of course."

Caterpillar eyebrows lifted in surprise. "You do? Yet you're devoted to the child who might well murder you in your sleep."

"She is part of the reason I let you keep your knife while you were in The Box. I wasn't convinced my influence on her was stronger than Aubrey's. She might kill me someday, but with a little luck and the tenacity of a patient father figure, nurture may prevail over nature. I believe I can mold the child; it is my fervent hope. I don't intend to stay here forever...my inner introvert will demand I leave at some point. I think Annabelle will be a fine leader when that time comes."

"Interesting. You may be right, if your nurture theory pans out. I have a question, one that has confounded me since I first discovered such a gentle, wise soul inside the body of Arnold Schwarzenegger's much larger brother."

"Let me guess. You wonder why I joined the Terminators to begin with, knowing of their nefarious practices."

"That's it exactly."

"Once I realized what I was dealing with, I thought I might effect change from within. There were many positive things happening here. Remember when I said I may have to dispose of the sisters? I hoped it wouldn't come to that, but in Aubrey's case, it did. I'm glad Annabelle was there to save you, tiny man. I would have done it if she hadn't...I had Aubrey and Annabelle both in the crosshairs of my firearm when we arrived at your execution. There will always be dragons, Fergus, even some with a benevolent side. Fortunately, there are people like us to slay them when they need slaying. I hope my answer makes sense to you."

"Perfect sense."

"And one dragon still remains. I expect her to return anytime now."

"You mean Zoey?"

"Yes."

Here was the second task: putting his friend's mind to rest in regard to the Zoey matter.

"Lester, you will never have to worry about that dragon again. She was placed on a magnificent sailing vessel against her will, and should be somewhere in the middle of the Atlantic by now."

Lester frowned. "I don't think she knows how to sail. That seems a bit cruel, even for one such as her."

"Not cruel at all. Tyler is the vessel's captain. You know the young man?"

"Ah, of course. Yes, Tyler is one of the good ones. I wish him luck. He'll need it to survive alongside Zoey on whatever island becomes their new home. And where are you off to? I assumed you would stay with your lady friend in the Colony."

"Alas, that is my desire, but I have other obligations."

"Let me guess. You're on a mission for the mysterious underground people."

Fergus noted the derisive tone and it comforted him. It was preferable for Lester to dismiss all that Amelia had told his friend back at the Jupiter Hills Golf Club.

"You don't believe our cover story then? What about the part where the magical little girl with the big green eyes cured you of the poison?"

"That was the most absurd story I've ever heard, and I've heard a lot of them in my time. The reason I survived the so-called poison dart is twofold: first, I'm still on the antibiotics for the gunshot wound, and second, I've spent the last few years building up an immunity to iocane powder."

Fergus laughed. "Arguably the best scene in *The Princess Bride*. Oh, Lester, I will miss you very much. The alliance you Terminators have with the Colonists will benefit everyone. It was a savvy move for you to negotiate the treaty. I'd like to drop by for a visit when I'm back in your neck of the woods. Promise I won't be shot on sight?"

"I make no such promises," Lester said with a rare smile. "I shall miss you too, my diminutive friend. Safe travels."

***

"Stop there. Not another step or I'll drop you like a buzzard off a shit wagon."

The high-pitched, trembling voice emanated from a copse of trees somewhere in the foothills of the Great Smoky Mountains. Autumnal color was beginning to creep into the verdigris foliage. In a few more weeks, the red, orange, and gold leaves would be even more prolific. It was enchanting country. Fergus wondered if he would still be there in the winter to behold those misty peaks blanketed with snow.

"You realize that makes no sense," Fergus replied to the trees. "A more logical phrasing would be, *not another step or I'll drop you like a ton of bricks!* The buzzard simile has to do with pungent, off-putting aromas, not the dropping of objects or people. Anywho, I come in peace, I am unarmed, and I have much to offer your community in terms of esoteric knowledge and specialized expertise. I'm also in possession of a few Snickers bars. Stale, yes, but even stale nougat, peanuts, and chocolate are better than no nougat, peanuts, and chocolate at all. Am I right?"

Seconds ticked by. Fergus continued to stand, arms raised skyward, waiting for the buzzard-dropping shooter to emerge from the thicket. When he finally did, Ferus extended his hand toward the old man wearing a weathered Tennessee Titans ball cap and holding an antediluvian shotgun.

"My name is Fergus. To whom do I have the pleasure of speaking?"

THE END

(Until the next time...)

Dear Reader,

I hope you enjoyed this book. I'd love it if you posted a review about it on Amazon and Goodreads. Reading a well-written book in the company of snoozing doggies is my favorite pastime. Receiving feedback and reviews from readers about my own books is my second favorite pastime. Which scenes did you like best? What character could you relate to the most? How do you think you'd fare in a post-apocalyptic world?

On a side note, if you've spotted a typo, please email me a nicki@nickihuntsmansmith.com. I hate those insidious little buggers as much as the next reader.

Follow me on Facebook at https://www.facebook.com/AuthorNickiHuntsmanSmith/ or read my blog (Eating the Elephant) at http://nickihuntsmansmith.com/.

I look forward to hearing from you!

Nicki Huntsman Smith

Made in the USA
Middletown, DE
01 June 2021